PRAY FOR RAIN

THE JAKE SAWYER SERIES (BOOK 4)

ANDREW LOWE

GET A FREE JAKE SAWYER NOVELLA

Sign up for the no-spam newsletter and get a FREE copy of the Sawyer prequel novella **THE LONG DARK**.

Check the details at the end of this book.

Email: andrew@andrewlowewriter.com
Web: andrewlowewriter.com
Twitter: @andylowe99

First published in 2020 by Redpoint Books
This edition April 2024
Cover photographs © Shutterstock
Cover by Book Cover Shop

ISBN: 978-1-9997290-8-0

For Tom and Josh

I reached my very edge. I was about to break down.
I was about to break through.

— TALISMANIST GIEBRA,
TALISMANIST: FRAGMENTS OF THE ANCIENT FIRE

PROLOGUE

He uncorked the wine.

'I don't normally drink on weekdays.' The man turned his head to the woman and gave her a lopsided smile. 'Special occasion, though.'

She said nothing. She had reclined into the corner of the sofa, head tilted, face in shadow from the tall floor lamp behind. Her bleached blonde hair spilled over both exposed shoulders; a few strands coiled into her pale cleavage.

'It's a nice white, this. Couldn't face red, or even rosé, in this weather.' He sloshed out two measures into long-stemmed brandy glasses, and glanced at the woman; no mention of his *faux pas*. The man flattened a palm onto his high forehead and swept away a film of sweat. His arms were hefty: inflated with muscle, embossed with protruding veins. 'You know what? I think it's getting hotter. They say we'll break the UK drought record on Saturday. Sixteen consecutive days above thirty degrees now.'

Still no response from the woman. He smiled, took a taste of wine.

'Hey! I can change this light, you know.' He took out his phone, opened an app, and drew his finger across the screen. The light from the floor lamp dimmed to a deep red. He laughed. 'Sorry. Bit porno, that one.' He selected another setting, and the hue softened to a diffuse pink.

He switched to his Spotify app and a string melody burst from a cylindrical smart speaker in the corner. Female moans, a four-four beat. 'Yes Sir, I Can Boogie' by Baccara. 1970s disco pop. He lowered the volume and smiled. 'There it is.'

He stepped forward, set the glasses down on the coffee table, and sank into a facing armchair.

'So, yeah. I'm a painter. Not the arty kind. Decorator. I do other bits, though.' He sipped his wine, dipping his head, peering at the woman over the top of the glass.

He sucked up the liquid, slurping like a child. Loud and shameless.

Another smile, his eyes still on the woman. 'Sorry. Where are my manners?'

He reached forward and lifted the woman's wrist. She wore a slender T wire bracelet, in rose gold. The man whistled.

'Is this real? You must earn a few quid to afford that, right?'

He put the glass back on the table and shifted round onto the sofa, next to the woman.

'That was gauche. Forgive me.'

He wore a light fitted T-shirt and linen shorts. He raised his bulky legs, propping both bare feet onto the coffee table. His calves were absurdly pumped and defined, and his swollen thigh muscles rippled as he crossed his ankles.

He gave the woman a side glance. 'I know what you're thinking. "This guy works out." You're right. And "work" is the key word. You put in the effort, you see the results. Right here.' He flexed his bulging bicep, slapped a hand onto it, squeezed; the muscle barely yielded. 'Some people might find this a bit vain.' He shrugged. '"All is vanity." Ecclesiastes 1:2.'

He drew in a deep breath through his nose and held it for a few seconds, savouring the silence, then made an 'O' with his mouth and exhaled, nice and slow.

'You're in good shape yourself, you know. But that's probably down to your genes. To stand outside the norm, to stand out... That takes work. I couple my fitness regime with a strict diet, and I never deviate. I don't let anything slip. That's the secret to achievement, really. All those compulsions, pulling you in different directions. You just have to tame them, balance the equation.'

The man slid his feet off the table and turned to the woman.

'Sorry. Am I boring you? I have to say, you're not giving me much to go on. But that's okay. I like submissive women. Silent types.' He reached out and slipped her into an embrace. He leaned in, hovering his open mouth close to her jawline, baring his teeth.

He pushed himself away and stood upright, looming over her. He watched, smiling, as the woman's body flopped onto the arm of the sofa and slid down, wedging her into the corner. Her head lolled to the side, and the man tilted his own head and stared into her empty eyes.

'Apologies, again. That was a bit intense. No need to rush things.' He bent forward, hitched one of his powerful arms into the crook of the woman's legs, and wrapped the other around the back of her neck. With no apparent effort, he lifted her off the sofa and slung her over his right shoulder. The woman's torso and arms slumped down his back and she hung there, limp.

The man closed his eyes, screwing them shut. When he opened them again, his gaze was distant, stolen away.

He moved off, out of the kitchen. 'Playtime's over.'

Outside, a muted dusk settled on the airless street. Another man sat in an open-topped two-seater, parked in a side road. He wore wraparound sunglasses, despite the relative darkness. He stared up at the window and watched the pink light fade to black.

PART ONE

THE SUN RISING

1

The visitors shuffled around the cramped walkways of the Yorkshire Wildlife Park. Most were dressed for the beach: shorts, sliders, floppy sun hats for the women, branded baseball caps for the men. The park had reached capacity for the third day running, and the entrance clerks had been told to operate a strict one-in, one-out policy. But all the popular enclosures—big cats, great apes—were hidden behind three-deep scrums, and the animals had either retreated indoors, or skulked in patches of distant shade.

A portly man in a red-and-white football top paused at the entrance to the *Project Polar* section and unfolded his park map. A young girl in a mottled blue summer dress wedged herself in front of him and stood on tiptoes, peering through the wire mesh fence. She held a hand to her brow, shielding her eyes from the midday sun.

'Please wear your hat, sweetheart.' A woman, barely taller than the girl, joined them. She was hunched forward, wilting in the heat, fanning herself with a folded map.

The girl took a wide-brimmed straw hat from the woman and pivoted to face her parents. 'Why can't we see him?'

The man squinted into his map. 'Blimey. Seventy acres, this place. Four hundred animals, seventy species.'

'You could be here all day and not do it all,' said the woman.

The man glanced at her, nodded. 'With these crowds, you'd never get round the bloody place in a day, let alone do everything.'

'Dad! I said, why can't we see him?'

He folded the map. 'Who?'

'The bear!'

The woman pressed the hat onto her daughter's head. 'There's more than one, sweetheart. And it's a hot day, isn't it? They're probably taking shelter. They like it cold.'

The man peered through the fence: a sturdy wooden base topped by several layers of mesh, wide enough for viewing and photographs. 'There's four bears in here.' He looked back at his daughter. 'It's like a park within a park. Ten acres. An eight-metre-deep lake. Let's move on a bit. We might see them further in.'

'They don't actually need it to be cold.' A boy spoke up from further back in the crowd. He was small and willowy, and wore an unseasonal black T-shirt with a yellow Batman logo. As he pushed his scruffy blond hair out of his eyes, his red-framed glasses glinted in the sun. 'They've just adapted to hunting on ice, in the wild. That's where they catch lots of seals. It's their main diet. They cut holes in the ice and wait for the seals to pop up for breath.' He shrugged. 'It's sort of like, they don't go after their prey. It comes to them.'

A young woman pushed through the group and laid a hand on the boy's shoulder. She was tall and elegant, with shining black hair pinned up into a high bun. She raised her Tom Ford sunglasses and looked the boy in the eye. 'Lolly or ice-cream, Luka?' She held up her phone. 'He says he's nearly at the front of the queue.'

'Lolly, please.'

She tapped something into the phone.

'He knows his stuff.' The portly man nodded down at Luka.

The tall woman smiled. 'He's a rare eleven-year-old. Loves school.'

'Not all of it,' said Luka. 'I just like learning.'

'Won't learn much here,' said the small woman, fanning herself with the map again. 'Whoever heard of an animal park without animals? Nearly sixty quid for the three of us, and that's booking online.'

The crowd surged a little, forcing the group back towards the entrance. The tall woman had to steady herself against the back side of the *Project Polar* sign. A few shouts came from further along the walkway, and she raised herself up, trying to catch the source of the commotion.

More shouting. The crowd rippled with greater force, pushing several people out onto the main park pathway.

'*Idiot*!'

'*What the hell is he playing at*?'

'*Get the keepers*!'

The portly man hustled his way along the walkway, trailed by his wife and daughter. Luka and his mother followed.

The crowd had compressed at a section of the fence that overlooked the narrow tip of the enclosure's lake. The movement had created space at the opposite side, and Luka climbed onto a litter bin, where he could see over the mass of people and down into the enclosure. A large man in a bucket hat and a tatty parka jacket had scaled the wire mesh and was scrambling down a steep verge towards a group of outbuildings. He slowed at the shore of the lake and sat down at the edge of a shallow ridge, feet dangling over the water below.

'It's a publicity stunt.'

'Was he with anyone?'

'Someone get the keeper!'

To the side of the outbuildings, an overhang of rock cast a patch of shade over three vast polar bears, sprawled on a bed of straw. A puddle of lake water lapped around their gigantic paws. The creatures seemed to be asleep: motionless and, apparently, oblivious.

Over at the far shore, a fourth bear emerged from a small cave carved into the raised wall of the lake, and wallowed in the grey water. A murmur of alarm bristled through the crowd, but the man in the parka made no attempt to conceal himself. He leaned forward, and hauled himself to his feet.

'Sit down, you idiot!'

'Stop shouting at him.'

'He must be mental.'

A teenager at the front of the crowd tore off his T-shirt and, with the help of a friend, hitched himself up onto the wooden base of the fence. He held on to the mesh and pressed his mouth to one of the gaps, calling out, in a strange mix of shout and whisper. 'Mate! Come on. You shouldn't be in there. You're gonna get hurt.'

Hands reached up. More voices, telling him to be quiet, urging him to get down, insisting the keepers were coming.

The man in the parka turned to the onlookers and waved his arms. 'They never come out!' He was loud, and the crowd cringed. 'They never come out to see me! Nobody ever comes to *see me*.' He sank down to his knees and shuffled round, resuming his position, sitting on the ridge at the edge of the lake. The topless teenager climbed down from the fence and stumbled back into the crowd.

The bear at the far shore surfaced and loped back towards the cave, tossing its head, sniffing the air.

'They only had these left.'

A touch on Luka's back. He turned and took a Strawberry Mivvi lolly from a man in a well-worn T-shirt with a screen-printed image of Bruce Lee, poised in a yellow jumpsuit. The man was slim, broad shouldered, and tall enough to be level with Luka at the top of the bin. He had glinting green eyes, and an untamed mop of inky black hair that gathered at the base of his neck.

He smiled, activating a dimple in his right cheek. 'Your mum's getting help. Better be quick, though.'

Luka frowned. 'What?'

The man nodded towards Luka's hand. 'Starting to melt already.'

He turned and forced his way through the crowd and scaled the base of the fence. He gripped the top of the mesh, and scrambled up and over.

Groans from the onlookers. A few shouts of anger and alarm.

He scrambled down the verge and sat at the edge of the ridge, a few feet away from the man in the parka, who stared forward, arms wrapped around himself.

Across the lake, the polar bear paced, agitated.

The man in the parka turned his head towards his new companion. 'I've seen that. *Game of Death.*'

The green-eyed man looked down at his T-shirt and nodded. 'It's not good. Most of it was filmed after Bruce Lee died. It's an exploitation film, basically.'

'So why do you wear that, then?'

A shrug. 'Saw the film, got the T-shirt. Listen. Sorry to interrupt. But I just wanted to say something.'

'I know. I'm putting myself in danger. It's irresponsible. I need to come out. I need to do this. I need to do that.' He scraped at his cheeks with filthy fingernails. 'I don't need to do *anything*.'

'No, no. I just wanted to say that I wish I'd thought of this.'

The parka man gave him a sharp look. 'You what?'

'Just look at it out there.' He pointed back at the faces by the fence. 'You can't move. This is the best place to be. Bit of shade. Trees. Water. Must be weird, though. Getting stared at all day.' He nodded to the bears slumped by the rocky outcrop. 'At least they can hide, I suppose.'

'Are you the police?'

The green-eyed man pushed back his hair, running his fingers over an albino patch at the crown of his head. He held out a hand. 'Jake Sawyer.'

The parka man studied the hand for a few seconds, then took it. Sawyer winced at the strength of his grip.

'My name is Daniel. Not telling you my surname.'

'See, you're already one point up on me, Daniel.' Sawyer sucked in a breath. 'Did you see we broke the record for the hottest July day today?'

Daniel dropped his head. 'I don't care.'

'Quite a time to be alive, isn't it? We're a weird species, don't you think, Daniel? We're a brilliant ape. King of the hill. Top of the food chain. We think of ourselves as successful because we can take what we need, when we need it. And none of the other creatures can do anything to stop us. The ones we find exotic or interesting, we stick them in places like this. The others... we farm them, eat them, enslave them.'

Daniel looked up. 'And we don't care how much we have to mess up the planet to do it.'

Sawyer smiled. 'Exactly. And then, when our actions cause extreme weather like this, do we call it out as a crisis? Set our brilliant ape minds to brilliant work, to balance things out? No. We call it a "scorcher", and we do deals with each other to exploit it. The tabloids, flogging two-for-one offers on tubs of ice cream.'

Daniel laughed, too loud. 'We're like, "We broke another record! Let's have another ice cream."'

Sawyer nodded.

The polar bear prowled back down to the lake, turned, and walked along the water's edge, towards Sawyer and Daniel.

Sawyer leaned forward, tracking Daniel's eyeline. He seemed to have noticed the bear's movement. Was reality dawning? 'Apparently, it sounds like paper ripping.'

'What does?' Daniel took off his parka, revealing a dirty white long-sleeved shirt, buttoned up to the top.

'When a bear attacks a human being, it often goes for the scalp, where the brain is, trying to scoop it out. Like the yolk from a boiled egg. And its claws are powerful enough to tear through the bone. The few people who've survived report that it sounds like paper ripping. Think of that sound, Daniel. A thick sheet of paper, torn in half. Only it's your skull.'

The bear stopped at the near shore and gave a low growl, almost a grumble. Its head swayed from side to side, nose pointed up high towards Sawyer and Daniel.

'They're short-sighted,' said Sawyer. 'But they can detect distant movement. He's come over to check us out, assess the threat.'

Shouts from the crowd behind. Sawyer glanced around. Three men in khaki shorts and park-branded polo shirts had entered the enclosure through a side gate. A fourth man in a Hi-Viz vest joined them, and waited off to the side. He held a rifle, barrel pointed up.

Sawyer turned back. The bear had started to plod up the shallow incline, towards the top of the ridge where Sawyer and Daniel were sitting.

'Will he eat us?' said Daniel.

Sawyer shook his head. 'Nah. He's well fed in here. He just wants to see if we're a threat.' He turned to Daniel. 'He will kill us, though.'

Daniel sucked in a breath, filling his lungs, and shuddered, as if he'd just stepped into a cold shower. He flattened his palms against the edge of the rock, bracing.

'But it's already too late to run, Daniel. He might look big and slow, but he'll catch us before we're even halfway back to the fence. So, what's going on with you? What's the plan?'

Sawyer looked back. The three men in park polo tops approached with caution, through a patch of trees. One took the lead, while the other two held back. All three had their arms low, carrying heavy objects that Sawyer couldn't make out at this distance. The man in the Hi-Viz jacket crouched at an elevated point near the gate and prepared his rifle.

Daniel turned to Sawyer, and for the first time, he seemed awake, in the moment. He scanned Sawyer, horrified. 'We've got to *go*. You...' He sprang to his feet, looked around: across the lake, back to the fence and the crowd, the raised phones.

The bear reached the top of the ridge, twenty feet away. It was immense: bottomless black eyes; parched, silvery fur; underbelly matted and dripping with lake water. Its smell drifted over: clean, earthy.

'Me?' said Sawyer.

'You... What are you doing? Getting in here?'

The bear stopped, and turned its head in a wide arc, assessing them both.

Sawyer grinned at Daniel. 'I'm here with a friend, and I don't want the day to be ruined by the sight of a polar bear tearing off someone's head.'

Daniel's knees buckled. He glared at Sawyer. 'You're crazy.'

'Stay where you are!' The lead keeper was close enough now to call over. They had all circled round behind, apart from the Hi-Viz man, who had stayed at the elevated point with his rifle.

Daniel stood there, trembling. Was he going into shock? A seizure?

Sawyer held his gaze and spoke low and calm. 'Daniel. Don't run.'

Daniel twisted round, scuffing a flurry of earth over the edge of the ridge. He broke into a strange, crouching scurry —bent forward, head down—and aimed for the far corner of the enclosure, near the *Project Polar* sign.

Shouts from the keepers. A scream from the crowd.

The bear took its cue, and pushed off its muscular hind legs. It cut across the back side of the ridge, gathering speed, giving chase.

Sawyer jumped up and set off sprinting after Daniel. But he angled his run directly towards the fence, crossing the bear's path. He turned to face it, and stood his ground, shouting and waving his arms.

The bear slowed and stopped, ten feet from Sawyer. It bowed its head, swaying.

Sawyer kept up the waving and shouting. The bear sniffed the air and let out a rumbling roar. It stayed in place, thumping its paws into the ground, throwing back its head.

Daniel reached the fence and clambered up and over the mesh.

The bear dipped its head, nose to the ground, as if searching for a signal to strike.

Sawyer waved and shouted. He took a breath and glanced at a movement to the side. The keepers had reached his position, all carrying small red fire extinguishers. The man at the front stepped across Sawyer and pulled the pin on his device. His colleagues did the same, and all three aimed their hoses down at the ground in front of the bear. They squeezed the levers, and the extinguishers hissed and spewed out dense jets of carbon dioxide, throwing a blanket of vapour across the creature's path.

It roared again, and stumbled to the side, stomping its paws. The men released a second burst from the extinguishers. This time, the bear turned and hurried away, back along the side of the lake, towards the rocky outcrop.

The keepers hustled Sawyer away, towards the side gate. The man in the Hi-Viz vest had secured his rifle and moved down in front of the gate. He smoothed down his trimmed, grey-black beard, and Sawyer caught the hint of a smile, and a barely perceptible nod.

Sawyer waited while the lead keeper unlocked the gate. Outside, two new arrivals in Hi-Viz jackets kept the crowd away from the fence. A few people applauded and shouted encouragement. Most held up their phones, pointing them at Sawyer. Luka and his mother had pushed their way to the front, at the edge of the walkway. Luka stared over, smiling, finishing off his Strawberry Mivvi. His mother's reaction was hidden behind her sunglasses.

The lead keeper opened the gate and ushered Sawyer through. He still hadn't spoken.

'I'm police,' said Sawyer. 'Where's Daniel? Is he okay?'

The man nodded. 'Been taken to the office.'

'You know him?'

'Danny Rawson. Soft lad. Lost his brother last year. Tried it before, but this is the first time he's gone in. Didn't recognise him in the parka.'

Sawyer nodded. 'Red flag on a day like today, though.'

He gave a strained smile. 'Danny will be alright. If I were you, I'd be more worried about myself.'

2

WARNING! A BOSS ENEMY IS APPROACHING! BATTLE STATIONS!

Sawyer steadied himself and adjusted his grip on the PS4 controller. Chunky lettering flashed red and black in the centre of the screen, as the *Bullet Symphony* announcer jabbered in frantic Japanese.

He had stripped down to his ageing Calvins and sprawled across the sofa. A desktop fan sat on the coffee table, wedged behind a salad bowl piled high with ice cubes. But the fan was noisy, and the stream of air only marginally chilled. He jabbed at the off switch, took a sip from a glass of rosé and refocused on the game, grimacing at the wine's acid tang.

His black-and-white cat, Bruce, mirrored his owner: splayed out on the cool tiles at the edge of the kitchen, just outside the spotlight of late afternoon sun that beamed in through the cottage's side window. It had been another endless hot day, with the scorched fields around Edale watered by farmers whose failing crops had exempted them from the emergency drought measures: hosepipe and sprinkler ban, no building or car washing, appeals for bath sharing. Now, after fifteen parched days of leeching from the reservoirs with not a replenishing drop from the sky, there was talk of rationing and mobile water tankers.

Sawyer's phone trilled: a trimphone ringtone.

Caller ID: *MAGS*.

He turned down the TV volume and jabbed at the reply icon, then set the call to speaker mode.

Maggie Spark's voice caused Bruce to twitch an ear. 'It lives!'

Sawyer smiled. 'Enjoying the summer?'

'I hope that's ironic. Are we really talking about the weather?'

'Why would we do that?'

On-screen, a vast alien mothership spat out a dense cluster of glowing pink projectiles. Sawyer jinked the core of his ship through the pixel-wide spaces in between.

'Because I'm willing to bet you're sitting there with the blinds drawn, watching something gloomy and existential, and eating Monster Munch.'

'You underestimate me. I've bought cookbooks. I took a Gordon Ramsay Masterclass. I follow an Instagram account called Doctor's Kitchen, manned by worthy Californians who show you how to make leek cassoulet and cream corn chowder.'

'And what's for dinner tonight?'

'Well...' Sawyer blasted the mothership with a barrage of arcing lasers from his ship's side turrets. 'Cold pizza. It's too hot to cook.'

'*MasterChef* application on hold until the autumn, then?' Maggie paused. 'Are you playing a videogame?'

'There's no such thing as undivided attention, these days.'

'And the blinds?'

He glanced over at the covered front window which would normally look out onto his orange-and-black Mini Convertible, parked this side of the driveway bridge. 'I'm topped up on Vitamin D. And I'm feeling indulgent. I've done my good deed for the day.'

'Which is?'

'Just... helping.' The mothership's outer shell fell away and Sawyer trained his weapons on a glowing inner core, which released a spinning spiral of counter-fire. 'The deal came through on Dad's house. All done.'

'Gone to a good owner?'

'Yeah. Retired couple. They hardly look old enough to be retired, though. Three dogs.'

Maggie whistled. 'That's a lot of dogs.'

'Proxy children. I suppose your kids grow up, move on, stop calling. But there's still that urge to nurture. Dogs are the ideal replacement.'

'In what way?'

'They don't judge, don't ask for money. They won't get anyone pregnant.'

'So why didn't you take your dad's dogs? Rufus and Cain, wasn't it?'

Sawyer eyed Bruce, now flat on his back in submission to the heat. 'Yes. I don't like to be relied on.'

'And has this come up with Alex?'

Sawyer finished off the mothership and gazed at the ludicrous pyrotechnic inferno which consumed its collapse. 'Haven't been for a while.'

'That is a big part of therapy, you know. You have to actually go. It's a game with a minimum of two players.'

'I was hoping I could go a few times, get the general idea, score some pills.'

She paused. 'Are you on medication now?'

'No. That's never gone well. Just made me feel worse.'

'And how *do* you feel?'

The on-screen explosion melting. Multiple colours, melting into one another.

Flashes.

The cellar ceiling. His father's blood and brains.

His father's painting. The central smear of red. The greys and whites at the edges.

Grey matter.

'Working on it.'

Maggie inhaled. 'On what?'

'Feeling.' Sawyer took a gulp of wine. 'How about you? Cycling through the dating apps?'

'Couple of things set up. I've only been separated for a few months, Jake. I'm not expecting someone to whisk me away anytime soon. How's your woman?'

Sawyer spluttered. 'My *woman*? If you mean Eva, then she's fine. It works.'

'Sounds pretty steamy.'

'Plenty of drama elsewhere.'

Car engine outside. The vehicle had slowed and parked up on the verge by the thin stream of reservoir run-off that separated Sawyer's cottage from the single-track Hayfield road.

'And your brother?'

He dug his fingers through his matted hair. 'He's better. Could hardly have been worse. I hired a speech therapist. Michael wouldn't see her at first, but he's more open to it now.'

Maggie clattered around. 'Sorry. Just cleaning. And are we allowed to talk about work?'

'You know as much as everyone else.'

'And that's quite a lot, now you're a celebrity.'

He paused the game and sat back, closed his eyes. 'I'm not a celebrity. The Pope is a celebrity.'

'Keating tells me they've been buried under interview requests.'

'Bloom manages that. I never see it.'

'Why not?'

'Because I don't say yes.'

A toilet flush, door slam. 'You said you were going to go away, after the Briggs case.'

'I did. Lanzarote.'

'Hmm.'

'That's your judging noise. You used to do it at Keele, when we'd been to see a film you weren't impressed with.'

'I'm not judging. Whatever works. Whatever settles you.'

'Now you're humouring me.'

'Jake, when was the last time we saw each other?'

He opened his eyes. 'Couple of months?'

'Since you tried to make dinner for me.'

'I thought I succeeded.'

'Debatable.' Maggie sighed, deeper this time. 'Don't push people away. Particularly the ones you need to keep close.'

'I find I don't have to push too hard. People generally don't need a lot of prompting to head in the opposite direction.'

'Self-pity doesn't suit you.' Her tone turned sharp. 'It's beneath you.'

He laughed. 'I'm better than that, right?'

'Right. Accept the help, but don't forget the self-care.'

'I'm seeing Alex tomorrow.'

'Good! I'm sure she misses you.'

A knock at the door. Two taps. A familiar rhythm. He

toggled the phone off speaker and picked it up as he hauled himself upright. 'Bored with the bedwetters, no doubt.'

'Well, that's you. Never a dull moment.'

'That'll look good on my gravestone.'

Sawyer pulled on his tracksuit bottoms and wriggled into an old Underworld T-shirt with the legend *INTO THE BLOOD* stacked down the centre. He peeked through the edge of the closed blind. A hefty man with an unkempt goatee stood on the porch; he spotted Sawyer and winked. A boxy, mustard-yellow Range Rover was parked down by the verge.

'I miss you,' said Maggie. 'I miss your... You-ness.'

'We've texted.'

'It's not the same.'

'It is for men.' He headed for the door, unhurried. 'So, am I still worthy of coverage? Has it died down a bit now?'

'Don't you follow the news?'

'I prefer the olds.'

'We've done this, Jake. You can't live in the past, or hide in your teenage 1990s.'

'I was happy then. Or at least I thought I'd worked out how to be happy.'

'It was just easier. Fewer complications. That's what you're pining for. Now you have to work harder for the happiness. You can't just stop trying and complain when it doesn't come to you.'

He opened the door and beckoned the man inside. 'One day at a time. Start with Saturday. Breakfast?'

'Usual place?'

'We're not being wire-tapped, you know.'

She laughed. 'Eight-thirty, at the Nut Tree.'

Sawyer hung up.

The man hovered in the doorway; he was vast and

rounded, with stout fingers and a sagging double chin, half concealed by the goatee. He nodded. 'DI Sawyer.'

Sawyer offered a theatrical salute. 'DS Ed Shepherd. Reporting for duty?'

Shepherd trudged over to the sofa but didn't sit. He nodded at the glass of wine on the coffee table. 'Drinking alone?'

'Not any more.'

'On duty. And too hot for it, anyway.'

Sawyer snatched up the glass. 'I agree.' He tipped the remaining wine into the kitchen sink and pulled two cans of Coke Zero from the fridge. He lobbed one, underarm, at Shepherd, who caught it and cracked the ring pull.

Shepherd nodded at the fan and the melting ice. 'Dare I ask what that's all about?'

'DIY air con. Saw it on YouTube.'

'Does it work?'

Sawyer hurled himself back into the sofa. 'No.' He took up the PS4 joypad again.

Shepherd squinted at the screen, at the swirling fighter craft, the pointillist mayhem. 'This is a *game*, yes?'

'It relaxes me.'

'How?'

'You see the objects, I see the spaces.'

'What spaces? It's mental.'

'There's always a way through. Even when it seems impossible.'

'So, are you back? In the real world? Taken your leave?' Shepherd walked over to the kitchen and bent down to ruffle Bruce's exposed tummy fur. The cat curled his paws around his fingers, drawing him in.

Sawyer glanced over. 'Now that is unusual. He's not normally so welcoming.'

Shepherd winced as Bruce dug in his claws. 'Too hot to

resist.' He withdrew his hand and headed back to the sofa, standing just off Sawyer's shoulder.

'Yeah,' said Sawyer. 'I'm back. There is no real world, though. It's all subjectively constructed.'

'Is that what you said when you were awarded that soft handball in the Champion's League final?'

'Spoken like a true bluenose.'

Shepherd knocked back his Coke. 'We'll get back to the top someday.'

'Not in our lifetime.' Sawyer paused the game, sat back. He rolled the ice-cold can across his forehead, waited.

'Lots going on,' said Shepherd.

'Like?'

'Your new best friend, for one. Dale Strickland.'

'Bizarre gardening accident?'

Shepherd crushed the empty can and flattened it, palm to palm. 'Running for office. Manchester mayor.'

'I heard. He won't get that. He probably knows it.'

'Angling for another job?'

Sawyer smiled. 'I don't think he sees himself as the King in the North. More like a Little Prince. Machiavelli.'

Shepherd raised an eyebrow. 'What?'

'Never mind. I thought he was working the war on drugs angle. Calling it an austerity problem. Social issues being criminalised.'

Shepherd shuffled his feet, distracted. 'Uhuh. So it really is poacher turned gamekeeper. Shaking up the political elite.'

Sawyer wrinkled his nose. 'Populism.'

'At least he's lost interest in suing you for harassment.'

'Yeah. It's almost as if I've got something on him, and he's decided it's wise to leave me alone.' Sawyer held Shepherd's eye. 'Go on, then. The suspense is killing me.

Why are you here? You don't text, you don't call. Unannounced visit. Always the drama.'

Shepherd puffed out his cheeks, ran a palm across his forehead. 'We've got a thing.'

'A thing you couldn't call me about?'

'A thing you need to see. I thought we could take my car. Better for the environment.'

Sawyer nodded, and sprang to his feet. 'A bad thing?'

'A very bad thing.'

3

Sawyer climbed down from the Range Rover passenger seat and gazed out across the blazing green meadows that blended with the base of Thorpe Cloud, a limestone hill inaccessible this side of Dovedale. The River Dove sparkled in the early evening sun; for almost its entire course it formed the babbling boundary line between Staffordshire to the west and Derbyshire to the east.

Shepherd got out and leaned over, elbows on the bonnet.

Sawyer turned back. 'You're making old man noises.'

Shepherd scrubbed at his goatee. 'It's this heat. It ages you. I feel like I've been slowly roasting for a couple of weeks.' He looked up, pointed towards the scatter of distant walkers at the peak of the hill. 'They're climbing a reef knoll. It used to be the sea floor, a long time ago.'

Sawyer eyed him. 'How long are we talking?'

'Oh, we're going way back.' Shepherd rolled up his shirt sleeves. 'Few hundred million years.'

Sawyer followed him along a dirt track at the edge of the river. He had changed into a fitted white polo shirt with indigo jeans and hardy, chocolate-brown ankle boots.

He wasn't officially at work, but Shepherd's escort told him that Keating would be lurking somewhere in the bushes, and he wanted to appear shipshape, on the outside at least.

They signed in at the outer cordon and ducked into woodland at the back of a modest caravan park. Sawyer cursed as he pushed past the parched branches. 'Surprised to see the river still flowing.'

Shepherd glanced back. 'It's practically immune to hot summers. The source is way up high. Axe Edge Moor, not too far from the office.' He stopped and turned, rosy-cheeked with the exertion. 'Did you know that limestone is the fossilised remains of sea creatures, back from when this was all underwater?'

Sawyer gave a strained smile. 'I do now.'

Shepherd shrugged. 'Been walking a lot this summer. Taking an interest in my adopted county.' He turned and pushed forward, working his way around a tangle of bramble. 'I know what you're thinking.'

'I hope not.'

'You're wondering why I've put on so much weight if I've been doing a lot of walking.'

'That's not what I was thinking.'

Shepherd turned, grinned. 'I think it's the cafés at the visitor centres.'

'Who can resist an iced carrot cake?'

They emerged onto a rugged lane, in sight of the crime scene tape marking the inner cordon. The passage was barely narrow enough for a single vehicle.

'This is sometimes used as a cut-through,' said Shepherd. 'Mainly by the tourists who have too much faith in their satnavs.'

Sawyer nodded and looked around. Farm buildings off behind the trees to the west of the river. 'They end up meeting tractors and have to perform extended reverse manoeuvres.'

'Yeah. So the tractor tracks are constant, and they tend to cover up standard tyre tread.'

'And at this time of year, with the Dovedale tourist traffic...'

Shepherd nodded. 'Exactly. Did you know—'

Sawyer rolled his eyes. 'Probably not.'

'Did you know that the word "dove" is derived from the Celtic word *dubo*, meaning "dark"?'

'And we're in the white Peak here, and not the dark.'

'Yeah.' Shepherd's reply was confused, almost a question.

'Interesting,' said Sawyer. He squeezed out another smile. 'Crime scene.'

Shepherd led the way, across a field on the other side of the tractor track, towards a group of yellow-and-blue squad cars, and a Scientific Services Unit van, all parked at the entrance to a broad patch of woodland. 'So. Previously on *Buxton Major Investigation Team:* Detective Constable Matt Walker is now Detective Sergeant Matt Walker, and Detective Chief Inspector Ivan Keating is now Detective Superintendent Ivan Keating. And DSI Keating is on holiday.' Shepherd glanced over his shoulder. 'But he's been called back. So I wouldn't expect the red carpet treatment. Still, the unit is now permanent for the area, and there's been a bit of a refit.'

Sawyer nodded towards the activity by the cars and van: a handful of uniforms, FSIs in Tyvek suits, plain clothes CID conferring in cliques. 'More bodies than usual.'

'We're going to have to play nice and share on this one. As I said in the car, a few regional forces have been looking into a series of murders committed over the last few months. MO and presentation patterns suggest they're linked. One in Nottingham last December, Yorkshire in February, Greater Manchester in May. And now this.'

'I remember reading about the Nottingham murder late last year. So what's the link?'

'Ground beneath your feet, sir. I want you to see this one pure, without my taint.'

A fiftysomething woman in a turquoise Tyvek suit stepped away from the group by the van. She hurried over to Sawyer and Shepherd, peeled back her hood and shook out a neck-length bob of peroxide blonde hair.

Sawyer dipped his head, no smile.

'DI Sawyer,' said Sally O'Callaghan. 'It's been quite a while since violent death last brought us together.'

'I've been in hibernation.'

'Ah, yes. Tenerife?'

'Lanzarote.'

Sally made a face. 'Don't they call that the ashtray of the Atlantic or something? Lanza-grotty?'

Sawyer shrugged. 'It's quiet. Just what I needed.'

She studied him, a flicker of concern. 'I can imagine.'

'What fresh hell is this, then, Sally? My colleague is being coy.'

Sally turned and strode away, back towards the van. 'That's for you to decide. It's a serious arse ache to set up here, though. I often fantasise about investigating murders in places with better infrastructure.'

Sawyer caught up with her, Shepherd trailing behind. 'But then you wouldn't have that unique blend of bleakness and beauty.'

She waved a hand. 'I don't know. There's something about a good multi-storey car park, don't you think? There's beauty in brutalism.'

'Beauty is the promise of happiness,' said Sawyer.

Sally smiled at him, raised an eyebrow.

They reached the group near the SSU van. Sally ducked inside, and a young detective stepped forward, holding out a hand for Sawyer to shake. He was short and slim, unseasonably dressed in a dark suit with a royal-blue tie in a tight, high knot. 'Good to see you, sir. How are you?'

'How long have you got?' Sawyer shook. 'DS Walker. Congratulations on the change of letter. How are *you*?'

Walker touched a finger to his tie knot. 'Barely a scar now, sir. You wouldn't know it had even happened.'

'Nobody would, with you dressed like that.'

Walker frowned. 'Keating is on holiday. But he's been called back. He's a DSI—'

'We've talked about that,' said Shepherd, irritated.

Sawyer nodded to the group behind. 'Talk me through the new faces.'

Walker turned, and pointed out the figures, moving from clique to clique. 'DI Sonia McBride. Nottinghamshire.' McBride was in her early thirties: girlishly slight, with blonde hair tied back in a ponytail, and a loose white blouse with a bright blue jacket draped over her arm. She stood at the edge of a group of FSIs: gesticulating, conducting, raising herself up and down on her heels as she spoke. 'Yorkshire. DI Paul Barlow.' Sawyer followed Walker's finger to a squat man in glasses with rounded silver frames. He was shaven headed, in a cheap-looking shirt with the sleeves rolled up. Barlow had angled himself away from the scene to talk into a mobile phone; he held his head low as he spoke, as if in mourning.

Shepherd took over. 'That pair are from Manchester.' Two men faced each other at the back of the SSU van. The smaller had a short back and sides: slicked up on top, and suspiciously thick and uniform black. He wore a grey summer suit with a blue shirt—no tie—and stood with his arms folded, gazing up at the sky, apparently listening to his burly, balding colleague.

'Little man is big man's boss, right?' said Sawyer.

'Yeah,' said Walker. 'Big man is a DS. Andrew Whittaker.'

'Adrian,' said Shepherd.

Walker nodded. 'Little man is Robin Farrell. DCI, no less.'

Sawyer took a gulp of air. 'I know him.'

'Friend or foe?' said Shepherd.

Sawyer grinned at him. 'He was one of my hosts in Manchester nick, last year.'

Walker gaped. 'You were arrested?'

'Wrongly,' said Shepherd, glaring at Walker.

Over by the van, Farrell shifted position. He spotted Sawyer, and tipped back his head, smiling, keeping his arms folded, holding Sawyer's gaze.

'How was his hospitality?' said Walker.

Sawyer set off towards Farrell and Whittaker; Shepherd and Walker followed. 'I'd give him two stars on Trip Advisor. He was delighted when he thought he'd bagged himself a career collar. Two for the price of one. A murderer and a lapsed copper. I wish I could have seen his face when they dropped the charges.'

Farrell strode forward. He raised his hand—flat, side on, thumb raised—and let it hang in the air. When Sawyer held out his arm, Farrell plunged his hand down to connect hard with Sawyer's, and followed the shake with a double-tap on the shoulder. 'Detective Sawyer. Nice to see you again. Could be better circumstances, but at least you're on the right side of the law, this time.' His voice was phlegmy and abrasive, in dire need of lubrication.

Sawyer held Farrell's hand, smiled, released. 'Never in

doubt, DCI Farrell. Surprised to see you out from behind your desk. Bit of an unnatural habitat for you?'

Farrell stepped in closer; too close. Designer cologne, sickly sweet hair wax. 'No, no. Nice to get out into the sticks. That big city excitement can get oppressive. It's interesting, to drop in on the rustic side of life.' He leaned in and lowered his voice. 'I was sorry to hear about your father. That must have been difficult for you.'

Ceiling.

Red and grey. Glistening bone, embedded in the gore.

'Not ideal for him, either.'

Farrell stood back. He tapped out a breath mint and rattled the canister at Sawyer, who shook his head. 'Indeed. You got your man, though. In the end, justice was served. I assume you've taken some time off.'

'Is it that obvious?'

Farrell opened his mouth, too wide, and flicked in the mint. 'You've hardly been hiding, though. Plenty of press.'

'I didn't seek it.'

Farrell frowned at Sawyer, studying him like a botanist faced with a wilting plant. 'I could never do that. Lay myself bare. I would just find it too stressful. I was always taught that a good policeman should be like a good football referee. Does the job so well, you don't notice he's there.'

Sawyer smiled. 'Looks like you've followed the advice, DCI Farrell. Nobody could ever accuse you of standing out.'

Farrell lowered his gaze to his shoes and nodded, smiling. He swept a hand towards Whittaker, not looking up. 'DS Adrian Whittaker. I think he was on leave during your... brief residence.'

Whittaker stepped out in front of Farrell and shook Sawyer's hand. Up close, it was clear that his Sunday-best clothes were too snug for his form: skinny fit trousers over unskinny legs, shirt buttons straining against a swollen belly.

Paul Barlow finished his call and stood at Farrell's side, waiting for Whittaker to finish his introduction. Farrell turned and clamped a hand on his shoulder. 'This is DI Barlow from South Yorkshire CID.'

On cue, Barlow stepped forward and wrapped a chunky hand around Sawyer's. 'How are you, son?' He grinned, completed the handshake with no eye contact, and stepped back again. Sawyer felt like a bemused royal being presented to a group of factory workers.

'DI Sawyer.'

He turned, to see McBride, next to Walker, smiling and holding out her hand. Her grip was surprisingly firm, and she was loud and clear, with an obvious Scottish brogue. 'Pleasure to make your acquaintance. I've heard a lot about you.'

'Who hasn't, eh?' said Barlow.

Farrell led them into the woodland, where a yellow-and-white forensic tent had been erected at the centre of a clearing. The soil beneath Sawyer's feet was crisp and grainy, starved of moisture, and the tree leaves were mottled green, with scorched rims.

Farrell stopped at the tent entrance and addressed the detectives. 'Ladies and gentlemen, I'm afraid we're faced with an extremely brutal killing. We have a young woman, I would say early thirties, with—'

'I'd like to assess for myself, DCI Farrell. If it's all the same to you.' Sawyer snapped on a pair of latex gloves and stepped across Farrell, unzipping the tent.

Farrell beamed at him. 'Of course you would.'

Sawyer ducked inside, followed by the others.

The woman's naked body had been laid flat out in the centre of a carefully arranged cradle of fallen branches. She had been covered by a thin, glittery, mesh-like fabric, tucked under her torso and weighed down at the corners by rocks. Her arms were laid out at the sides, dipped down at thirty-degree angles, mirroring the shape of her long legs, which were splayed out in an inverted 'Y'.

Never the face first. He always tried to get a general sweep, an impressionistic snapshot, before going to the face.

The woman's long bleached blonde hair had been swept out to form a fan behind her head. Her cheeks and jawline were stained by dark blue bruising and her features lay disfigured behind a mask of crusted blood. Her slender neck was bruised and blistered, and her eyelids had been closed, with a few dabs of violet eye shadow applied to each. Her mouth, shining with rose red lipstick, pouted out from the centre of the violation.

Flower petals—white, yellow, red, orange—had been scattered around the outline of the body, forming a vibrant natural border, or frame. A tiara of pink and white daisies and carnations had been placed across the woman's forehead.

Sawyer crouched and lifted away the fabric. No obvious torso wounds. 'Who reported it?'

'Dog walker,' said Farrell.

Shepherd spoke, from somewhere behind. 'Fella called Damien Mount. Late forties. Works for the National Trust in Hope. He's down here visiting his mother in Thorpe, walking her dog. He's been interviewed. Bad shakes.'

'DNA and shoe prints taken,' said Sally. 'For elimination.'

Sawyer leaned in to the dead woman's face. He touched a finger to the roots of the splayed hair. Nicks and slash marks dotted her skin. 'He chopped off some of her hair. Probably with a razor. Bite marks around the neck and face, too.'

He lifted the woman's arm and examined the rose gold T wire bracelet around her wrist. A date had been engraved on the inside. He walked around to the legs and crouched, lifted the fabric. 'Bite impressions here, too. Buttocks, thighs.'

'Looks like he tried to eat her,' said Barlow. 'We haven't got Hannibal the bloody cannibal running round, have we?'

Sawyer ignored him. 'Looks like she's been cut with something, too. Vagina, inner thighs. Maybe the same blade he used for the hair.' He stood up. 'Who is she, Sally?'

'No match on IDENT1 or NDNAD, but she fits the description of a misper from Ashbourne. Reported by her partner two days ago. He'll do the formal ID once we get her out of here, but it looks conclusive. The bracelet has their wedding date.'

'Looks like strangulation. Any sexual abuse?'

Sally sighed. 'My team is still conducting—'

'My guess is that we'll find some,' said Whittaker. 'Lacerations around the vaginal area. He's not shy.'

Sally kept her eyes on Sawyer. 'We'll need Drummond to confirm.'

'Who's Drummond?' said Farrell.

Sawyer looked at Farrell; the question had been addressed to him, not Sally. 'Pathologist. How long do you need the scene open, Sally?'

'We've completed preliminaries, done the photos. But I'd like to get the body to Drummond and—'

'You should focus on hand searches,' said Whittaker.

'—and complete the hand searches before it gets dark.

Inward spiral of the inner cordon. Outward spiral of the outer cordon and beyond tomorrow.'

Whittaker shook his head. 'I would start with a parallel search of the outer cordon. Seal off the inner and save it for—'

'Can you muzzle your DS, Farrell?' said Sawyer. 'Just while I speak to my SOCO?'

'*Your* SOCO? We know you'd qualify for a blue tick on social media, Sawyer. But this isn't your private gig. And as your colleagues have demonstrated towards your good self, it's customary to address a superior officer as "sir".'

'It's not your gig, either,' said Shepherd. 'Sir. It's DSI Keating's. You and the Yorkshire and Nottinghamshire forces have been given courtesy access, but the scene is inside the Derbyshire jurisdiction.'

Farrell didn't falter. 'And when is DSI Keating likely to grace us with his presence?'

Ignoring him, Sawyer crouched and studied the bracelet again.

'He's due back at Buxton MIT within the hour, sir,' said Walker. 'We've all been called in to a meeting.'

Sawyer stood up. 'I'm sure the all-important roles and reporting lines will be on the agenda, DCI Farrell.'

'A suggestion,' said Sally. 'How about we establish which of you fine gentlemen has the largest penis later, and focus for now on this poor young woman and who did this to her?'

4

‘I like it,’ said Sawyer, surveying the new headquarters from the window of Shepherd’s office. ‘Feels like an upgrade. Like they finally have a bit of faith in us.’

‘I think so,’ said Shepherd, at his desk. ‘Even the tech works. Air con is a bit choppy, though.’

The Derbyshire Major Investigation Team unit had been established on the top floor of Buxton Police Station barely a year earlier. It was open plan, with the senior detective offices built along the windowed walls, and support rooms—victimology, intel—lined up at the near side. In Sawyer’s absence, the furniture had been levelled up, from flatpack and Formica to glass and steel. For the junior staff without offices, the cubicle spaces had been replaced with nominal partitions and meeting pods, and a section of desks at the far end had been reserved for civilian support staff.

The central space was dominated by a glass-walled, soundproofed conference room, with a twenty-seater oblong table, video conferencing, and a monitor on the far wall. Each of the seats had its own touchscreen monitor wired up to the main terminal, which was controlled by whoever was sitting in the head chair.

'Can we listen in?' said Sawyer, nodding to the conference room, where Farrell sat at the head of the table, in discussion with Whittaker, and the Yorkshire and Nottinghamshire DIs.

'No.' Shepherd blew on his coffee. 'And I doubt even you could find a loophole.'

'I see even Rhodes has been evicted from the batcave. What's down there now?'

'Storage, I think. A few woodlice.'

The lift door opened, and a man in full police uniform strode out and headed for the large corner office. He took off his flat police cap and fanned himself with the brim, smoothing down his tidy crop of white hair. He spotted Sawyer at the Shepherd's window and jerked his head towards the corner office.

'I've been summoned,' said Sawyer.

Shepherd sucked in a breath. 'Let's be careful out there.'

As Sawyer crossed the floor, Farrell emerged from the conference room.

'DI Sawyer.' He slapped a hand onto Sawyer's shoulder and squeezed. 'I hope we can put our previous encounter behind us. I just wanted to say how delighted I am that a man of your stature is involved in this case. I'm looking forward to you working for me.'

'*For* you?'

Farrell leaned in and mock-whispered into Sawyer's ear. 'I do outrank you, remember?' He stood upright and, finally, released Sawyer's shoulder. 'I know a few things might have changed since your break, and you're well known for your flexible approach, but we do still run things on rank, you know. The titles aren't advisory.

They don't change in relation to column inches or profile.'

'DCI Farrell.' The uniformed man stood at the door of his office. 'I was hoping I could borrow DI Sawyer for a moment, before the main meeting.'

Farrell smiled and swept a hand up and out, in a 'be my guest' gesture. 'Absolutely, sir.'

Sawyer sauntered towards the corner office. He stopped to note the new legend on the door, raised in pristine white against the door's walnut-brown surface.

DETECTIVE CHIEF SUPERINTENDENT
IVAN KEATING

Keating stood aside to allow Sawyer to enter, and closed the door behind him. 'Making friends?'

Sawyer walked to the window. 'I'm the wrong side of thirty-five. I don't need any new friends.'

'Farrell is good.' Keating perched on his L-shaped desk: folders and document tray at the front; monitor and keyboard a short swivel away at the back. 'I know he was involved in your detention, but he was just doing his job at a time when we didn't have all the information, and we had to treat you as the major suspect. He can be abrasive, but he's on our side. It's rare you find a DCI who's loved by all.' Keating's tone had already switched to his default shop mode: a roll of Welsh with an Irish swish.

'I'm sure we'd find his boot prints on plenty of bodies.' Sawyer looked out across the road, down towards the Tarmac Silverlands Stadium, home of Buxton Football Club. The evening sun was fading, and two floodlights cast long shadows beneath the players in a small-sided game on the Astro training pitch. 'Pre-season already?'

'Local walking football club.'

'I thought they looked a bit old for it. Doesn't look like there's much walking going on.'

Keating laughed. 'That's the thing about getting older. You age physically, but you still feel twenty-five in your head.'

Sawyer turned and lowered himself into one of the low-slung grey chairs facing Keating's desk. He squeezed the arms. 'Nice. So, did I miss much?'

Keating took his seat and tossed his cap onto the desk. 'Had a drowning up at Mermaid's Pool. Misadventure.'

'Ah, summer madness. People diving in after drowning dogs. Train delay rage due to buckled lines. Brawls at the Waitrose barbecue section. You been away? Freemason's convention?'

'Anglesey. Bloody baking, but a bit of relief with the sea breeze. Dropped in on a couple of cousins. I assume you've been hiding? You never liked the sun. I always used to think you were a closet Goth.'

Sun-flash.

His mother's hands, reaching out.

Sawyer sprang to his feet and paced, plotting a path to the window and back to the chair.

'Have you been recharging?' said Keating. 'Relaxing?'

Sawyer stopped and looked at him. 'Oh, you know. Joining the teenagers up at Nine Ladies Stone Circle, smoking dope, watching the sunsets.' He set off again. 'I don't mind sunshine. It's just the heat. Only lizards could truly enjoy this weather.'

'Did you sell your father's place?'

'Yes. He left some money. More life enhancing than life changing. Congratulations on the promotion.'

Keating nodded. 'It'll help us all. Another stripe. Bit more money. The main thing is that this place is now taken seriously.'

'It's quite an upgrade. Smart of you to keep your office more or less the same, bar the fancy chairs.'

Keating sat back. 'You think I've taken the credit for finding the man who murdered your mother.'

Sawyer stopped at the window. 'He murdered my mother *and* my father.'

'Harold committed suicide, Jake. We both watched it happen.'

The footballers gathered around an elderly player who had taken a tumble. A couple were gesticulating, pointing.

'It was slow-motion murder. You didn't grow up with him. You didn't see what it did to him. When Caldwell murdered my mother, he poisoned my father.'

'Do you mind if I ask you a personal question?'

Sawyer turned and looked at him, exasperated. 'I hate that. Just ask the question. Better to be sorry than safe.'

'Why didn't you do it? Why didn't you kill Caldwell? You had a gun on the man who murdered your mother, and, as you say, was indirectly responsible for the death of your father. What stopped you from killing him?'

Sawyer turned back to the window. The elderly player had been hauled to his feet. 'I found forgiveness in my heart.' He pulled away and returned to the chair. 'Parental obligation. My mum wouldn't have approved. And I wanted to continue my dad's work. Deny Caldwell his freedom.'

Keating poured out a couple of tumblers of water and slipped on a pair of black, thick-framed glasses. 'They gave him life, despite his age. I know the judge. Bob Juckes. Decent man.' He took a folder out of a drawer. 'Your doctor recommends a staged return. Occupational Health suggests a couple of hours a day.'

Sawyer raised an eyebrow. 'It's not a healthy occupation.' He sat again. 'I'm okay. I'm owning it.'

Keating squinted at him, nodding. ‘On top of it all, there’s your new celebrity status.’

‘I’m not a celeb—’

‘You are. After Logan’s article went viral.’

Sawyer smiled. ‘Do you even know what “viral” means?’

‘Lots of people read it. Lots of people now know you and your story. Is that right?’

‘I’m okay.’

Keating turned to his computer, Googled something. He tapped the screen with a pen. ‘Hero cop. Brave bystander. Talking down a disturbed man from suicide by polar bear. It says the keepers used fire extinguishers.’

‘Standard procedure. There was a marksman on hand, but the keepers know the animals. Extinguishers will spook a bear enough to put doubt in its mind, make it back off. It’s a prize asset and they don’t want to just give up and shoot it.’

Keating turned away from the computer screen and eyed Sawyer over the top of his glasses.

‘I’m okay, sir.’

‘I need you more than okay. We’re facing something we haven’t seen in a long time. Sustained, organised, spread over a wide area, multiple forces. You will need to cooperate with multiple senior detectives, some of whom you might not like very much. You don’t need to make friends, but you will need to influence people.’

‘Why the big love-in? If we think there’s a link between the killings, why aren’t we just investigating the Derbyshire murder and consulting with the other forces?’

Keating shook his head. ‘It’s more complex than that. A formal network will help with all the cases. Past, present and future. Cure and prevention.’ He took off his glasses and cleaned the lenses with his shirt sleeve. ‘I don’t expect you to be settled and adjusted and cracking jokes with the likes of Farrell, but you're here because I believe in you. I believe in your instincts and abilities. So, could you at least return that respect by giving me your full attention?'

Sawyer sat back, nodded. 'I'm okay. I'm good. I'm centred. I'm a happy camper.'

Keating forced a smile. 'Back in the tent.'

'Pissing out.'

5

'Thank you all for coming at short notice.'

Keating took his seat at the head of the conference table. Sawyer, Shepherd and Walker sat next to each other along one side, across from Farrell, Whittaker, McBride and Barlow. Two other male detectives flanked Keating: one scrawny with silver-framed spectacles, the other closer to Shepherd in size, with tall, slicked-back hair. They all sat before an embedded touchscreen which connected to Keating's master console.

Farrell rolled a ballpoint around his fingers. 'Appreciate you cutting your holiday short, sir.'

Keating nodded, but didn't look at him. 'I would like to spend a little time making sure we all know each other and we have a grasp of how this is going to work. You are all now senior members of a cross-country task force. This is a coordinated effort with one aim: to apprehend whoever is responsible for the murders of four young women. We'll cover the details of that in a second.

'This station's MIT will be the nerve centre of Operation Orca. There's a rough equidistance from here to all of your bases, but we'll use videoconferencing for daily briefings and only meet in person when necessary. Effectively, it's a regional Incident Room.'

'A Northern coppers' brain trust,' said Barlow, grinning.

'Please bear in mind that we're trying to catch a dangerous killer, not score points over each other. I want judicious resource management, and no details revealed externally without my sign-off. All evidence and action records go straight into the HOLMES database, which we will all be able to access. Share and share alike.'

'Sharing is caring,' said Barlow, drawing a polite laugh from McBride. Shepherd gave Sawyer a side-eye.

Keating continued. 'I'm sure you're all familiar with the HOLMES system. We've set up a dedicated HOLMES team here, and I want an airtight record of everything filed. Every statement, document, exhibit. All intelligence, big and small.' He held out a palm towards the detective with the slicked-back hair. 'DC Stuart Myers will be the Officer in the Case. His is the single voice I want the CPS to hear. No lobbying on the side. When we find a suspect and build the case, DC Myers will be the link between the CPS and the prosecutor. Hopefully, that will happen very soon.' Keating looked to the skinny detective on his other side. 'DC Ross Moran is the Disclosure Officer. He will look at every single document that goes into HOLMES, assess its relevance and coordinate actions out to junior officers on our teams. He will also work directly with the team of civilians here.' He nodded to the group of desks in the corner outside. 'Most are retired officers, and they will flag things up to DC Moran, who will filter the actionable elements into our briefings.'

'EO?' said Farrell.

Keating held a palm out towards Walker. 'The Exhibits Officer is DS Matthew Walker. This is usually more of a

DC job, but DS Walker is recently promoted and I believe his instincts will serve the role well. Every exhibit will be logged by DS Walker, and he will work with our SOCO, Sally O'Callaghan, on forensic strategy.'

Farrell took out his notebook and scribbled something. 'Sounds pretty tight, sir. I assume we're on short leads?'

'Yes. I've cancelled all leave for six weeks. Any issues with that, come and see me privately. Family Liaison, at least in the most recent case, will be handled by our regular FLO, Maggie Spark, assisted by DC Patricia Highfield. Both are highly capable, and will serve as the sole links to advise the family and gather intelligence. Maggie is a psychotherapist, which helps with this work, but as you all know, Family Liaison isn't about counselling. It's light on support, heavy on intelligence.' Keating activated his console and the individual touchscreens synced with the imagery on his screen. He looked around the table, covering all the faces. 'In short, you all work together and you find me the bastard who's doing this.' He tapped an icon, handing control to one of the other touchscreens. 'DS Shepherd.'

Shepherd swiped at his screen, revealing an image of a young woman, standing on top of an overhang of gritstone rock which overlooked a Y-shaped reservoir and viaduct in the valley below. She beamed into camera, her blonde hair tamed by a purple bobble hat. 'We've formally identified the deceased who was discovered early this morning, near Dovedale. Angela Holt, thirty-six. This is a picture of her taken at Bamford Edge a couple of months ago. Angela ran her own business. High-end scented candles, on a subscription model. Hot Wax. It was a big success, and she'd started to add soaps and other beauty products. Her husband says she went out for a drink with a friend on Tuesday night but didn't return. We found her wearing the bracelet you can just see in the picture. Rose gold. Tiffany. She bought it herself on the first anniversary of the business. It's engraved with their wedding date. Three years ago next week.'

Keating cut in. 'We're waiting on pathology, but the initial report suggests that Angela was strangled, by hand, probably some time late on Tuesday night, and her body was discovered by the dog walker two days later. She was most likely left there in the early hours of this morning.'

'No ligature marks?' said Sawyer.

Shepherd shook his head. 'Up close and personal. There's no evidence of rape, pre or post mortem, but Angela had been pretty badly beaten, her vagina had been slashed, and some of her hair had been cut off. She was also presented in an unusual way, similar to the previous victims. She had been placed on a bed of fallen branches, body covered by a thin, mesh-like fabric, and surrounded by flower petals. Her hair had been splayed out around her head, and a hand-woven crown of pink and white daisies and carnations had been placed across her forehead.'

Shepherd swiped his screen. 'To avoid copycats and cranks, the detail of the presentation has been withheld, as with the previous victims. Laura Bertrand, thirty-four, was found in Wollaton Park in Nottingham last December.' The screen showed a crime scene photo of another blonde woman, presented in the same way: similar pose, long blonde hair fanned out around her head, torso covered in thin fabric, tiara of pink and white flowers, frame of petals surrounding the body. He swiped again, showing a similar image with a different blonde woman. 'Dianne Walton, thirty, found in February, in woodland off Winscar Reservoir in Yorkshire, at the north-eastern corner of the Peak District.' Another swipe, another similar image. 'Hannah Lane, thirty-two, also blonde. Found in May at the base of a shallow ridge on open moorland up in Saddleworth.' He nodded to Farrell and Whittaker. 'Manchester. All three previous victims were strangled, and show no signs of direct sexual contact. All apart from Laura Bertrand were beaten and their vaginas were...' Shepherd struggled for the word. 'Brutalised.'

'Eye shadow applied to them all?' said Sawyer.

'Yes. All a similar colour. Violet.'

McBride cleared her throat. 'This guy does not prey on the vulnerable. Sex workers or addicts. All these women were what we would call successful. They either owned their own businesses or had high-paying jobs.'

'We should manage the press,' said Farrell. 'They're already starting to call him "the new Yorkshire Ripper".'

'Fits well,' said Walker. 'Except the killings aren't all in Yorkshire and he doesn't go for easy targets.'

'And he's not using a hammer,' said McBride.

Sawyer took a sharp breath. His mother's voice.

'Jake! Run, my darling.'

'Or a knife,' said Shepherd.

Her hand, broken and bloodied, reaching out.

'Don't look back!'

'Never let the facts get in the way of a good story,' said Barlow, tipping back his head as if expecting praise for a novel observation.

'Still,' said Keating, 'I take it you're all familiar with the Ripper enquiry? Early 1980s. Thirteen victims. The perpetrator, Peter Sutcliffe, was captured through sheer luck.'

'I think they teach it to recruits,' said Barlow.

Sawyer nodded. 'As a textbook catastrophe. How not to conduct a task force-style enquiry. Decisions made based on personal rivalries. Unreconstructed attitudes and sexual politics. Credulous senior officers driven by their career prospects.'

'I know human nature hasn't changed much in forty years,' said Keating, 'but let's at least show them that major enquiry policing has sharpened up since then. I'll get our Media Relations Manager, Stephen Bloom, to set up a press conference and announce the operation.'

'The gaps are interesting,' said Sawyer. 'December, February, May, July. Weeks separating each killing. He's relaxed, takes his time. Maybe it's tricky, acquiring a certain pedigree of victim. Maybe the times are dictated by other factors. And why the adornment? The flowers, petals, body covering. The contradictions will lead us somewhere. Vaginal mutilation but no rape, no semen. An almost tender attitude to the bodies, but also violence and contempt. Is it guilt?'

Sawyer caught a large house spider in his peripheral vision, scuttling across the light blue floor tiles, towards the table. DC Myers saw it, too, and raised a foot to stamp on it. Sawyer jerked his chair to the side, blocking him.

'Don't!'

Myers startled, and pulled his chair away from Sawyer. The spider changed direction and ran back to the side of the room, disappearing into a groove at the edge of the tiles.

Sawyer held up a hand to Myers. 'Sorry. It's just... What kind of maniac kills a spider?'

Farrell smiled and leaned forward. 'DI Sawyer. I know you've been away, and you might be a bit rusty. But can we stay focused on the kind of maniac who kills young women?'

Sawyer caught a smirk from DC Moran, as Myers regained his composure. He looked at Keating. 'Any leads on the other murders?'

Keating threw his head back. 'Ah, yes. No meaningful

trace evidence from any of the previous three scenes. Nothing on victimology, either.'

Sawyer nodded to the other detectives. 'Passive data? Have you all coordinated before?'

'They have,' said Keating. 'The best we've got is a shop CCTV showing the second victim, Dianne Walton, buying something from a newsagent just outside Sheffield city centre. Nothing on any of the others. Last pings of their mobiles nowhere near the deposition scenes.'

Shepherd checked his notes. 'Angela Holt's phone last spoke to a mast at 8:30pm on the night of her disappearance. Then, nothing.'

'Drummond will have more tomorrow,' said Keating. 'Nothing from the scene, so far. Sample results tomorrow, too. Usual story with the tyre tracks. Too many on the nearby lane. Tourist traffic.'

Sawyer spoke to Shepherd. 'I assume we've cross-reffed the shot prints and track marks from the previous scenes?'

'Yes. It's all in HOLMES. No matches.'

'Probably varying his footwear,' offered McBride. 'Different vehicles, probably stolen.'

Sawyer tapped an icon on his screen and reverted back to the image of Angela Holt. 'Might he work in a job where he has access to lots of cars? Cabbie?'

'Like Christopher Halliwell,' said Walker.

'Not the same species. Halliwell killed sex workers.'

'The presentation reminds me of Steve Wright,' said Shepherd. 'The Suffolk strangler. He was a kerb crawler, too, but he displayed some of his victims in the shape of a cross.'

McBride shook her head. 'That was to put police off the case.'

'Yes,' said Sawyer. 'It wasn't his MO. He got his kicks from the killing. The presentation was just mind games.

Nothing to do with his need.' He pinch-zoomed the image on his screen, focusing on the rose gold bracelet. 'Behaviour reflects personality. Is our killer here doing that? Is the presentation part of his killing personality, or is he just fucking us around?'

'He?' said Farrell. 'That's an assumption.'

Sawyer looked up. 'You really think a woman might have done this?'

'So you're saying that he might be mocking us?' said McBride. 'Hideous violence presented with lots of—'

'Garnish?' said Barlow.

Sawyer shifted the close-up image to Angela Holt's bruised neck and beaten face. 'No. I don't think that.'

The hammer. Crashing down. Heavy.

An ocean of blood. The afternoon heat, tainted by the tang of copper.

He jerked his gaze away. 'Have Rhodes check recurring CCTV and ANPR on major roads near to the deposition sites.'

'For all four victims?' said Shepherd.

Sawyer smiled. 'Let the sharing begin. Give him a couple of the civvies to work with. They can cover the ANPR, but I want his eagle eyes on the CCTV.'

'We've been working on a profile,' said Farrell.

Sawyer nodded. 'We?'

'Myself and DS Whittaker, in association with DI McBride and DI Barlow.'

Sawyer glanced at Keating. 'Is it in HOLMES?'

'Not yet.'

'So it's your own little secret? Been watching *Mindhunter*?'

'Sawyer...' Keating eyed him.

'I'm guessing you're the Holden figure, and Whittaker is Bill? In your head, anyway.'

Farrell glanced at Whittaker. 'I think this is in *your* head, DI Sawyer.'

'Profiling is sexy,' said Sawyer. 'But it's flawed, because it's based on interviews with psychopaths. Psychopaths lie. Instead of building up a composite bogeyman, I would suggest a more scientific approach. Go back to training college and focus on five key areas. One, the scenes. The murder scenes, the deposition scenes. Two, the nature of the attacks themselves. The MO, the unusual presentation. Three, the forensic evidence. Pure science. Four, the medical examinations. Five, the victimology and victim characteristics. Who were the victims and why were they targeted? And on point five, are there any similarities in victim acquisition?'

Barlow waved his pen in the air. 'All were missing for a couple of days before being found. The Manchester and Yorkshire victims both told their partners they were meeting friends. But I don't believe that was the case with the Nottingham woman?'

McBride spoke up. 'The Nottingham woman, that is, Laura Bertrand, went out to walk her dog and she didn't come home. The dog was found limping around the edges of her walking spot with blood on his collar and a couple of broken ribs. Must have been spooked and ran. The DNA test on the blood showed that it was human, but not Laura's. No match on NDNAD. No matching DNA retrieved from the other scenes.'

'Not much hope of a voluntary DNA drive for all the men,' said Barlow. 'Bit of a wide catchment area.'

'The dog must have bitten him,' said Sawyer. 'Looks like he gave it a kick and it bolted. At least we have the DNA profile in case we get a suspect to match.'

'Interesting that he changed his acquisition strategy after that,' said Whittaker. 'Too risky?'

'Refining his fantasy,' said Sawyer. 'You see it in most serial cases. The first one is messy, and they get better with each subsequent victim.'

'Let's do the conference first thing tomorrow,' said Keating. 'Get busy now, though. I would like to be able to offer something to our esteemed scrutineers.' He held a palm out to the four detectives. 'You're all working on your individual cases. My team here will focus on Angela Holt.'

'The freshest kill,' said Barlow.

McBride rolled her eyes. 'Please.'

Keating got to his feet. 'As I say, full cooperation. Strict process for all evidence, intelligence and actions.'

Sawyer swiped through the individual victim screens. 'They all look the same.'

Farrell scoffed. 'Bravo!'

Sawyer smiled, kept his eyes on the screen. 'Similar age, hair colour. They're not random. He went to them. He picked them out. But why them?' He looked up. 'We need to know more about these women. They're not just bodies. They used to be living, breathing people with loves, losses, hopes and fears, messy relationships. Like all of us.' He looked up. 'The murders ended their lives. They didn't define them.'

'Sir,' said Farrell, 'before we close, we do need to cover an uncomfortable aspect of this operation. One of the senior detectives has a significant media profile, and it's public knowledge that his stability has been brought into question. Is that not likely to compromise the investigation?'

Sawyer was back on the image of Angela Holt. 'Why didn't he take the bracelet?'

Keating leaned forward on the desk. 'I appreciate the comment, DCI Farrell. But I don't see why DI Sawyer's... eminence would be a matter of concern. We're all capable civil servants, and I suggest we stop worrying about past events and focus on stopping future crimes.'

Sawyer looked up from his screen. 'He wants this.'

'Wants what?' said McBride.

'He's killing hard targets, not easy prey. He's not interested in side benefits like jewellery or money. He's making it hard for himself, and hard for us to stop him.'

Whittaker nodded. 'By killing in different areas? Jurisdictions?'

'Or at least by depositing the bodies in different areas.' Sawyer swept a hand around the table. 'He wants *this*. The task force. He wants the best and brightest. He wants multiple forces working on him.'

'Why?' said Keating.

'He thinks he deserves it,' said McBride.

Sawyer looked at her. 'He thinks he's better than us.'

6

Julius Newton gathered his staff in the small meeting room in the basement of Sheffield's Institute of Arts Gallery. There were three men and three women: unpaid volunteers and students from nearby Hallam University.

Newton stood behind the seat at the head of the gleaming white central table and gestured towards the orange-and-white chairs. The volunteers all sat, apart from Newton, who leaned forward, resting his hands on the back of his chair. He was early thirties, bald by design, with a trimmed black beard. He wore khaki shorts and a loose black T-shirt with high sleeves that showed off his broad biceps.

He reached into his pocket and pulled out a large pair of glasses with heavy black frames. He slipped them on, and kept his eyes on the table as he spoke. 'Thank you all for your punctuality. The purpose of this evening is for you to familiarise yourself with the work we are presenting here next week.' Newton raised his head. 'You are all pioneers. This exhibition is the first of its kind in the north of England, and it's expected to draw plenty of visitors during its two-month run. You're all aware of the works themselves, and their origins, but I want you to experience them face to face, in the flesh, on the opening press night. It's crucial that you don't preload with analyses and assessments, which will all become diluted when expressed on the night. As Picasso said, "Art is the lie that makes us realise truth."' Newton thumped the spread fingers of his right hand down on the table, causing a few of the volunteers to startle. 'The truth must be revealed to you there and then.'

He stepped to the side and nodded to a transport trolley next to a large plinth, mounted on a corner table. The object on the plinth was several feet tall and wide, and hidden behind a white sheet that ran down to the floor.

'Outsider art can be challenging. The artists are all marginalised because of many factors. Mental health, transgressions, the political regimes in which they are forced to operate. Some are incarcerated, some have stolen to finance their work, or used stolen material to produce the work. This blanket obscures the centrepiece of the exhibition. A devastating piece produced by Hungarian artist, Ferenc Lamos.'

An older volunteer near the back raised his hand.

'Brad?'

'Isn't he the guy who does nothing but repeated renderings of the deposition of Christ?'

A colleague to his left nodded. 'Uses tar and etching, on reclaimed wood.'

Newton sighed. 'Indeed. Lamos sadly took his own life last year, but he donated his work to the foundation that is funding our exhibition. I am keeping this centrepiece under wraps for now, because it carries an extraordinary potency, and I would like you to be able...'

He paused. All of the volunteers had their phones out. Newton drove both his hands into the table, palms down.

'*Please*!'

This time, they all startled, and put away their phones.

'I'm sorry. I would ask you not to preview or pre-judge this work. It absolutely has to be seen first time, up close. Do not diminish its power by reducing it to just another Google image search. For now, I would like two of you to carefully position the piece in the section I've marked out on this floor.'

'I'll do it.' Brad rose and strode over to the corner table. He was tall and sinewy, with an elaborate neck tattoo.

'Me, too.' A younger, shorter man sprang up from his chair and joined Brad.

Newton shook his head, raised his hand. 'No, no. Rueben. Perhaps Anna—'

'I'm good.' Rueben steadied himself by the side of the plinth; Brad took the other side.

Newton edged around them, watching and waving his hands. 'Please, please. The artwork is securely fastened to the platform beneath, but you must be so careful.'

Rueben felt for a grip. 'It's hard because of the cloth. Can we just move it and cover it once it's in position? Like all the others.'

'Looks like an exhibition of old-school ghosts out there,' said Brad.

'*No*!' Newton was red faced and shrill, almost shrieking. 'I have to insist—'

Brad lifted his side of the plinth, testing it for weight. As he did so, Rueben tried to do the same, but tilted his side back too far and the cloth caught beneath his trainer. It fell down, revealing a huge block of scruffy dark wood with a plate of lighter wood hammered into its centre. The image, rendered in black oil or tar with flecks of amber, showed a crowd of anguished women and disciples taking a lifeless Christ down from a crucifix that had been scratched into the wood's surface and highlighted with a rich red substance that looked suspiciously like blood. It was a crude but effective sight, elevated to a disturbing degree by the expression on Christ's face: eyes impossibly wide and anguished, mouth open; a frozen rage against his agony and betrayal.

'Sorry, sorry.' Rueben struggled to gather up the cloth and re-cover the picture.

Newton stared at it for a few seconds. He raised his hands to cover his eyes, then dragged them down his cheeks in unison, as if wiping away tears. He repeated the motion several times, and gave a low moan of despair, rising in volume with each swipe. 'No, no, no, no!' He was breathing deeply, too quickly, almost hyperventilating.

The volunteers looked at each other. Brad stepped forward. 'Julius. Are you—'

Newton spun away and crashed through a side door, out into the muggy evening. He hurried down a passage to the back of the gallery and crouched by a line of recycling bins, facing the wire mesh fence that looked out across Pond Street. With shaking fingers he lit a menthol cigarette, taking short, frequent drags, fixating on the red and blue lights of the sports centre, waiting for the trembling to stop.

7

‘Ladies and gentlemen.’

The room fell silent. Keating shuffled in his seat at the centre of a table cluttered with microphones and mini recorders. He was in full uniform, flanked by Sawyer and Shepherd, with the other detectives seated at two separate tables, either side. Four poster-size photos had been fixed to the wall behind. The victims smiled down on the scene: a forward scrum of photographers, several rows of seated reporters, and a tight cluster of TV cameras and junior officers near the media room double doors. Stephen Bloom, the tall, Nordic-looking media relations manager stood at Keating’s shoulder, in a fitted powder-blue suit with pink polka dot tie.

‘Thank you for your attendance today,’ said Keating. ‘We are here to announce a major police initiative, which I hope will receive your full cooperation. In the early hours of Friday morning, the body of thirty-six-year-old Angela Holt was found in woodland near the Dovedale and Thorpe Cloud area of Derbyshire. We are treating this as a murder enquiry, and we have strong reason to believe that the perpetrator was also responsible for similar crimes committed over the past year in Yorkshire, Nottinghamshire and Greater Manchester.

'As a result, we are today launching Operation Orca, a multi-area task force comprising senior detectives from those jurisdictions, as well as key staff from the Major Investigation Team here in Derbyshire. We believe that pooling our resources and intelligence will lead to the swift apprehension of the person responsible.'

A familiar voice rose up from the front row. 'Dean Logan, *Derbyshire Times*. What makes you believe the crimes are linked?' Logan was large and loud; an ex-Wapping hack who had bagged the exclusive interview which had sent Sawyer's story national. He rose slightly from his seat as he spoke, and stayed half-standing, compelling Keating to address him directly.

'Dean, you know I can't compromise the investigation by answering that question at the moment. We are channelling the expertise of four major police forces into this operation. We'll be collating, consulting, sharing everything. I'm confident that we have some of the best brains in English policing at our disposal, and we will soon be able to apprehend the person behind these appalling crimes.'

A female voice from the back. 'Roz Hudson, *Mirror Online*. When will you be giving updates?'

Keating brushed something off his uniform jacket. 'When we have something to report. For now, I would like to issue an appeal to everyone. Ask yourself about the people you share your life with. Family, close friends. Are they behaving strangely? Are they out at odd hours, with unconvincing explanations? I would of course particularly appeal for information in the case of Angela Holt, as her murder is the most recent. Did you know Angela? Have you seen her or had contact with her over the past few days? Are you aware of anyone who might have wanted to harm her? Please come forward with any information on this case and the others, no matter how small. Contact details will be provided, and you can also find them on the dedicated website we have set up at Operation Orca dot com. All contact will be treated with the utmost confidentiality. These crimes have taken the lives of four women in the prime of their lives, and they have devastated their friends and families to a degree most of us here can barely imagine.'

Sawyer's phone vibrated in his pocket.

Logan rose again. 'What progress have you made so far?'

Keating screwed up his face, staying just the right side of flippant. 'We have only just set up the operation, Dean.'

'Of course. But the detectives from the other forces who have joined you. What progress have they made?'

Sawyer glanced at his phone screen beneath the table. Message from Eva Gregory.

Saturday? Dinner? x

'We have several lines of enquiry that we're currently pursuing and I really can't say any more at this stage. If any of you would like access to the individual detectives, then please speak to Stephen. For now, we ask that you let us focus on apprehending a dangerous criminal, and we will keep you fully informed of all developments.'

Sawyer tapped out a reply.

Busy Saturday. Wrestling lions. Monday? I'll call. x

Another reporter waved a hand. 'Taylor Fenway, *The Guardian*. How can we help if you can't give us any information on why you're linking the crimes, or any detail on the recent case?'

Keating nodded and pondered for a second. 'We're all helping each other. We owe it to these women to put aside agendas and work together. The police, the public and you guys in the way you report the crimes.'

Logan scoffed. 'And how would you like us to report the crimes, DSI Keating?'

'Ignore them,' said Sawyer, still looking down at his phone.

Logan turned to him. 'What?'

Sawyer raised his head and took a breath. 'Don't glamourise the crime. Drop this idea that some of you have already raised: the New Ripper.'

'We can't just ignore the similarities,' said Logan. 'As you well know, DI Sawyer, the media is still a powerful tool.'

Sawyer set down his phone and smiled at him. 'In my case, the media exposure has been centred on events that were out of my control. This is different. Although we don't quite have the full picture yet, it's clear that we're dealing with someone motivated by ego. He's a narcissist. That means the more press reports he reads that elevate him to some kind of folk devil status, the more you feed his ego, and the more young women you put at risk. Don't make him exotic or notorious. Don't give him a nickname, an alias. Just call him what he is. A murderer.'

He turned his head and addressed the BBC-branded TV camera at the centre of the room.

'To whoever is responsible for these killings. Hand yourself in. Give up. There's still time. You've committed horrendous acts, but if you stop now, then you will at least be seen as someone who did the right thing in the end. You are unwell, and whatever inner demon is compelling you to violence, the first step in silencing its voice is to remove yourself from temptation and submit yourself to professional help... while you still have the freedom to make that choice for yourself.'

8

Dale Strickland shouldered his way through the bodies packed into the tiny corporate office in the Rainbow Rooms Community Centre. He was shorter than average, fortyish, with heavy-framed glasses and an even crop of grey hair. Dale was suited, but the heat of the morning had pre-baked the building, and he had pocketed his tie. The audience parted as he passed through, helped aside by a huge, square-jawed assistant.

'Good morning to you all!' He raised his hands in the air and applauded, like a footballer acknowledging his fans. A group near the door returned the gesture with applause and a few whoops. As Dale reached a desk at the front of the room, a blond man in a fitted suit stepped forward and shook his hand. Dale turned to face the room, and the blond man stood beside the hulk, adjusted his tie and mopped his brow with a light blue handkerchief.

A young woman in a pink T-shirt handed Dale a black plastic crate. He beamed, flipped it over and settled it on the floor in a patch of space by the desk. He caught the blond man's eye for a second, then stepped up onto the crate, raising him several inches above most of the audience.

'Friends. I'll keep this short.'

Camera clicks and whirrs, a few flashes.

'I'm here to begin a journey. It is my hope and aim that this journey will end with nothing less than a once great city being born again.'

Applause and whoops from the back, and now a few of the other observers close to Dale.

'And, of course, I do not use the term lightly. Your charity, Rebirth, has an incredible record of support and rehabilitation for those afflicted with substance abuse issues. Your work reaches out much wider than the Greater Manchester area, and you shame the nation by setting a standard that cannot be matched, even in the capital. If elected Manchester mayor, I will model that standard and ensure that it's fully applied to the acute areas of need here in the city centre, and I will also take it out to the boroughs. Bury, Oldham, Rochdale, Stockport.'

He paused, and rubbed two fingers through the groove between his frown lines.

'Why?' He lowered his voice for effect. 'Because I am tired. I am tired of party politics. Politicians gaming the system for the good of themselves, for the good of their parties. I want to do what's good for the people. I am tired of those who find themselves at the fringes of our society being demonised for wanting to escape a reality that has been created by draconian government policy.'

Murmurs of assent.

'Labour. Conservative. Liberal. These are outdated ideologies with outdated ideas. Ideology is for the privileged few to argue over, as they swan around their elitist Westminster circles, serving nobody but themselves.'

The large man leaned in to the blond man and whispered. 'He already made that point.'

The blond man smiled. 'Repetition is good.'

'We need to move away from left and right, and focus on everyday people and everyday struggles. I fully accept that I have made mistakes in my personal life. I have struggled with the consequences of poor choices. Who hasn't? But this is why, unlike the other candidates, I am uniquely qualified to address this rotten system from within, and build something stronger and *enduring*.'

He pointed towards a sandwich board set up at the side, which carried a bright campaign poster: an image of Dale looking regal and inspired, above the legend, *FOR LASTING CHANGE, CHOOSE STRICKLAND.*

'I am not an idealist. I'm not saying that we can create a perfect society. There will always be people who choose to work outside of the law, who don't care about the law. And for those, we have to give the police the resources they need to do their jobs properly, like solving the terrible local murders we have seen recently, and highlighted by the police at their conference yesterday.' He beat a fist onto his chest, over his heart. 'I have masses of respect for our police. I've encountered many police officers in my time.' He angled his head, gave a sheepish smile. 'Perhaps a few too many. The vast majority are wonderful, hard-working people. But there are too many who seem more interested in their own careers and media profiles than they are in the lives of the citizens they are paid to serve.'

He glanced back at the blond man, who made a subtle wind-it-up gesture with his finger.

'So, I promised I would be brief. And I'll close by saying that I'm not here to change the whole world. But we have to start somewhere. And I choose to start up here in the north of England, which is too often dismissed as backward and irrelevant by the London elites who base their media companies here to take advantage of cheap rents, but give nothing back into the local economy.'

Loud applause.

Dale lowered his voice again. 'I stand here today as an independent candidate. But I hope to visit you again soon, as the new mayor of Greater Manchester, where I promise that I will be the one who gives something back. I will pledge fifteen percent of my salary to homeless and abuse charities like Rebirth, to make sure that the work I start will be seen through. To help those in their time of need, to give them the strength and strategy to help themselves, and to make our city, up here in the north of England, the envy of our failing leaders in the south. Thank you.'

A sustained burst of applause. Dale stepped off the crate and handed it back to the woman in the pink T-shirt. The large man held back the audience and made way for Dale to walk through to the exit, shaking a few hands on the way. The blond man followed, handing out promotional cards.

Outside, the blond man held open the back door of a white Mercedes. Dale gave a short wave to the crowd and ducked inside. The large man stepped in to the driver's seat, and the blond man took the passenger side.

When the doors were all closed, Dale took a sip from a bottle of water and gazed at the branch of Betfred outside his window.

The big man glanced up into his rear-view mirror. 'Where to?'

Dale caught his eye. 'Far, far away, Hector.'

The blond man fiddled with his phone. 'Salford Quays. Business school meet and greet. Get the fucking air-con on, will you? I'm sweating like a rapist.'

The car pulled away. Dale kept his eyes on the street, at the crumbling pubs and takeaways, the hair salons and bait shops. An ambient chill seeped around the interior. He tipped back his head and closed his eyes. 'Any word from Fletcher?'

The blond man looked up from his phone. 'Haven't seen him since late last year. We had a tip that he's back in the country, though.'

Dale opened his dark eyes. 'You sound more Scottish when you're sugar-coating, Marco.'

Marco pocketed his phone. 'We haven't heard anything else.'

'I'd like a word. Find him. Whoever gave you the tip, find out who told him. Repeat until Fletcher.'

Marco nodded. 'Sawyer still has that gun. And he knows that we know. We're fucking hog-tied. It connects you, us, to Shaun. It's insurance. He probably has the location in his will or something, so if we do get to him, he can fuck us from beyond the grave.'

Dale closed his eyes again. 'And we're certain that they can match bullet to gun? You didn't just see it on *CSI: Las Vegas* or something?'

'Rifling,' said Hector. 'Each gun barrel is unique. They get the gun, they fire another bullet. They compare.'

'It's still not enough to connect it to me personally,' said Dale.

Marco shrugged. 'Maybe not. But any investigation will compromise the campaign. Shit sticks. He might be saving it up for a crunch moment. He'll know you're running.'

'Find Fletcher.' Dale's voice took on a flinty tone. 'We know he wants to finish the job, and he's probably been tracking Sawyer for a while now, to make sure he gets it right the second time.' He took a long slug of water. 'Follow Sawyer. He should lead you to Fletcher.'

9

Shepherd hauled himself out of the Mini. 'You're definitely improving.'

Sawyer locked the car and led the way up the cobble-edged path to the faded red front door of a three-storey house. 'A patient, better driver?'

Shepherd looked at him. 'I wouldn't go that far.' He rang the bell. 'And I take it back. I am worried. You're quoting Radiohead.'

They waited. The house was upscale and recently built, slightly out of character for the surroundings: the storage outbuildings of a working dairy farm. A detached annexe housed a popular local farm shop, and a promotional board for Bradwell's ice cream lay flat outside the closed door of the shop.

The faint sound of a fussing child escaped through an open second-floor window. It was mid-morning, but the temperature had already reached the point where any prolonged exertion brought on a light sweat.

'Storms forecast for next week,' said Shepherd.

Sawyer rolled his phone around in his pocket. 'And where's this? Fantasyland?'

'No. Seriously. They're saying it's going to break.'

Sawyer nodded up at the piercing blue sky, and flinched at the sunlight. 'Right.'

Shepherd shouldered off his jacket. 'Christ, I feel like an ant under a magnifying glass.'

The door opened, and an elderly man in a saggy white shirt peered around the gap. 'More police?'

They fumbled for warrant cards, but the man let the door swing open, and was already halfway back down the hall by the time they entered.

'It's quite alright. I know police when I see them. In there.' He pointed towards a room to the left, as he began a slow ascent of a central staircase.

Sawyer and Shepherd walked through into a huge, but under-furnished sitting room. An open bay window looked out on the farmland that tilted down to Alstonefield and Milldale.

In the centre of the room, three artisanal armchairs sat adjacent to an expensive-looking vermillion sofa. A balding fortysomething man sat in one of the armchairs, tapping at an iPad. He was drawn and haggard, barefoot in shorts and T-shirt stretched over an ample girth.

'Lewis Holt?'

The man startled at Sawyer's voice. 'Yes? Hello. Can I... We've just spoken to the police. Well, the family liaison people. Patricia and Maggie. They were... I appreciate their...' He looked down at the iPad screen for help.

Sawyer stepped forward. 'I'm Detective Inspector Jake Sawyer. This is Detective Sergeant Ed Shepherd. I'm so sorry for your loss.'

The man stared at Sawyer, curious. A few long seconds passed before he found his voice again. 'Of course. Thank you. What can I do to help?' He spoke in guttural Glaswegian, and his diction was scattered and halting, as if the words tasted strange in his mouth. 'Can I get you something to drink? Tea? Water? Something stronger? Oh, but you're on duty—'

'Thank you,' said Shepherd. 'We're fine. Would you mind if we asked you a few questions?'

Holt sighed and hung his head. 'What more do you need to know? The lasses before, they were lovely. But I'm all talked out.' He waved a hand. 'I'm sorry, I'm sorry. No problem. Of course. Take a seat.'

Sawyer parked at the head of the sofa, nearest Holt, while Shepherd took one of the chairs opposite. 'I know this is incredibly difficult, Mr Holt. But you can help us to catch the person who harmed Angela, and make sure it doesn't happen to—'

'I keep hearing this!' Holt threw back his head. 'I don't give a *fuck* about the other people it doesn't happen to, yes? I gave a fuck about Angela, and now she's dead. It's already too late to help her.'

Shepherd inched to the edge of his chair. 'Mr Holt. I'm—'

'Exactly,' said Sawyer.

Holt looked up. 'What?'

'Exactly. It's too late for Angela. You can't help her. But you can help the person, just like you, who will soon be in the same position if we can't catch the perpetrator. You have the power to control what happens to whoever caused her harm. So you should give a fuck, Mr Holt. Surely Angela would want you to?'

Thrown, Holt glanced at Shepherd, then scowled at Sawyer.

A thud from upstairs, and the sound of the child again. Full-throated crying, this time.

'Is that a relative who answered the door?' said Shepherd. 'You have a young daughter, right?'

'Yes. Rosie. She's eight. She's autistic. That's my dad, trying to keep her calm. She's not good with change. No lamb curry for dinner on Friday. A different-shaped glass for her bedtime milk. Mummy not coming home. Angie's parents moved to the US a few years ago. They can't make it back. So it's just me and my dad. My sister is coming to help tomorrow. I could pay for someone, but...'

Something in the tone of the crying tugged at Sawyer: the way it peaked and waned like a siren, from screaming to sobbing and back again. He had heard it before, long ago. As the noise settled, he felt a pang so physical he had to deflect with an empty question. 'Is this your house?'

Holt squinted at him. 'Yes. We built it ourselves a few years ago. Angie's business took off when we got it online, and we bought up a few farm shops. She liked this one best, so we settled here.'

'On Tuesday, the night when you say you last saw her, did Angela say where she was going?'

Holt turned his attention to the iPad again. 'No. She never did.'

Shepherd caught Sawyer's eye. 'So this wasn't unusual?'

'She said she was having a drink with friends. That's what she always said.'

'And the next morning,' said Sawyer, 'you reported her missing. So it wasn't unusual for her not to tell you where she was going and then not come home—'

'No!' Holt jerked his head up. 'She always came home. Sometimes pretty late, but she always came home. That's the unusual part. I was a bit worried when it got late, but I'd had a few drinks, must have dropped off.'

Sawyer shifted position. 'Were you happily married, Mr Holt?'

Holt scoffed. 'Y'don't miss much, eh? We had what you might call an open relationship. We saw other people. It was mostly her seeing the other people, but I suppose these things never work out equal. Since the wee one was born, I put on a bit of weight.' He looked out of the window. 'Things change, y'know? We wanted to stay together. Still there for each other, but just not *together* together.'

Shepherd took out his notepad. 'And you were both happy with that?'

Holt shrugged. 'We agreed, yeah. I suppose one person always wants more of one thing than the other person. But like all relationships, you meet somewhere in the middle.'

'And yourself?' said Sawyer. 'Are you seeing anyone at the moment?'

'No, I'm not. There's been a few complications with the business. New franchise not happening. Just admin. It's been taking a lot of my time.'

Sawyer moved to the side, trying to get a look at Holt's iPad screen. 'I'm sure you can appreciate that I'm wondering about potential jealousies. Complications with partners you might have had. Were you always honest with people about the situation? Did you both let them know you were technically with someone?'

'Depends.' Holt rocked back on his chair and pushed himself forward, just about making it to his feet. He took down a bottle of Black Label whisky from a shelf and poured himself a measure. 'You can find people who don't care either way. Usually they're the ones with something to lose if the truth comes out. There are ways of meeting people in that situation. It keeps it sort of... equal.'

'Ways of meeting people? You mean online?'

'Of course.'

'Do you know how Angela met people?'

He sipped his whisky. 'No idea. That was part of our arrangement. We never talk about it.'

'So, "having a drink with friends" was a euphemism.'

'Yes. Sometimes it could just be having a drink with friends, though.'

More sobbing from upstairs. Sawyer took a breath. 'I'd be keen to know how Angela met people, Mr Holt. Did she have a personal computer?'

'Yeah. Laptop. But it's passworded.'

Sawyer pushed out a smile. 'We can work around that.'

On the drive back to Buxton, Sawyer and Shepherd were silent for the first few minutes. As they slowed for a crossroads, Sawyer turned to Shepherd. 'Work with Maggie, and Walker. Find Angela's friends. Maybe she did go for a drink with them, but then met someone else. Just find out more about her. Who she was, how she lived. The unfiltered version. I'll drop you at the station.'

Shepherd nodded. 'And where might I find you?'

'A few things are bothering me. I'm going to seek some answers from an old friend.'

10

The lift rattled down the shaft at Sheffield's Northern General Teaching Hospital. It wheezed to a halt at the basement level and the lift doors jerked open. Sawyer stepped out into the warren of joyless corridors—flaking paint, fossilised fittings—and followed a familiar route, past the chemical storeroom into a refurbished lobby area lined with unlabelled side rooms and admin offices. His nose twitched at the smell of cooked food: something meaty.

A young woman in sharp business dress looked up from a tidy desk and beamed at him. 'Hello! I remember you.'

Sawyer smiled. 'Haven't been down here for a while.'

'Oh, I remember everybody.'

'Gina?'

'That's right! Isn't it lovely when someone remembers your name, Detective Sawyer?'

'Makes you think we might not be living in a simulation, after all.'

Gina glanced up to the left, then back again at Sawyer. 'I've never really thought of it like that, but yes. I see what you mean. Are you down here to escape the heat?'

'No, but it is cooler.'

'Oh, it's a joy, isn't it? We're obliged to maintain a certain temperature, but it's obviously an advantage to be so far beneath the surface. Frazer is in his office. I'll let him—'

'He knows I'm coming,' said Sawyer.

She reached across to her desk and handed Sawyer a brown McDonald's bag. 'Would you mind taking his lunch? It should still be warm, but let me know if he wants me to give it a blast in the microwave.'

Sawyer took the bag and headed down the corridor. He stopped at a door marked *F. DRUMMOND* and tapped out a light knock. No answer. He tried the handle and the door opened to reveal a small austere office with a single desk and chair, a row of filing cabinets and a corkboard propped against the wall by the desk. A window in the connecting door revealed the mortuary and autopsy room: overhead lamps, metal gurney, a wall of body drawers. An immense man stood before a rack of coat hooks near a metal sink. He wore a short-sleeved brown shirt, and was shiny-bald, with a dense grey beard and semi-rimless glasses. He removed an apron, deposited something into a chemical waste bin and washed his hands.

Sawyer set down the McDonald's bag on the desk and took a seat. He opened an app on his phone: *Mario Kart Tour*. The game ran through its opening copyright and credit screens and gave a loud ping as the Nintendo logo appeared.

Frazer Drummond walked through from the autopsy room into the office. He grunted at the sight of Sawyer. 'Still playing kids' games, eh?'

'Just young at heart.'

Drummond gave a weak laugh. 'This is big news, Sawyer. You have a heart?' He slotted a folder into one of the cabinets. 'I'd always thought of you as a bit of a tin man.' He pivoted, and trained his pale blue eyes on Sawyer, staring down from close to seven feet. 'It fits, actually. I'm feeling unusually paternal towards you today.'

Sawyer closed the game and leaned back in the chair. 'To what do I owe the honour of your affection, Frazer?'

'The milk of human kindness.' Drummond took out another folder and closed the cabinet. He strode over to his desk, the footfalls rippling through Sawyer's chair legs, then yanked over his own chair and fell into it. 'I would respectfully suggest that you have a fucker of a job on your hands here.' He tore open the brown bag, unwrapped his burger, and scattered the fries over the paper.

Drummond demolished almost half of the burger with his first bite.

'Friday treat?' said Sawyer. 'Or a regular order?'

'Sophia's gone vegan; Ben and Emma have followed. I play along at home and get my reptile pleasures here. You've had quite the time. Catching killers and child abductors.' He smeared some ketchup over the paper and scraped a few fries across it. 'I was sorry to hear about your father. Hell of a story. And extraordinary how you managed to put it all together.' He tossed in a mouthful of fries, spoke as he chewed. 'I take it you've been on leave? State-sponsored shrink?'

Sawyer nodded. 'Couldn't stay away forever, though. I missed the glamour. Good to hear the family is well.'

Drummond raised his head from the papers and glared at Sawyer over the top of his glasses.

Sawyer leaned forward, angled his head. 'I thought we might be drifting into the arena of forgiveness by now.'

Drummond took a few sheets of paper out of the folder. 'Only God forgives.'

Sawyer sat back, nodded at the folder. 'Angela?'

'The hair was removed quickly. Pretty crude. Sharp knife. No stab wounds, though. Couple of nicks on her shoulder but no defensive wounds.'

'The hair is his trophy. He took some from the other three victims.'

Drummond took another bite of his burger. 'Ah, yes. Operation Orca. Where do you get these crazy names from?'

'There's a database. It randomises from hundreds of options. We check for any unfortunate connotations and go with it.'

Drummond chewed, stared at Sawyer. 'Your man, Farrell. He's given me access to the HOLMES section on the other three victims. Haven't had a chance to look yet. I'll pop any findings into the system. You know, you probably think I'm a bit of a dinosaur at heart, but this really does it for me. Private database. Shared intelligence. Keeps the human contact to a minimum.' He turned back to the folder. 'Lacerations. Anal and vaginal. Not the same blade as he used for the hair. The tearing isn't neat. He used something on her. Something corrugated. Maybe a candlestick.'

'Time of death?'

'Rigor, lividity... Not too long before he dumped her. If she went missing on the Tuesday but was found on Thursday... Judging by stomach contents, he didn't bother to feed her.'

'Cause?'

Drummond shook his head. 'Asphyxiation. He strangled her. Thumb impressions plus evidence of cerebral hypoxia. Also, regional venous obstruction. Pinpoint haemorrhages in the skin. Conjunctiva of the eyes and the organs above the point of constriction. Major bruising around the front of the neck, trachea partially crushed. She would have lost consciousness in twenty seconds or so, depending on the pressure and severity of the strangulation. Then, after two or three minutes keeping up the pressure, you get brain death, and the lights go out for a good minute or two after that.' Drummond frowned. 'He broke her jaw. She also had a few dislocated neck vertebrae, probably from the force of the blow or blows. The knuckle impressions show he hit her with his fists, not an object. And he was wearing gloves. There's a few tiny fragments that look like brown leather embedded in her skin, but I doubt it's anything you could work with.'

Sawyer nodded. Drummond's office was starting to feel small, enclosing. 'What about the bite marks?'

'Oh, yes. Some around the face and neck, quite a few around the thighs and buttocks. Given their depth, I'd argue they were established post mortem. And don't get excited about matching bite impressions to dental records. Those forensic odontologist fuckers... They're as bad as homeopaths. It's pseudoscience. Catnip for the credulous. A bite impression isn't unique. It's not like your fingerprint or your DNA, and it's been shown that people have been convicted and even executed on faulty bite mark evidence.'

Sawyer's breath quickened. He knew the flashes would come soon, and hoped he could get out of this subterranean shoebox first. 'Could you take a look at the other cases later today? See if anything stands out or doesn't match?'

Drummond nodded and took another bite of burger. He consulted one of the papers. 'There are deep impressions around the back of the neck, bruising to the back left and right side. I'd say he beat her until she was either unconscious or senseless, then gripped the back of her neck.'

An overlay of his brother, right there in the room, crawling through the blood-spattered grass.

'So, he strangles her...'

His dog, terribly wounded, but still barking. Hoarse and hopeless.

'...and he violates her with this object...'

His mother, reaching out. But he can't help.

'...then he cuts off her hair...'

He can't get to her.

Drummond crumpled the paper bag in a loud, single motion, shocking Sawyer out of his reverie. 'And here's the really strange thing. Not a drop of semen. No excitement. No obvious evidence of direct sexual contact, at least not in a specific sexual context. I'll get toxicology to Sally tomorrow, just to be sure, but that must tell you something about our new friend.' Drummond took off his glasses and screwed up his eyes, pinching at the bridge of his nose. 'There's a lot of violence here, Sawyer. Excessive.'

Sawyer forced himself to take slow, steady breaths. 'Is there a right amount?'

'I mean, there's more than he needs to use to subdue. I'm not a psychologist, but I'm going to take a wild guess and say we're dealing with someone who isn't too keen on women.'

11

Keating took his seat at the head of the MIT conference room. Sawyer and Shepherd sat along one side of the table, while Walker, Myers and Moran took the other. The individual monitors showed Keating's video and audio feed in a large box, which dominated the upper half of the display, while smaller boxes containing the feeds of the other five sat in a row across the bottom. Keating tapped and swiped at his screen, and the faces of the four virtual attendees joined the row: Farrell, Whittaker, Barlow and McBride.

Keating squinted into his screen. 'Gentlemen, and lady. Are we all hearing and seeing each other okay?' Nods and waves. 'I assume you've all had time to digest the response to the press conference?'

As Farrell spoke, his feed box replaced Keating's as the largest. 'Looks like your grandstanding had quite an effect, DI Sawyer. Plenty of splashes about "The New Ripper" and how we're "baffled". I see your own Mr Logan has filed a piece in the *Derbyshire Times*, focusing on Angela Holt, and another for *The Mirror*. Both pretty light on our pleas for public vigilance, but heavy on speculation about methods, who might be next, et cetera.'

McBride's feed box replaced Farrell's. 'The info twisted and taken out of context, of course.'

Keating sighed. 'We have to get used to an uncomfortable truth here. We need the media. I can't have any hint of antagonism or any sense of us and them. It's more asymmetric than symbiotic, but a mutual trust can only help us. We should keep the channels open, and offer regular feedback. I don't want to give anyone the impression that we're conducting this investigation in a vacuum. That was one of the mistakes made by the Yorkshire Ripper enquiry.'

A few seconds of silence. The nine boxes beneath Keating's feed seemed momentarily suspended. A silent chorus.

'We spoke to Angela Holt's husband,' said Sawyer. 'Their domestic situation was colourful, and there could be something in the people they've encountered as part of their open relationship.'

Walker shuffled in his seat. He glanced at Moran and Myers. 'I'm filing this into HOLMES after this meeting, but I spoke to a couple of Angela's friends, who say she arrived in a taxi at The Manifold Inn on Tuesday evening, around 7pm. They had something to eat and a few drinks. She left early and wouldn't tell them where she was going. They say they teased her about a hot date and she was coy about it.'

'No CCTV there,' said Shepherd. 'Barely any internet down in the valley.'

'What did Angela drink?' said Sawyer.

Walker looked around the faces. 'Uh... glass of wine, I think. Pretty sure. I'll double-check when I file it.'

'We have her laptop,' said Sawyer. 'And we've been

looking for possible connections, contacts. According to our data ninja, Karl Rhodes, she spent a lot of time on a website called *Secret Encounters*.'

'Dating?' said Barlow.

Sawyer nodded. 'Sort of.' He glanced at Keating. 'Extramarital dating.'

'Yeah,' said Walker. 'It's for people who want to meet up, but privately.'

Moran frowned. 'To have affairs?'

'I suppose you can get anything online, these days,' said Sawyer.

Shepherd cut in. 'We need to check the previous victims' device histories for matches from Angela Holt's activity. Rhodes is trying to break through some encryptions, but I'll make sure it goes into HOLMES as soon as he's finished.'

Walker raised his hand, lowered it. 'I looked through the victimology interviews from Laura Bertrand. No parallels there.'

'He changed his acquisition method after he attacked her,' said Sawyer. 'After the dog bite.'

Walker nodded. 'Dianne Walton and Hannah Lane are more interesting, though. Dianne's boyfriend was away and she hadn't been to their flat for a couple of days. She messaged him and he was worried, but thought her phone might have been broken. When he got back, she wasn't there.'

Whittaker spoke up. 'Yes, and Hannah's husband said they'd been having problems with the relationship, but they were having counselling, trying to make it work. We found a couple of similar websites on her computer. *Extramarital*, and something called *Dark Strangers*.'

'It's the usual problem, though,' said Farrell. 'The sites

are based internationally, so there's no chance of getting login details or access to message histories.'

'And Angela Holt didn't visit those sites.' Sawyer swiped at his screen and accessed the forensic report section of HOLMES, maintained by Sally O'Callaghan. 'CCTV? ANPR?'

'Rhodes is still working through it,' said Shepherd.

Sawyer nodded. 'Sally's toxicology report for Angela Holt shows no alcohol, no drugs, no direct sexual contact. But she had a glass of wine with friends. So even if she drank more after leaving the Manifold, she must have been alcohol-free for a few hours before she was murdered. So where did he take her? Where did he keep her?'

'What else did Sally get from the site and searches?' said McBride.

Sawyer shook his head. 'Not much. The flowers were picked wild from nearby, and the material for the fabric has no distinguishing markings or anything that could help us source it. Line search uncovered a flattened cigarette end. Hard to call on its freshness, but we've taken a DNA profile. The smoker isn't in NDNAD and the profile doesn't match the Laura Bertrand dog-bite blood.'

One of the civilian volunteers—a squat fiftysomething man in a clammy-looking polo shirt—tapped on the conference room door and entered. 'Sorry to disturb, sir. But as you're all meeting, I thought you should hear this immediately. We've just received an anonymous email at the Operation Orca address, with a YouTube link. I'm the only one who has heard the file. I've checked it for malware and forwarded the link to the conference message centre.'

Keating nodded. 'Thank you, Phil.' He tapped on the red figure '1' that had appeared by a speech bubble icon at the bottom of his screen. He accessed the link in the message, and the system's browser opened a YouTube page with the title *Greetings!* and a blank thumbnail image.

'It seems to be audio only,' said Phil, before retreating and closing the door behind him.

Keating selected the *Broadcast To All* option and played the video.

'Good evening.' A male voice sounded from the conference table's central speaker. It was deep and confident, but heavily distorted by digital processing. 'I'm sorry to be the bearer of bad news, but I must confess, I'm quite enjoying myself and I have no intention of stopping anytime soon. But now you've all got together, you probably think it's only a matter of time before I slip up or you find a way to track me down.' The speaker paused, and took a few slow breaths. 'Well. I'm sorry to say, that isn't going to happen. You see, I won't be slipping up, and you're not going to track me down. Not even with the help of your "hero cop".'

Sawyer raised his head and caught Keating's eye.

'Detective Inspector Jake Sawyer. It's an honour to know that a man of your pedigree is on my trail. I hope you're listening to this, because I've got a special request, and with such a special policeman like yourself on the case, I feel confident that my request will be fulfilled. I've included the details of how to do so in the description text of this audio, but in brief, I will require a Bitcoin payment of ten thousand pounds by ten o'clock tomorrow morning. I may be many things, Detective Sawyer, but I'm not greedy. I see this as an insurance payment. If it is not forthcoming, then...'

The speaker paused for a few seconds; the conference room was quiet but for his slow, juddering breaths.

'If I do not receive this payment within the given time limit, then I will soon be taking another... bite.'

12

Sawyer and Shepherd stood before Keating's empty desk. A scrawny man with a tidy moustache sat at the table by the window, peering into a laptop screen, taking occasional taps at the keyboard. Sawyer edged to the left, stealing a little of the overhead air con stream from Shepherd.

Keating bustled in from the conference room. 'We'll take another remote briefing tomorrow morning, and they're all coming in person on Monday.' He crashed down into his seat and spoke to the man in the corner. 'Anything from the video?'

Karl Rhodes didn't look up. 'It's only audio, on top of a blank image. He took it down half an hour after uploading, but I've cloned it and captured the details he left in the description.'

Sawyer walked over to Rhodes and peered over his shoulder at the screen. 'Strange that he would ask for money now. If money is his motivation, why not do it after the first murder?'

'Is he a chancer?' said Keating.

Rhodes shook his head. 'Pretty sharp for a chancer. His

instructions for the Bitcoin transfer show that he knows his way round the systems.'

'The reference to taking another "bite" seemed specific,' said Shepherd. 'The marks on the bodies. That's a detail we've never made public.'

Keating sighed. 'Could be idiomatic. A coincidence.'

'He paused before he said it.' Sawyer moved to the window and looked down at the football stadium, the green turf muddied by late afternoon shadow. 'He wanted us to hear the significance.'

'Do we make it public?' said Shepherd. 'Someone might recognise the voice.'

'Good luck with that,' said Rhodes. 'Sounds like he's put it through quite a few filters. YouTube reprocesses audio file uploads to limit memory use. And they don't keep the originals. I'll do what I can to clean it up, but it's like trying to rebuild a shredded document while wearing boxing gloves.' He snapped the laptop shut and sprang to his feet.

Sawyer turned. 'It's more like the payment demand is part of his taunting. Like he doesn't want the money. He just wants to show us that he's the boss. And he'll know that we'll be concerned about him going public, because of the pressure it would put on us. That's probably his next move if we don't pay.'

'He mentions you by name, Sawyer,' said Rhodes. 'Could this be someone you've pissed off in the past?'

'We'd need a whole new task force to examine potential suspects on that theory,' said Keating.

Rhodes paused at the door and surveyed the office, the civilian volunteer desks. 'Anyone want a look at the passive data? I've been raking through the details for all of the victims so far. The old computers are still down in the batcave. Stinks a bit, but it's cool down there.'

'Hell of a sell,' said Shepherd.

Keating tapped his desk. 'You go, Sawyer. I want a quick word with Shepherd.' Sawyer caught his eye. 'About the in-the-flesh meeting on Monday.'

Rhodes grinned. 'Just the two of us, Sawyer. Like old times.'

Sawyer and Rhodes took the lift down to the ground floor, then shuffled down a narrow stone staircase to Rhodes's old basement office.

Rhodes unlocked the door and flicked on the pale light. The room was cramped and musty, with the continuous hiss of server cooler fans. Most of the equipment had been boxed up for the short journey to Rhodes's new office on the top floor, but he had retained a temporary workstation at a wall-mounted desk in the corner.

He wheeled out a rickety office chair and fired up a boxy PC. 'Grab a pew. Sorry about the mess. Transferring data. I don't want to disconnect everything until it's done.'

Sawyer pulled out a chair and sat down. He winced at the clutter on Rhodes's desk: takeaway coffee cups, empty Doritos packets, a Krispy Kreme bag. 'Coffee and doughnuts. Really?'

'One of my minor crimes down here. I've got the whole world in my hands, remember? And we're a long way from Google Search, I can tell you. The things I've seen.'

Sawyer looked inside the Krispy Kreme bag. 'I can imagine. Celebrity sex tapes, cartel chainsaw massacres. And don't think I haven't heard about your *Prisoner: Cell Block H* secret shame.'

Rhodes gave a wheezy laugh. 'Have one of them, if you like. Still fresh from yesterday.'

'Not fresh, then. I'm good.'

Rhodes swivelled in his chair, wide-eyed. 'Jake Sawyer? Turning his nose up at sugar? Haven't seen you with your sweets lately, either.'

'Trying to eat more like a grown-up.'

Rhodes turned back to his screen. 'You've changed, man. I could always tap you up for a cola cube. You don't win friends with kale.'

Sawyer grunted. 'Passive data. Go.'

'Well, I've found a fucking treasure trove of ANPR and CCTV related to the four victims.'

'Really?'

'Of course I haven't. Precisely fuck all. Nothing from shops, nearby businesses. No repeat vehicles near the deposition scenes at the relevant times.'

'He'll be using stolen cars. We're cross-referencing for vehicles that have been taken and then found a few days later. That'll be a dead loss for DNA on the first three cases, but we might get lucky with the car he used for Angela Holt.'

Rhodes sniffed. 'Probably still got that somewhere, though. If he's planning to do more.'

'Any digital trail from the message today? The volunteer said he received the YouTube link in an email.'

Rhodes held up a finger. 'Good question. Message was sent from a burner Gmail account, and from behind a VPN. Now, you can trace the computer IP address from an email header, even if you use a burner account like Gmail. But because our man sent it from behind a VPN, the IP is masked.'

Sawyer took out a pink doughnut and picked at the sprinkles.

Rhodes turned from his screen and caught him. 'Stay in the room, Sawyer. This is important. So, if I try to trace an

IP address without a VPN, I could at least find the server the email bounced off, which would give us a fix on the sender's location.'

Sawyer nodded. 'And we could make a legal claim to Gmail to let us know the actual IP address, which would give us the computer ID.'

'Yeah. But the VPN makes all that impossible. Even if we did trace the computer IP address, we wouldn't see the Google server, and no matter how politely we requested the IP, Google couldn't give it to us.'

'Uhuh. Because they wouldn't have it.'

'Exactly. They'd only have the details of the VPN service the sender was using. And all that data is encrypted and undisclosable.'

Sawyer tossed the doughnut back into the bag. 'So what about the victims' devices? I know the marital dating sites are shady, but surely they wouldn't have gone to the trouble of paying for VPNs?'

Rhodes smiled. 'Well... I checked the data reports from the other victims' devices on HOLMES, and our illustrious colleagues found nothing. But they didn't look hard enough. Everyone has secrets, right? If you haven't got secrets, you're not doing life properly.'

'A hinterland.'

'Indeed.'

'But the two dating sites visited by Hannah Lane...'

Rhodes nodded. '*Extramarital* and *Dark Strangers*.'

'They're based in the US and there's no hope of getting login details or chat history.'

Rhodes rubbed his eyes. 'Angela Holt's site, *Secret Encounters*, is based in the Netherlands. That might seem easier, but they're under no obligation to give us her password so we can check her message history. Particularly now we're not in the EU.'

Sawyer leaned forward, resting his elbows on his knees. 'What about that hack from a few years ago? When all the logins and passwords were shared.'

Rhodes grinned, bearing a rack of nicotine-stained teeth. 'Ashley Madison? That was the wake-up call. Now all the dating agencies use strong VPNs and practically unhackable encryption.'

Sawyer took out his phone and rolled it from hand to hand. 'Password.'

'What?'

'You said *Secret Encounters* was under no obligation to give us Angela Holt's password. But do we know her login name? Her alias?'

'I know it, yes. It's not in HOLMES yet, though.'

Sawyer frowned at him. 'Why not?'

Rhodes took a breath, weighing it up. 'Something in her emails. I haven't logged it with the civvies yet, and, as you know, we shouldn't even be discussing it until it's in the system.'

Sawyer sat up. 'You know her login name and her password, don't you?'

'I'm not at liberty to disclose that.'

Sawyer laughed; Rhodes dropped his gaze. 'Come on. It'll be out there later today, anyway. You'll get the credit. What did you find?'

Rhodes turned to his screen and brought up a page of data. 'Angela Holt, aka "Miss Chievous". *Secret Encounters* sends a notification email whenever an account receives a message or a thing they call a "nudge", which is like an acknowledgement without a message. A bit more enigmatic, I suppose. They also let users send a "virtual gift". Basically, a blank message with an inline image of a champagne bottle, flowers, chocolates.' He scrolled the screen using a wired two-button mouse. 'Angela was careful not to leave any of these virtual gift or nudge emails accessible in her inbox. She was using a Gmail burner account, with no VPN.'

'So, how did you get into her emails?'

Rhodes shifted in his seat. 'We're nearly there. I need you to *really* focus on the next bit. Have a doughnut or something.'

Sawyer shook his head, lowered his voice. 'How did you get into her emails?'

Rhodes grinned again, but didn't turn round. 'I was considering digging out some software that performs a cryptoanalytic brute force attack. It churns through every possible combination of password based on a few initial parameters. But that's too, y'know, tippy-tappy.'

'You mean tiki-taka,' said Sawyer.

'Same thing. So I went route one.'

'You guessed it.'

'Yes, I did.' He turned, raised an eyebrow. 'It was "Password85". You'd be amazed by how many people try to use "password", and then when they're told to add numbers, just stick their birth year on the end. She did make the "P" capital, though. Tricky.'

Sawyer rolled his chair closer. 'I don't suppose she used that for her *Secret Encounters* login, though?'

'No. And that'll all be encrypted by VPN. I can explain it again for you, if you like.'

'That's okay. Just hurry up and tell me what you found in her emails.'

Rhodes scrolled again. 'So, she deleted all the emails from *Secret Encounters*. All the messages, virtual gifts, nudges. But she didn't empty the trash. Schoolgirl error. She'd been messaged by quite a few people, and I can't see the content of the actual messages. Just the notification emails and dates they were received. I checked the ones that arrived across the two weeks before her disappearance, and she'd been contacted by three different accounts. We can't get into those accounts, but we can search for the profile details, based on the login names.'

Sawyer closed his eyes. 'And the profile details will let us research the users' likes and dislikes.'

Rhodes nodded. 'And we could set up a fake profile—'

Sawyer opened his eyes. 'And try and tempt them into meetings.'

13

Dale Strickland jerked open the first-floor sash window. The rattle and squeal of Deansgate traffic filtered up through the summer fug, and he pushed his head out and lingered for a moment, inhaling the evening. Frying food, sweltering asphalt, exhaust fumes, candied vape smoke.

He turned and faced the huddle. 'Sincerest apologies. My office isn't really designed for conferences, and we are still waiting on air conditioning.' He leaned forward on his desk and smiled. 'Other priorities at the moment.'

The room was a sweatbox, and Dale was dressed down, in lilac linen shirt and blue shorts. The local journalists shuffled in place, fanning themselves.

In the corner, Marco looked up from his phone. 'I hope you've got everything you need. I know it was only a short tour, but I'm sure you can appreciate that Mr Strickland is tired after a busy day of campaigning.'

A thickset man in a saggy short-sleeved shirt elbowed his way to the front. 'How many of the Players clubs are you planning to open?'

Dale smiled. 'As I said, the clubs are my attempt to put something back into the local communities.'

The man nodded. 'They're not charities, though, are they?'

'No. I never said they were. But I'm hoping they will be the beginning of a long-lasting franchise which will create jobs and give local teens a focus. Something to do, somewhere to go. A social life that isn't based around toxic illegal activities or pointless turf wars. As any GCSE Physics student will tell you, nature abhors a vacuum. And I believe that a great deal of our social problems involving young people stem from a lack of belonging, or meaning. The digital culture means they are more virtually connected than ever before, but it's no substitute for face-to-face relationships. The cold connections of social media keep them in touch, but same-room contact keeps them human, and gives them something to look forward to. If I'm elected, then I will fight hard to establish incentives for similar local businesses.'

Hector squeezed through the group and whispered something into Dale's ear.

Dale held up his arms and headed for the door. 'I'm so sorry. Urgent business. If you need any more detail on the clubs, please speak to Marco.' He bustled through the group, walking backwards out into the busy snooker room. 'Apologies again for the discomfort. I'm a prospective politician. I can work towards changing policy, but there's nothing I can do about the weather.'

Dale turned, and Hector followed him through a door marked *STAFF ONLY*. They climbed a narrow side staircase and, as they exited through a second door on the top floor, Dale's nose twitched at the hint of something pungent.

A man stood just inside the entrance to a carpeted office at the end of the corridor. He had his back to the half-open door, and was veiled behind a swirl of dense grey smoke.

Dale entered the office and walked to the wide, glass-topped desk by the closed window. As Hector took his place in the centre of the room, Dale lowered himself into the revolving chair, keeping his eyes on the man. He was tall, well over six feet, and broad shouldered, dressed in white T-shirt and fitted blue jeans, with heavy, unseasonal ankle boots. His blond hair had been tied into a stubby ponytail that dangled over the back of his muscular neck. A soft, mud-grey briefcase lay on the chair at his side.

His pinhole eyes drifted across to Dale. 'Ashtray?' He raised his unfiltered cigarette in redundant clarification.

Dale sat back, nodded towards the end of the desk. 'Use that.'

The man walked to the desk and double-tapped his ash into an oversized mug.

Dale beamed. 'Always a pleasure, Austin. You should have told us you were coming. What are you doing here?'

Austin Fletcher touched a finger to the mangled flesh around his left ear. He lowered his head, obscuring his gaze behind an overhanging brow. 'Unfinished business.' The voice was low and flat, untroubled by emotion.

Dale caught Hector's eye. 'It's stalemate. Sawyer has the gun.'

Hector nodded towards Fletcher. 'Thanks to him.'

Dale held up a hand. 'What are you proposing?'

Fletcher dropped his cigarette into the mug and reached down to the briefcase. He took out a slim folder with a black plastic cover and tossed it onto the desk. 'Enough waiting.'

Dale took the folder and flipped through the pages. It was a collection of maps: marked locations, highlighted waypoints, plotted movement patterns. The pages were labelled with date ranges and times, some colour coded. A few locations had been underlined: *EDALE, UPPER*

MIDHOPE, ROSEMARY HOUSE, BAKEWELL, STANSHOPE. Dale looked up; Fletcher's eyes were on him. 'Very pretty. Gold star for effort. I know a few of these. But... Rosemary House?'

'Brother,' said Fletcher.

'Stanshope?'

'Shrink.'

Dale turned to a section devoted to the Bakewell location. 'Not so many visits here recently.' His eyes flashed to Hector. 'Trouble in paradise?'

Fletcher took a step towards the desk. '*Now.*'

Dale stood up and tugged open the window, keeping his back to Fletcher. 'I'm working on something new, to get him off the board. I can't risk anything yet.' He turned and smiled. 'So, no. Not *now*. Soon. I'm trying to be a man of the people. It's not a good time.'

Fletcher retrieved the folder and slid it back into the case.

Dale darkened. 'It's almost Saturday. The run-off vote will be decided on Monday. I'm an independent, and it should be between me and the Labour guy. Just a little longer.'

Fletcher zipped up the case and strode past Hector, out of the office. Dale and Hector stood motionless, listening to the diminishing clunks of Fletcher's boot heels on the stairs.

'He's a problem,' said Hector. 'I can solve it.'

Dale flopped into the chair. 'He's a pain, but now we know where he is. Keep him in sight. Make sure he doesn't solve the real problem before we're ready.'

14

Sawyer pushed through the double doors and hurried across the car park. He glanced up at the cloudless sky: at close to 6pm, the sun still hung like a midday spotlight, scorching the earth. He touched a hand to the bonnet of a police Land Rover, and flinched at the heat.

'Frying tonight?'

He turned. Dean Logan squeezed between two civilian cars, and popped out in the channel between Sawyer and his orange-and-black Mini. Up close, Logan was just shy of Sawyer's height, but he was twice the width, in a worn grey suit and limp red tie. He dug a handkerchief out of his pocket and mopped his brow. 'Could pop a couple of fucking eggs on there.'

Sawyer sidestepped him and aimed his key fob at the Mini. 'I'm a fan of pans. Tried and tested.'

Logan spluttered. 'Doesn't sound like you, at all. You been away? Let me guess. A pilgrimage to the dojo.'

Sawyer paused at the car door. 'Winter sun.'

'I'd kill for a touch of winter now.'

Sawyer opened the door. 'Ambush in the car park. A page from your old Wapping playbook?'

'Just a quick one. Didn't want to make it too obvious to your fine co-workers. I assume Keating has got Occupational Health on speed dial.'

Sawyer sighed. 'A very quick one.'

'Angela Holt,' said Logan. 'And the others.' Sawyer stayed silent. 'Rumours.'

'About what?'

'The presentation. The way the bodies were dumped.'

Sawyer eased past Logan and slipped into the driving seat. 'I'm aware of what you mean by "presentation".'

Logan leaned down, holding the door open. 'Is it unusual? Is it the thing that's giving you the link between the four victims?'

Sawyer stared ahead. 'And where are you getting this information?'

'I'll take that as a yes.'

Sawyer waggled the door, forcing Logan to step back. He closed it, and drove away.

'Long time, no see.'

Alex Goldman shuffled into the sitting room and headed for her throne-like mauve armchair. As usual, a tray sat on the curvy-legged side table with a plate of assorted biscuits, and the standard teapot and cups replaced by a jug of iced water and two glasses. Alex was shrunken and slow moving, recently seventy, with a neat helmet of blow-dried, battleship-grey hair and colour-drained clothing that blended with the functional furnishing.

Sawyer took a seat on a black *chaise longue* tucked into the near wall. 'Six or seven months.'

Alex made it to the armchair and flopped down with a

satisfied grunt. 'Not long for you. An eternity for me. You missed my birthday.'

'The big six-oh?'

Alex smiled. 'Don't. Really, don't.' She poured two glasses of water. 'It's hardly like you've been a stranger, though, Jake. There was a time around Christmas that I could hardly get away from you.'

'Big case. Lots of coverage.' Sawyer reached over to the coffee table and set down his phone and wallet.

Alex passed over his glass. 'The abducted children, or your own?'

'Both. Hence the time off.' He took the drink. 'No tea?'

She puffed out her cheeks. 'In this heat? Although I do love a cup of tea on a hot day.' She sipped again, smiled. 'That's such an old person thing to say, isn't it? And there's no getting away from it. I'm old. I turned seventy.'

'You sound surprised.'

'Yes. I was hoping to slip back to sixty-eight or so, but it didn't happen.'

'Time only moves forward, I suppose.'

Alex raised a finger. 'Ah! That's what your father was telling you, when he gave you the *Memento Mori* medallion, before his death.'

Sawyer took a drink. 'Did I show that to you?'

'I may be slow on the outside, Jake, but my connections are still firing up here.' She tapped her temple.

Sawyer gazed up around the walls. Alex had moved some of her landscape pictures and pet portraits in from the hall, but the biggest picture still dominated the wall behind her armchair: an elaborately framed, slow-shutter photograph of the waterfall at Lumsworth, the water froth shining white, caught in a suspended cascade. 'I wasn't the happiest the last time I was here.'

Alex offered him the biscuit plate. 'Yes. The winter

solstice. The longest day. A lot's happened since then, though. You tracked down the man who murdered your mother. And your father took his own life. I'm so sorry, Jake.'

He waved away the biscuits. 'Thank you.'

'When we last met, you said that optimism is unrealistic, and hope isn't necessarily a good thing. Are you following your father's advice? The philosophy implied by his coin? Are you moving forward?'

'Working on it.' Sawyer braced, expecting a flash, a sound.

'And stopping your sessions with me. Is that part of the work?'

He sighed. 'I wasn't sure I needed this any more.'

'Wasn't?'

'I'm worried again. About my thoughts and behaviour, over the last few months.'

Alex set down her glass on the side table and sat back, taking her time. 'Did you get away? I assume you were signed off work for a while?'

'Canary Islands. Peace and quiet. I stayed on an island off the mainland. La Graciosa. It didn't turn out to be as peaceful and quiet as I'd hoped.'

'Do you feel responsible for your father's death?'

He looked up, glared at her. 'In what way?'

'We've talked about your faulty fear response. How it puts other people in danger. From what I read, your investigation solved your mother's murder, but your actions revealed your father's crimes. And, to avoid—'

'I didn't pull the trigger.'

Alex held the moment, took another sip of water. 'You say you're worried. What about?'

Sawyer smoothed a palm across his hair. 'I'm seeing it all again. Feeling it all again.'

'Flashbacks?'

'More than that. It's like it's happening in front of me again. As real as... reality. My mother. My father.'

'We need to revisit the reliving therapy we started last year, to take you through the events and reframe them as unpleasant memories, to free you from this pain that sits behind you, always at your back. Use your mother's influence for your own growth. And we may need to do some work on what you witnessed with your father.' She leaned forward. 'Remember? We said it would be like going down to the underworld, like Orpheus and Eurydice. Retrieving the pain of your loss and turning it into something the adult version of you can process. You are carrying around the influence of your mother and father. We have to make that a positive: from unwelcome legacy to an ever-present inspiration.'

Sawyer swished the water around in his glass. 'I understand all of that, intellectually. It's just... It's like this weather. This heat. It's constant, no respite. There's no relief. You know, like the bit in *Taxi Driver*? I just want something to come and wash it all away. Like a sluice. Purify me. Rinse it all off me. Start again.'

'It sounds like absolution. You are still an atheist, right?'

He gave a grim laugh. 'I don't feel like a sinner. I spent some of my time off reading. I read a book called *The Psychopath Whisperer*. Studying people who report no sense of regret, limited empathy.'

Alex clasped her fingers together and rested her hands in her lap. 'We've been here before, Jake. If you're worried that you might be a psychopath, then by definition, it means you're not one.'

He looked down at the thin green carpet. Dog hairs, a vaguely worn channel from the door to the *chaise longue*.

'Three main psychopath traits. One. Glib interpersonal style. Dishonest, manipulative, arrogant, deceitful.'

Alex nodded. 'Glibness can also be a defence. To deflect from internal pain. The old thing about the loudest guy in the room being the most damaged.'

'Two. Sensation seeking. Impulsive, reckless, seemingly having no thought for your own safety.'

'No fear.'

He looked at her. 'You can't deny that one fits for me. I need to be busy, occupied, distracted. It turns down the volume on everything else. I play videogames that seem insanely hostile to others. I feel calm when things are stressful—'

'And stressed when things are calm?'

He nodded. 'Three. Defective emotional response. Lacking remorse, finding it impossible to understand why others might view my behaviour to be unacceptable.'

Alex sipped her water again. 'Surely you can put yourself in other people's shoes? You wouldn't be able to do your job if you couldn't.'

'I have to work at it. Like an act.' He gazed up at the fountain picture again. 'It doesn't come naturally. Is that normal?'

Alex took a long breath. 'Everyone's on a spectrum for all their behavioural responses. Maybe you're a bit closer to the darker shades than you'd like to be. And this is why we have to continue the work. Get you closer to the centre. It's all progress.'

Sawyer scoffed. 'A journey.'

'Of course. I'm sure you're aware of Alan Watts. He was a British philosopher. He said that life isn't all about a quest for successively greater achievements. He said it's about the journey itself. The constant work in progress.'

'A quest for meaning.'

'Precisely. And that meaning doesn't have to be some grand revelation. It might be just about making the journey of life as pleasant or as happy as possible for yourself.' She leaned forward again. 'All we're doing here is trying to make your journey smoother, to help you to understand yourself better. Like your issues with fear. Have you felt the tingling sensation since we last met? You've reported it happening when you've been in situations with limited oxygen, maybe even just high-pressure situations. Have you been in any of those recently?'

Sawyer smiled. 'One or two.'

'And do you have the brain scans you told me about last time? The ones you retrieved from your father? The ones conducted after the attack on your mother, and on yourself? The concerns about lesions in your brain, possibly impeding your primal fear response.'

'They seem too old. Like a different version of me.'

'You should get some new ones. A fresh approach. Look into your own head. The brain is fascinating. So mysterious. It could be helpful to look at your physiology with someone else, while we work on the psychology.'

Sawyer took a deep gulp of water. 'Someone else?'

'I know someone. A neurosurgeon. He's very good. Get some new scans, discuss them with him. He may have some insight into the tingling sensation. This sort of proxy fear you sense but don't really feel. Jake, for the record, I don't think you're a psychopath. But I am concerned that your mental state is increasingly leading you to make inappropriate choices. How do you *feel*? Day to day? Moment to moment? Is there contentment in you? How do you feel about the idea of hope now? Has it changed? Do you feel in any way optimistic?'

He drained the glass, and gazed down at the carpet. 'It's not *how* I feel. It's what I feel. We've been worrying about whether or not I can feel fear. But I'm not sure I really feel anything.'

Sawyer left Alex's and drove out of Stanshope village, plunging into another stale and stuffy evening. He opened all the windows, and slotted the Mini into the single-track Stable Lane that wound down towards Wetton and the Manifold Valley. The last embers of sunlight glimmered at the fringes of the fields, and he cued up a favourite nineties playlist—Olive, The Beloved, Faithless—hoping to ease the ache of all the self-examination.

He parked on the familiar roadside verge near Ecton Mine and transferred the playlist to his phone, slotting in his earphones as he walked along the old railway track carved through the valley. The path was busy with late walkers and cyclists, but Sawyer kept his head down and, after half an hour, climbed the steep stairs that led to his childhood retreat.

He paused at the top, removed his earphones, and peered up at the ten-metre-high circular front entrance to Thor's Cave, a natural karst cavern at the top of a limestone crag overlooking the river and steep-sided valley.

Murmurs far below. A faint rushing of water. Keening birds, the hoarse bleating of sheep on the other side of the crag. Over the years, Sawyer's ear had been tuned to the echoes of human sounds from within the cave, and now all was silent.

He clambered up the stone slope and used his phone light to navigate through the narrow passage that led to the unvisited far end.

Another pause. Listening. Still nothing.

He found the deep ditch that ran beneath the slitted

window in the crag face and crawled further inside. The stone was cool and dry, and, after a little rummaging, he found the large, smooth rock, dug deep beneath the overhang of the ditch.

He lifted away the rock, and his phone light picked out a metallic glint from the contents of the transparent evidence bag: a semi-automatic Glock G17 handgun.

15

Sawyer stripped down to his underwear and settled himself before the training dummy in the corner of his bedroom. The movable struts of the 'wooden man' were intended to replicate limbs and joints, and Sawyer could practise his striking and blocking techniques, while working out his arms and legs. He passed through a few drills, rotating the struts with his palms, driving his forearms across their length to simulate blocking and immobilisation. The evening heat exhausted him after only a couple of minutes, and he switched focus to slow and steady accuracy and technique, following his Jeet Kune Do principles: efficiency, directness. Nothing extraneous or classical. Nothing for show.

He dropped down on the side of the bed and dipped his head, saturated in sweat. The muscles across his back rose and fell with each breath, distorting the tattoo that spanned his shoulders: *Κατά τον δαίμονα εαυτού* ('True to his own spirit'). He showered and settled on the bed with his laptop. As he navigated to the *Secret Encounters* website, Bruce padded in and flopped out on the cool windowsill.

He found the three profile names identified by Rhodes from Angela Holt's notification emails: DrFox, PlayWithFire99 and Bikerboy. All three had opted for one of the site's default avatars: a close crop of a suit and tie for DrFox; a silhouette of a fisherman casting a rod for PlayWithFire99, and a point-of-view shot from a vehicle windscreen in a country lane for Bikerboy.

Sawyer flicked through the profiles. All were claiming to be mid-thirties, and their introductory messages were littered with the standard self-deprecating details: never write a profile after a few glasses of Rioja; my relationship is now a friendship; imbalance in sexual desire. Bikerboy claimed to have no physical preference but was keen on 'the kind of woman who eats ice cream in bed'. DrFox insisted that life was too short to 'drone on about how his partner doesn't understand him'. PlayWithFire99 listed 'rudeness' among his dislikes. All three emphasised the importance of 'discretion'.

He marked a tab in his browser for each of the main profile pages, then opened a new tab and searched for the article Keating had pulled up on the zoo incident. Sawyer's stomach lurched as he read the quotes from the observers about his 'bravery'. Jackie Mullins (38) visiting with her husband and young daughter, was convinced that Sawyer was 'crazy' and made it clear that she couldn't possibly have done 'anything like that'. As far as Erik Brewer (52) was concerned, the whole thing was 'a publicity stunt', despite the park's record attendances that summer.

Sawyer clicked on an in-line gallery, dismissed a disclaimer about disturbing images, and scrolled through a few tame pics of Danny and himself sitting side by side on the edge of the ridge. The final shot showed Sawyer and Danny being ushered out of the enclosure by the uniformed keepers. Sawyer dragged the image onto his desktop and double-clicked it to open it in his image preview software. The man with the rifle and Hi-Viz jacket was just visible behind the main crowd; Sawyer zoomed in on his face and smiled.

He snatched up his phone from the bedside table and made a call. It rang for a long time before it connected.

'Yeah?' Male voice, broad estuary accent.

Sawyer glanced at the clock as it flicked over to 10:45pm. 'Tony Cross?'

'Depends who you are.'

'It's Jake. Jake Sawyer.'

A pause on the line. Barely suppressed laughter. 'I was wondering how long it would take for the penny to drop. How are you, my friend?'

'Better than you. Is the zoo marksman gig business or pleasure?'

'Freelance. Good money.'

'It's like Lewis Hamilton driving a cab.'

Cross laughed: loud and jarring. 'My options are limited. Listen. We should catch up properly.'

'Busy now?'

Cross whispered to someone. 'Yeah. I do a bit of work up at the Thorpe Cloud rifle range. Could meet you there?'

'I'd rather stick to civilian spots. I'll have a think and send you a suggestion.'

Another whisper from Cross. 'Fair enough. Good to hear from you, Jake.' He faltered. 'You've had a busy one, mate.'

'You could say that.'

Sawyer hung up, switched on his electric fan and lay flat out on top of the bed, tired and aching after his workout. He had developed a dread of sleep: it was a surrender to the nightly retelling of his tale, each time with a painful new twist.

The whirr of the fan.

The purr of the cat.

And then he was running, at top speed, through the heat of the day that had defiled his childhood.

He wanted to leave it all back there on the verge: the pleading and screaming.

The bloodstained grass.

Contains images that some people might find...

He wanted to leave it all far behind, to will it out of existence.

He ran, but he wasn't running away.

He wasn't scared.

He was being good. He was six years of age, and he was doing what his mother wanted.

'Jake! Run, my darling. Don't look back.'

He ran and he ran. Across the radiant fields, towards Wardlow. Reaching for the comfort of home, calling for his father.

Swishing through the long grass, as it grew heavier and heavier.

Wetter and wetter.

Redder and redder.

He slowed, wading not running now. The field like a paddy: the soil a sludge, flooded with blood.

'Don't look back!'

And then, the basement room. His father in the corner: older, torn apart by time.

'Help me, Jake.'

The voice. Rich and reassuring, as he wedged the shotgun under his chin. 'Help me with this. I can't reach.'

His father was older, but Sawyer was still the boy. The six-year-old.

He tugged and twisted at the gun, trying to change the angle, divert the aim. But he'd been here before, in this lucid nightmare. He knew that he could only brace as it played out.

He was powerless to change anything. His intentions shone like steel, but his hands were liquid, spilling over the gun barrel.

His father grew impatient with his fumbling and pushed him away, stretching his finger down to the trigger, saying he was useless, saying he might as well just do it himself.

The click, the turning away.

But no bang in his dream this time. Just that sudden stop.

And awake.

The whirring of the fan. But no purr from Bruce.

The usual unholy hour. Earlier than normal, though: 2:40am.

Somehow, for the first time, he had wrenched himself out of the nightmare.

Or something had woken him.

He rolled off the bed and guzzled some tepid water direct from the tap in the bathroom sink. As he stood upright, his nose tingled, and he turned his head back to the bedroom, to the open window.

A smoky aroma: acrid but fragrant.

And familiar.

Sawyer burst back into the bedroom and tugged on a T-shirt. He ran, barefoot, through the sitting room and crashed through the front door.

Tail lights from further down the lane.

He pelted forward, giving chase as the car rolled off the verge into the road, gathering speed. It slowed for a moment, then screeched its tyres and streaked away.

Sawyer squinted into the gloom, but it was too far to catch a number plate. He walked back to the house, retrieved his phone from the bedroom, and crouched by the Mini passenger door.

He shone a light underneath, around the tyre rims and undercarriage. Nothing.

16

Keating took his seat at the head of the conference table and tapped at his screen, then polished the lenses of his glasses with a bespoke cloth as they waited for the other detectives to log in.

'Morning, all,' he said, without looking up. They mumbled a response: Sawyer, Shepherd, Walker, Myers, Moran, and Rhodes, sitting next to Sawyer. 'We're honoured by your presence, Karl.'

Rhodes grinned and tugged at his moustache. 'Sir. DI Sawyer asked me—'

'I see you filed a data report into HOLMES.'

'This morning,' said Moran, glaring at Rhodes. 'Early.'

Keating put on his glasses and smiled at Rhodes. 'Conscientious. But do bear in mind that we're handling intelligence gathered by other forces, and we should keep focus on... due diligence.' He glanced at Sawyer. 'I appreciate that it's hardly a symmetrical enquiry, but we should give our colleagues plenty of time to assess any analysis or recommendation well in advance of these briefings. Let's not get too cosy.'

'Share and share alike,' said Sawyer.

'Precisely.' The remote feed boxes appeared across their screens: Barlow, Farrell, McBride, Whittaker. 'Morning, all. We're joined this morning by our Digital Media Advisor, DC Karl Rhodes. Let's get to it.' He shared a document to all the participants: a static PDF of an email. 'We have another message from our friend. Please read and digest.'

A moment's silence as they read the short message.

'No video link?' said Farrell.

Rhodes shook his head. 'Not this time. Same as before with the email, though. Encrypted behind VPN. No chance of tracking back to the originating server.'

'So he wants us to hurry up and pay,' said McBride.

Sawyer read from the message. '*If you're struggling for money, you can always put the rose gold bracelet on eBay.*'

'Another detail we haven't made public,' said Shepherd.

Sawyer continued. '*If the Bitcoin payment is not transferred by 10am, I will claim my fifth soon after.*' He looked up. 'We should call his bluff.'

'Not pay it?' said Walker.

'If he's bluffing, that's okay. If he does kill again, then we have another body to work with. Richer data.'

Shepherd turned to look at Sawyer. 'You're not serious?'

'Of course I'm not serious.' He shuffled in his seat. 'This ransom is a red herring. It's just part of his pathological need for control. These killings aren't about *money*. If we pay, we play his game by his rules. I've got a better idea. Our game, our rules.'

'I assume we're staying inside the law, though, DI Sawyer?' said Farrell.

Sawyer nodded at Rhodes, whose face filled the main feed box as he spoke.

'I discovered Angela Holt's login details for *Secret Encounters*.'

'How?' said Whittaker.

'It's technical,' said Rhodes.

'He guessed her password,' said Sawyer.

Rhodes continued. 'I also found *Secret Encounters* notification emails in her trash. She had made contact with three user profiles in the two weeks before her death.'

Sawyer shuffled in his seat, impatient. 'We set up a dummy profile, with a picture of a thirtysomething blonde woman. We use it to contact these three profiles, see if they bite. They all use generic pics, but there is an option to hide real face photos behind a password. Most people make initial contact because they like the sound of the profile description, and then ask for a photo password so they can see what the person actually looks like.'

'But...' McBride's face took over the largest window. 'What's stopping people keeping those photos and exposing the users as potential cheats?'

'Mutually assured destruction,' said Sawyer. 'Angela Holt's husband told us that the affair websites all thrive on that concept. Most of the users want to stay in their current relationships, usually marriages, but are just looking for—'

'A bit on the side,' said Barlow.

Sawyer nodded. 'So, at first, there's an element of tension and trust. But once you have each other's picture password, the stand-off ends. If we can get these profiles to react to our contact, exchange picture passwords—'

'We might be able to set up meetings and monitor them,' said Walker.

'It's a cunning plan, Sawyer,' said Farrell. 'But it's a bit like getting a number of a group of sheep by counting the legs and dividing by four. There's an easier way.'

'Already tried it,' said Rhodes. 'Getting the profiles' details from *Secret Encounters* direct. Client privacy concerns. This isn't just a regular dating site. They see any kind of identity revelation as potentially catastrophic for their business.'

'Lot of suicides after the Ashley Madison leak,' said Shepherd.

'They say they are willing to release details of the identities...' Sawyer paused for effect. 'But only if the clients themselves consent.'

'Well, that's not going to happen,' said Barlow. '"Hello. It's the police. Do you mind if we get your secret identity and look into your nefarious online activities?"'

'Can we get legal on their asses?' said Whittaker.

'It'll take too long.'

'Still,' said Keating. 'Belt and braces. I'll raise a court order, and a reciprocal court order for INTERPOL.'

'With respect, sir...' Farrell's face filled the screen. 'That kind of legal mire will take weeks to wade through. Maybe months.'

'And, isn't this entrapment?' said McBride. 'If we set up this fake profile and he bites? They call it catfishing.'

Shepherd shook his head. 'You'd need a pretty creative and optimistic lawyer to bring that into the fight.'

'It is catfishing,' said Sawyer, 'but it's not entrapment. Because we wouldn't be leading him into a crime. Just a situation he thinks is a date. Then, we arrest, check his alibi, cross-ref DNA from Laura Bertrand's dog-bite blood and the cigarette we found in Dovedale. That would put him at two of the scenes.'

Keating pondered for a few seconds. 'Make it happen.'

'Rhodes can set up the alias,' said Sawyer. 'They have these things called "nudges". Coy acknowledgements to let someone know they've been noticed. He can send out a few of those to each of the three profiles.'

'I'll write the profile,' said McBride. 'If we're posing as a thirtysomething blonde woman, we might as well get a thirtysomething blonde woman to do it.'

'We should use fresh images,' said Walker. 'We can't use DI McBride because her profile in the case is too high. But it needs to be a real person, in case he tries to use Reverse Image Search and rumbles us for a model pic or something.'

'And we have to make her a success at what she does,' said Sawyer. 'She owns her own business or has a high profile job. "I have money, would love to spend it on having fun. All work and no play..."'

'Sounds like you should write this yourself, son,' said Barlow. 'You got experience posing as a woman, have you?'

Sawyer closed his eyes. 'I'm in touch with my feminine side.'

'Aye,' said Rhodes. 'He doesn't see gender.'

As the meeting broke up, Sawyer followed Keating back into his office and closed the door behind him.

Keating settled himself at his desk. 'No secrets, DI Sawyer. Remember?'

'Just a quick private conversation. I spoke to Logan.'

'Your biographer.'

Sawyer forced a smile. 'He asked me if the presentation was unusual. Said he'd heard a rumour that we're linking the killings based on that factor.'

Keating looked up. 'We've never made it public, any information on the presentation.'

'To avoid copycats, yes. But it seems that someone isn't too worried about it leaking. Either it's our man, contacting Logan anonymously for some reason, or...' His eyes found the window.

'Or it's from someone on the inside,' said Keating.

17

Sawyer sidestepped into the window booth at the Nut Tree, a homely café in a one-storey grey brick building just outside Hartington. Maggie Spark stood up and leaned over the table; Sawyer returned the kiss on the cheek, but the hug was limp.

'I took the liberty...' She gestured down to the table. Large jug of orange liquid packed with ice cubes and lemon slices; two glasses; and an elongated bread bun, topped with thick, unnaturally white icing.

He filled a glass. 'Thank you. What's this?'

'Iced tea. Citrus.'

He sipped, raised his eyebrows in approval.

They sat. Maggie had chopped down her rust-red hair into a boyish pixie cut, and wore a low-cut summer blouse: yellow, with flecks of white petals. She angled her head and inspected him. 'You're looking better than I expected.'

He laughed, caught her eye. 'Is that your idea of a compliment?'

'Yes. Feel free to return it. I'll try to cope.'

'I like the hair. It's a little bit...' He took a breath through his nose.

'Careful.'

'Carey Mulligan.'

She poured herself a glass of tea. 'I'll take that.'

Sawyer picked up the bun, peeled off a section of icing. 'How's single life?'

'Couple of dates here and there. Nobody exciting. One guy just wanted to talk about the cricket. I tried to hold my own for a while but... it just ran out of road.'

'That's your problem. You spend your professional life assessing people, working them out. Your bar for emotional intelligence is set too high.' He laid the chunk of icing back on the plate.

'Not hungry?'

'Had breakfast before the briefing.'

'Is the case moving ahead?'

He sipped his drink. 'Angela Holt made contact with three profiles on a dating site a couple of weeks before her death. We've set up a fake profile, trying to tempt them into meetings. One of the DIs from the Nottingham case wrote the profile and we've used an image of one of the civilian volunteers for the pic. We sent virtual nudges to the profiles we're interested in.'

Maggie nodded. 'Just a case of waiting, then. See if you get a hit.'

'The profile was only online for twenty minutes before we got a message.' He took out his phone and turned the screen round to face Maggie. 'Didn't even have to ask him for his picture password. He volunteered it.' The image showed a sun-flared beach shot of a short, flabby man in his mid-forties. He was topless, smiling into camera.

Maggie grimaced. 'Unnatural crop. I know the tricks. Someone was standing next to him.'

'Some guy in Aberdeen. So he says. Doesn't seem like a fit. We're just waiting on replies from the other two now.'

'Horrible case. I spoke to Lewis Holt. Strange sort. Seemed genuine, though. Still the most likely suspect, I suppose?'

'Technically, yes. But he didn't do it.' Sawyer swept his hair off his face.

Maggie smiled. 'You're looking rather leonine at the moment.'

'Are you about to make a joke about wild animals?'

She sipped her drink, held the moment. 'That was stupid, Jake. They would have got him out of there without you. Don't believe your press. And don't overcompensate.'

'For what?'

'You know what I mean. For the people you've lost.'

He stared down at the jug. 'It was a new experience. And it's reconnected me with an old acquaintance.'

She nodded. 'Did you see Alex?'

'Yes. Back on the couch. Well, the *chaise longue*.'

She reached her hand across, rested it on his. 'That's good. You've had a hell of a time.'

He drew back his hand. 'How's Mia? Freddy?'

'They're good. We're cycling near Ladybower tomorrow. Mia is prematurely teenage. She spends most of the time complaining about the heat. I tell her she never complains about it when we go on holiday, but she just does that big shruggy sigh and says that it's "different".'

Sawyer cracked a smile. 'I saw the lost villages were visible now, up in Derwent.'

'Yes! We're going to see them. Isn't it incredible? Sort of sad. What a story, though. How those people were turfed out of their homes to make way for the reservoir. We've had such little rain you can see whole buildings now. Limestone cottages from the old Derwent village.'

'The past poking through.'

Maggie took another drink. 'Well. That's the trouble

with the past. You can never quite keep it down. As you can imagine, it comes up a lot with my clients.'

He looked up. 'Sorry, but I can't stay. We can catch up again after the case is clear. I wanted to quickly ask you something, though. Have you ever worked with anyone who showed worrying signs of misogyny?'

'Nobody comes immediately to mind. Why?'

Sawyer's phone buzzed in his pocket and he took it out. Shepherd. 'Just an angle on the case. Something I want to understand.' He leaned over for a hug.

'This you leaving, then?' said Maggie.

'It is.'

Outside, he took the call. Shepherd spoke as soon as he connected. 'Another message. Our man is not happy about the lack of payment, but he says he's not ready to kill again yet. He's willing to give us some more time, but he wants an "insurance payment".'

Sawyer hurried to the Mini, parked across the road. 'Or what?'

'Or he'll release details about the bodies' presentation to the press.'

———

Sawyer drove into Buxton town centre and found a lucky parking spot in a side street by a line of three-storey terraced guesthouses. He walked back up towards town, and slipped into a coffee shop at the end of the street. Dean Logan was already there, halfway through a latte, hunched over a pile of newspapers. He had grown flabbier since their last meeting, and his T-shirt wasn't quite roomy enough to conceal his paunch.

He raised a hand at Sawyer's entrance. 'Morning! Coffee? Tea? A fucking chai infusion, whatever that is?'

Sawyer dropped into the sofa opposite. 'I'm good.'

Logan grinned. 'I was just thinking. It's a bit on the nose to be meeting with a journalist in a coffee shop called The Source.'

'Only if the meeting actually proves to be fruitful in some way.'

Logan slurped at his latte, retaining a puff of milk froth on the end of his flat nose. He swiped it away. 'What kind of fruit were you hoping for?'

'Forbidden. Who contacted you about the presentation of the victims?'

Logan gave a theatrical shrug. 'As you say, forbidden.'

'If you won't tell me who told you, can you at least tell me *what* they told you?'

'But then that would be giving away all my sweets.'

Sawyer sighed. 'Did they approach you anonymously?'

'Yeah. Email.'

'Burner account? Gmail?'

Logan tried on a teasing smile. 'Yeah. I had a geeky pal take a look but he says it's all encrypted. Don't understand all that. I'm old school. Face to face. I used to meet anonymous sources in the snug of this pub in Westminster. The landlord—'

'He's been in touch with us, too. He's threatening to release details about the bodies' presentation unless we pay. I assume he's planning to use you for that purpose. But here's what you're going to do…'

Logan raised an eyebrow.

'…if you'd be so kind. You're going to run a story about a "police insider" who has informed you that we are receiving crank calls from someone claiming to be the killer. Make it clear that we think it's a hoaxer.'

'But won't he just read that and make the details public in another way? I'm not the only journo in town.'

Sawyer leaned forward. 'I hate to say this, Logan, but I think you're important. You're part of his power play. He's mentioned me by name, and he'll know we have a connection. Maybe he wants you to leak the presentation details because it's a minor fuck-you to me, to the police.' He lowered his voice. 'And if he does react to your insider story by releasing the presentation details, that tells me he's not the killer.'

'How?'

'Because the killer would kill. He would be way too pathological to stand for a betrayal like that.'

Logan gave a wheezy laugh. 'So you want me to wind up someone who knows who I am, who has contacted me already, and who might have already killed four people. What if he targets me to show he won't be fucked with?'

'Like I said, he's pathological. There are many consistencies across the victims. I don't think he'll deviate and switch from young blonde women to middle-aged men.'

Logan took a long slug on his latte. 'Sorry to break this to you, Sawyer, but you might be wrong. And what if you are, and I run this story, and it pushes him to kill again?'

'I'm not wrong. I wouldn't do this if I wasn't certain.'

Logan ran a hand across his thinning hair, revealing a scalp reddened by sunburn. 'He has details only the killer could know.'

'Only the killer, and the investigation team.'

Logan gaped. 'Do you think he could be an insider? One of the good guys?'

'It's possible,' said Sawyer. 'Or a bad guy with access to one of the good guys.'

18

Sawyer hustled the Mini through the tourist traffic in Tideswell town centre. It had just gone midday, and the in-car thermometer showed the outside temperature at eighty-five degrees. He cranked the air con, cued up his favourite album—*Loveless* by My Bloody Valentine—and sped over the packhorse bridge at the fringe of the town. He swung past a cluster of double-parked cars, and joined a narrow, rising lane, flanked by dry stone walls and thirsty farmland.

The swirling soundscape of dipping and swelling guitars always cleared his head, amplified his focus.

He turned the case over in his mind. You joined up the facts, but you paid closest attention to the disconnects, the unusual details. You always learned more from the extraordinary.

Terrible violence, but almost respectful presentation.

The disfigurement of the biting, the adornment of the make-up.

The control and domination, but no obvious sexual release.

The hot frenzy, the satiation, but then the cold demands for money.

The last one was particularly unbalanced. Extortionists were usually transactive, and rarely killed to cement their credibility. The killer was acting out a fantasy, refining it. The killings would take over his life: planning them, removing the evidence, covering his tracks. Logan's story should flush out the truth behind the contact, but if humiliating the police *was* part of the killer's power trip, then his demand for payment would continue, and escalate.

Rosemary House was a shabby, three-storey manor set in modest grounds on the edge of Bradwell village. The gardens were well tended, with tidy pathways and herbaceous borders layered with vivid summer colours: lemon, magenta, red, orange. But the house itself seemed gloomy and aloof. A casual observer might mark it as a boutique country hotel: fine dining, four posters, weddings and wine tastings. But its guests were not there by choice.

Sawyer signed in at reception and used a temporary pass to open the heavy double doors that led to the residential rooms, either side of a featureless corridor with a skylight picking out the bland colour scheme: tepid greens and browns. A couple of landscape watercolours hung at either end. It was an arid airlock between the messy outside world and the rigorous modulation beyond the doors. Nothing primal or arousing. Nothing that could be read as a challenge.

He paused outside Room 38, wincing at the faecal whiff from the communal toilet opposite.

Two taps on the door.

A woman's voice from inside. 'Just a second.'

He waited in the unconditioned air and gazed into the nearest watercolour: rolling hills, a lake beyond. The painting was barely twenty inches square, marooned in the centre of the end wall: a wilderness of off-white.

A young woman in a fitted grey blazer opened the door and smiled: friendly but wary. 'Are you Jake?' Sawyer dug out his warrant card; she laughed. 'Oh, no need for that.' The woman opened the door wide and stepped back into the room; Sawyer entered.

Despite the open window that overlooked the back gardens, the room was stuffy and smelt of stale socks and detergent. It was budget hotel chic: small and functional, with a single bed, wall-mounted TV, en suite bathroom, tea and coffee-making facilities. A burly man in a long-sleeved white T-shirt sat in the corner armchair, focused on a handheld gaming device. He was pushing forty, with closely cropped grey hair and a grown-out salt-and-pepper beard. A few posters had been tacked to the walls since Sawyer's last visit: a white image with single stacked lettering —*PINK FLOYD: THE WALL*—over a background brickwork effect; the 1980s Liverpool footballer Ian Rush, all in red, striking a ball; above the bed, a computer-rendered image of a middle-aged man holding a shotgun, with a young girl at his side, below the legend *THE LAST OF US*.

As Sawyer entered, the man looked up briefly, and returned to his game. The volume was too loud, and the blipping and trilling clashed with the birdsong through the window. Sawyer approached him and leaned down, hugging him around the shoulders. The man didn't return the hug, but dug his head into Sawyer's body as he kept focus on the handheld screen. Sawyer turned to face the woman, who had stayed near the door.

'So, I'm Sue Bradbury-Lane. I believe you were told that I was a speech therapist. Actually, I'm a speech and language therapist.' She faltered. 'I wonder... Could we speak in private for a few moments?'

Bradbury-Lane stepped out into the corridor and led Sawyer into a small, stifling break room next to the toilet: coffee table, low-slung chairs, mini-fridge, sink, side shelf with kettle and cups. She had a brief go at opening the window, gave up, and closed the door behind them. 'Goodness, this heat!' She picked up a laminated food menu from a pile near the fridge and fanned herself. 'Last year, my sister went to Menorca. It was good timing because we had such a terrible summer, of course.' She took a seat; Sawyer did likewise. 'But this year, it's actually hotter here than it is there.'

Sawyer gave a polite laugh and peered out of the window. A man in overalls stood over one of the flower beds, sprinkling them with water. 'I might need to make an arrest.'

Bradbury-Lane looked alarmed. 'Oh?'

He smiled at her. 'Hosepipe and sprinkler ban.'

She leaned over and looked out of the window. 'Ah! Doesn't apply to watering cans.'

Sawyer nodded. 'Not really my field, anyway.'

She grinned. 'Quite. So, I've had quite a few sessions with your brother now. Your father... Oh. I'm so sorry for your loss.'

'Thank you. Did he ask you to look into Michael's specific issues with speech and expression?'

'Ah! He did, and this is the reason why I called you. I don't actually think that I'm the right person for the job. Speech and language is my area of expertise, but Michael's problem isn't speech and language. He has rarely spoken out loud to me or anyone else since I've been working with him, but he has no difficulty with expression or word acquisition. He can write down responses to my questions.'

'He's spoken to you?'

'Oh, yes. A number of times. Mostly one-word responses, but I don't feel the issue here is selective mutism. That normally sits alongside social anxiety, and we usually see it in younger people.' Bradbury-Lane paused. She rubbed the fingertips of one hand over the palm of the other: up and down, up and down. 'I... understand that you and Michael were involved in a most appalling event when you were young children. And your mother was—'

'Don't forget the dog.' Sawyer rifled through the magazines on the coffee table. *Esquire, Radio Times, Country Life*.

Bradbury-Lane clasped her hands together. 'The dog?'

He opened the *Radio Times*. 'Our dog was killed, too. We were ambushed, on our way home from school. 1988. I was six, Michael was nine. My mother was having an affair with a man called William Caldwell, a senior police officer at my father's station.' Sawyer raised his eyes from the magazine and looked at Bradbury-Lane. 'She wanted to end it, so he murdered her. And he tried to murder me and Michael. And our dog. We survived, the dog didn't.'

Bradbury-Lane leaned forward. 'Yes. I read about—'

'I tracked down Caldwell late last year. But my father had got there first, long ago. He was keeping Caldwell captive in a purpose-built basement prison.' He slumped back in the chair and sighed. 'In my father's eyes, it was a fate worse than death. You've got to hand it to him. He was fucking *committed*.'

She dropped her gaze, letting the tension roll away. 'So... As I say. I don't think Michael's issues are with speech and language. Selective mutism is rarely related to trauma of that magnitude. I'm sorry to say, Mr Sawyer, that I don't think I'm qualified to give Michael the help he needs.'

———

Back in Michael's room, Bradbury-Lane took a seat and wrote up the handover paperwork, while Michael kept focus on his game.

Sawyer paced. He leaned in at the bedside table and studied the untidy batch of photographs Michael had taped to the back edge. A young Michael lying at a fireside, pretending to be asleep, while Henry, their Jack Russell terrier, licked at his face. A faded Polaroid of the two of them in a garden paddling pool: Jake as a chubby baby, barely able to hold himself upright, while toddler Michael paraded around in sky-blue trunks and a rubber ring with a protruding giraffe's head.

And in the centre, Michael had positioned a black-and-white photograph of their mother, Jessica, windswept on a rainy seaside promenade; her long black hair held upright at the side, as if in supernatural suspension. Her smile—flustered but indulgent—caught Sawyer off guard, and a familiar pain knifed through his heart.

'Remember Llandudno, Mike? I was obsessed with making these elaborate sandcastles. A bigger kid kicked one over and you said you'd "do" him, so he ran off and told his mum.' He glanced at his brother and saw the hint of a smile on his lips. 'And she came over and had a go at Mum. But Mum said she needed to tell *her* son to stop bullying people. You remember that?' He looked again, and saw Bradbury-Lane look up, too. Michael gave a slight nod. 'It was so hot. Dad told us to keep our T-shirts on, but we ignored him. And we were sick from the sunburn.' He laughed. 'Then we were peeling the skin off each other, seeing who could take the longest slice.' Sawyer sat down on the bed. 'And from then on, you just wanted to stay in the arcade. You used to play that game all the time. Sit-down thing, in a cubicle.'

'*Space Harrier*,' said Michael. His voice was low and steady, close to a whisper.

'Fuck, yes. *Space Harrier*. And you found a bag of tenpence pieces and gave it to Mum and Dad. They said they'd hand it in, and they gave you a bit of money for being honest. But they didn't really hand it in.' Michael looked up from the game. 'Mum once told me that they'd asked the police, but they couldn't be bothered with it. There was only a few quid in there. They just rationed the money out to you. And then, on the last day, I was on the beach with Mum and Dad, and I've never felt rain like it, Mike. It was like slabs of solid water, hammering down into the sand. Turned my sandcastle to sludge. We all ran into the nearest shelter. The arcade. You were playing your game. Dad had a go, saying he wanted to see what the fuss was all about. Mum and I were on the Penny Falls.'

'Mint lollies,' said Michael.

'Yes! We both had one. And I remember Dad dragging Mum outside to take this picture. It might as well have been last week, Mike.'

They sat there for a while. Michael had paused the game; he stared down at a patch of worn carpet near to Sawyer's feet. Sawyer's phone buzzed in his pocket, breaking the moment.

'Caldwell,' said Michael.

Sawyer looked into his brother's eyes: green on green. 'What about him?'

'The women. I saw you on TV.'

'It's not Caldwell, Mike. He's in prison.'

Michael returned to his game. 'Someone like him.'

The door opened and a hefty, misshapen man with a scraggy ginger beard bustled into the room. He settled a pair of half-moon spectacles over his eyes, and looked from Sawyer to Bradbury-Lane. 'Mr Sawyer. It's a pleasure to see you, of course, but I would have appreciated the opportunity to introduce Ms Bradbury-Lane more formally, as I've been delighted with her work.'

Sawyer checked his phone. Text from Shepherd.

Urgent briefing in an hour.

'Sorry, Mr Hill,' said Sawyer. 'I appreciate that you're the Operations Manager here, but this is more of a freelance arrangement. And we've made the mutual decision to bring it to a close.' He walked to Michael, leaned down for another awkward one-way hug. 'I'll be looking into alternative options.' He smiled at Hill. 'I'll keep you informed.'

'I understand that. But it's time for Michael's lunch now, and I would be grateful if—'

Michael rose from his chair and hauled himself into the bathroom, taking slow, heavy steps.

Hill called after him. 'Please wash your hands thoroughly, Michael. We need to be diligent with hygiene in this weather.'

Michael turned on the taps, not bothering to close the bathroom door. He rolled up his sleeves and lathered soap onto his hands. Sawyer stepped closer to the door. 'Bye, Mike.' Michael raised a hand in farewell, revealing a ladder of fresh, jagged scars that spiralled down the length of his forearm, front and back.

19

Keating logged everyone in at the MIT conference table: Sawyer, Shepherd, Myers, Walker and Moran in the room, with Farrell, Whittaker, McBride and Barlow on remote. 'Afternoon, all. Thank you for standing to attention at short notice. Also present today is Stephen Bloom, our Media Relations Manager.'

Bloom spoke in response to a nod from Keating. 'We have a potentially troubling story which was uploaded to the *Derbyshire Times* website earlier today.'

Sawyer had never been able to place Bloom's accent. Today, he sounded like a politician: public school, but with an edging of Scandinavian. He swiped at his screen and shared a link to the story; Sawyer tapped it. His home screen was overlaid by a browser window featuring the short article, attributed to Logan. According to the time stamp, it had been uploaded barely half an hour after their meeting at the coffee shop.

The headline blared out beneath a composite image of the four victims.

RIPPER: PAY UP OR I'LL KILL AGAIN

Sawyer skimmed the copy: Logan had jumped through all the right hoops. It spoke of an 'insider source' who had confirmed that the task force assigned to the case had been in contact with a man claiming to be the killer, who was demanding payment to suppress 'confidential details that might compromise the enquiry.' He had overcooked the jeopardy as he saw it, tabloidising it for effect, but had inadvertently hit on the messenger's direct threats. The story continued with a manufactured police quote dismissing the contact as 'probably inauthentic', and signed off with a pompous note about how the story was 'developing' and promised more soon.

Keating pinched the bridge of his nose. 'Thoughts?'

Sawyer dismissed the browser window, just as Farrell's face filled the main feed box.

'It doesn't sound like he's got any audio,' said Farrell. 'I assume he would have released it as a media file within the story if he'd got hold of something like that.'

'Strange that he's claiming a big exclusive,' said Walker, 'but then suggesting the police think the contact is a hoax.'

Keating sighed. 'Again, shades of the Yorkshire Ripper enquiry, only in reverse. They were contacted by a man who claimed to be the killer but who turned out to be a hoaxer. The detectives were so eager to believe they were onto their man that they wasted valuable police resources chasing him down, and in that time, three more women were murdered by the real killer.'

'Peter Sutcliffe,' said Shepherd.

Keating eyed him. 'I don't suppose anyone has any idea about the identity of this "insider source"?'

'One of the volunteers?' said Moran. 'Do they all check out?'

'Of course they do,' said Keating. 'They're mostly retired officers, but they've been rigorously screened.'

'And if it is one of them,' said Walker, 'they now also know about this story, and they'll be worried that we—'

'Myers,' said Keating. 'Since you're covering CPS diligence, and we don't actually have a suspect to build a case against right now, run a double-check on all the volunteers.'

'Check for any with financial problems,' said McBride.

Myers made a note, clicked his fingers. 'Thanks for that. It never occurred to me.' He glanced up at Moran and they exchanged a smirk.

Keating stared up at the ceiling. 'The immediate concern is what our man might do when he sees this story.'

Farrell's face filled the screen again. 'Sir. I hate to raise this, but it is the elephant in the room. There is one among us who is a known associate of the writer of this story. I wonder, does *he* have any idea about the identity of this "insider source"?' He smiled, sweet and deadly.

'No,' said Sawyer. 'He doesn't.'

'Is it worth asking nicely?' said Keating to Sawyer. 'Use your connection to Logan to ask him to reveal the source.'

Barlow scoffed. 'Blood from a stone. The hacks won't give us anything, but they're the first to complain when they don't feel they're getting enough from us. Parasites.'

A moment of awkward silence; Bloom broke it. 'We could go official with details of the presentations? Rob the caller of his leverage, hoaxer or not.'

'Let's see how he reacts to this first,' said Shepherd. 'It should give us more information about him.'

'See if he kills another one?' said Whittaker.

'Of course not. But at least this story might make him see that we're not going to play his game.'

'And it's deniable,' said Walker.

Sawyer's phone vibrated with a silent email alert. He took it out.

‘DI Sawyer,’ said Farrell. ‘Are we interrupting your game of *Candy Crush*?’

Sawyer smiled, didn’t look up. ‘DCI Farrell, if you’re going to do the passive-aggressive dad thing, at least update your references.’ He held up the phone. ‘Update from Rhodes on the *Secret Encounters* profiles. Mr Keen from Aberdeen, aka DrFox. He’s tried to reel us in with a dick pic, taken with a flash. It’s not him. We replied, but he hasn’t even read the message.’

‘Maybe he met his match,’ said Barlow. ‘I do love a happy ending.’

Sawyer continued. ‘The second contender, PlayWithFire99, has sent us a photo, too.’ He opened the attached image from Rhodes and studied it. ‘Standard-looking bedroom, blinds drawn behind him. Tracksuit trousers, no top. Well muscled. Clearly gets to the gym. And he’s an articulate guy, too. He left a message. “U like?”’

‘Sounds like a charmer,’ said McBride. ‘What about the third guy, Bikerboy?’

Sawyer looked up from his phone. ‘He replied a few minutes ago, with a virtual nudge. He’s online now.’

Rhodes met Keating, Sawyer and Shepherd in Keating’s office and set up his laptop at the corner table. Walker hovered outside, and Sawyer waved him in.

Rhodes navigated to the online chat area of the *Secret Encounters* site and made way for Sawyer to sit down before the laptop. ‘Time to show us that feminine side you mentioned.’

The others stood behind Sawyer as he opened a private chat with Bikerboy. He glanced at the green text beside Bikerboy’s name: *ONLINE NOW*.

Sawyer typed.

got your nudge

'Why all in lowercase?' asked Keating.

Sawyer shrugged. 'Feels more direct. Chatty.' He looked up at the unconvinced faces. 'It's a chat window, not an academic paper.'

A message came back immediately.

nice

Then another.

liked your profile. any more pics?

Sawyer typed.

show me yours and I'll show you mine

A pause. Then...

LOL Such a tease

'See?' said Shepherd. 'He's found the shift key.'

Sawyer sent the password, which gave Bikerboy access to the three extra pictures of the police volunteer. After a few seconds, the reply came back.

VERY nice

Sawyer typed.

Password?

A pause, for almost a minute.

'This is unbearable,' said Rhodes. 'Like a fucking reality show reveal.'

Another message.

Harley85

Sawyer typed the password into Bikerboy's picture section. There was one image: a tall thirtysomething man, slim and broad shouldered, crouched by a gleaming motorcycle, smiling for the camera. He wore aviator style sunglasses and a black biker jacket with red and white stripes across the shoulder pads.

Sawyer waited. Another message came through.

All good?

He typed.

love the bike!

The reply was immediate.

Take you for a ride?

Sawyer paused for a few seconds, then typed.

too nervous

Again, the reply was immediate.

LOL I'll go easy. You can sit on it first. See how it feels.

Sawyer typed.

we still talking about the bike?

A long pause. Sawyer drummed his fingers on the desk, glanced out of the window.

'You've spooked him,' said Walker. 'It's too early to introduce double entendres into the relationship.'

Another message came through.

LOL You're good! You free tonight? Drink? See how it goes?

Sawyer pondered, then typed.

yorkshire bridge inn?

Another immediate reply.

I know it! never been though. good thing I suppose LOL. 8? I'll wear the jacket in the pic. might be a different bike though. got more than one.

'Oh, he's interesting,' said Walker.

great! see you there

He paused, typed another message.

can't wait!

The green text next to Bikerboy's name switched to red, and the message changed to *OFFLINE*.

Rhodes reached over and snapped the laptop shut. 'Well, *I'd* meet you.'

20

Maggie Spark took an afternoon train from Edale to Sheffield. It was crowded, but blissfully air-conditioned, and she savoured the half-hour of downtime, catching up with her book: *Peacehaven*, a contemporary romance set in Brighton. In between chapters, she gazed out at the sunlit slopes of the Hope Valley, scrolling by in peak bloom, overlooked in the distance by Stanage Edge, a four-mile shelf of gritstone. Justin would be there now, with Mia and Freddy. A day of hiking, horse feeding, local ice cream, futile attempts to convince Mia to take off her headphones. She had accepted the end of the relationship, but still pined for her part in the makeshift solidarity of dual parenting on these endless, aimless summer days.

She took a cab from the station to the Institute of Arts Gallery. The exhibition, *Outsiders*, was sparsely attended. There were better things to do on an eighty-degree Saturday in July than wallow in the creative expression of the marginalised, the mentally unwell, the neurodiverse.

In the main hall—cavernous and brilliant white—she paused at a small painting fixed in the centre of a larger frame. It showed a burning forest, the flames leaning to the right, devouring the trees. Fleeing, smouldering horses; panicking humans. Maggie leaned in close, and noticed that the human figures were all angelic girls in flowery dresses, some with the skirts cut high to reveal stubby penises.

'These artists don't seek to be discovered, you know.' A man appeared at her side, smiling. 'Someone discovers them.' He was early thirties, with a shining bald head and a thin shadow of black beard. He wore white knee-length shorts—designer looking—and a tight-fit white T-shirt that emphasised his toned biceps. He held out a hand. 'Julius Newton. I'm the curator.'

She shook. 'Maggie Spark. Nice to meet you.'

Newton beamed. 'Of course! We have some of Desmond's work here. I understand he's a client of yours. Did you patronise?'

'Oh, no. Well. Maybe in an abstract way.'

'He is quite a talent. His work is in storage, I'm afraid. The exhibition is running until September, so we'll be cycling the display pieces. I could take a contact, and let you know when Desmond's work will be on view?'

Maggie smiled. 'Thank you, but I'm seeing Desmond in a couple of weeks, so I'm sure I'll find out from him.'

Newton didn't bother to hide his irritation. 'Ah. Okay. If you insist. Were you interested in any particular pieces?'

'Not really. I'm meeting a friend soon and thought I'd drop in to see if Desmond's work was here. Nice to get out of the heat, too.'

Newton nodded and dropped his gaze to the stone tiled floor. 'The piece you're looking at is by Francis Darger. He was a solitary character. A caretaker. He lived in the same one-room apartment for his entire adult life, from the 1930s to the 1970s. He was known for attending Mass sometimes five times a day.' Newton gestured towards the painting, but didn't look at it. 'When he became too infirm to look after himself and was moved to a nursing home, his landlord discovered hundreds of artworks like this. I find the trouble with the mainstream art world is that the pieces are too self-conscious. They try too hard, they pander. They have the observer in mind. The thrill with outsider art is that it's pure. Art for art's sake. For the artist's sake.' He slid on a pair of heavy-framed glasses, keeping his eyes on Maggie.

'I suppose...' She turned back to the painting. 'All art is a form of therapy. Many see it as frivolous and unnecessary. But for some, it's practically lifesaving.'

He waved his arms wildly. 'Oh, absolutely! We are vastly complex creatures, and we express our inner thoughts and pain in many ways.'

Maggie leaned in to the painting. 'The detail is incredible. He seems interested in subverting gender expectation. He was ahead of his time.' She looked back; Newton had turned away, keeping his eyes down, as if avoiding the painting.

He took a step back, hesitated. 'Yes. I'm sorry. I try not to become too closely acquainted with the works. I do find some of them a little... overwhelming.'

He offered a thin smile, and dug a packet of menthol cigarettes from his shorts pocket. Maggie looked down at Newton's hand; he was trembling.

'It was a pleasure to meet you, Maggie. I hope to see you again soon, perhaps when Desmond's work...' He trailed off, and hurried away.

Maggie spent another twenty minutes in the gallery, then headed to a nearby bookshop where she had planned to meet an old university girlfriend. The city centre was cloaked in mid-afternoon heat, and heaving with partially clothed bodies.

She ducked beneath a street vendor's awning, bought a bottle of water, and lingered in the shade to take a long drink.

Across the street, Austin Fletcher turned towards the window of John Lewis, keeping sight of Maggie's reflection.

21

Beverley Swift took a seat at the head of the MIT conference table, next to Keating. She was mid-thirties, with shoulder-length golden blonde hair pinned into a bushy ponytail. She flushed red as she sat, and rolled her gold band wedding ring up and down the base of her finger.

Sawyer glanced at Shepherd. 'Beverley. You won't need to do anything other than take a seat in the pub, have a drink, look at your phone. The landlord will be aware of what's happening, and we will have officers stationed outside and inside.'

She shrugged. 'I want to help. That's why I was okay with you using the picture. I'm not scared of him. I know I'm a trainee detective, but I'm also a woman. And like all other women, I want this bloke off the streets.'

Keating cleared his throat. 'The aim of the operation is to make an arrest. Once we're clear on his identity, we'll move in and your involvement will be over.'

Beverley nodded. 'How will you take it from there?'

DCI Farrell's face filled the main video screen feed. 'He might refuse DNA.'

'That would go down as adverse inference,' said Myers. 'His brief would advise him against it.'

'The meeting is set for 8pm,' said Sawyer. 'It'll still be light. There's a beer garden, so it'll be easy to settle in a couple of hours before and keep an eye on comings and goings. We know what he looks like, more or less, and so the moment he shows, we can arrest. But I would prefer for him to approach you, Beverley, as it makes it easier to link him to the website and will give us a strong case for his connection to Angela Holt.'

'Be there for seven, Beverley,' said Keating. 'We'll set up outside and inside at six. Do you have any questions?'

She shook her head, forced out a smile. Keating nodded. After a moment of silence, Beverley got the message. She rose and left the room.

'She seems terrified,' said McBride. 'Do we really need her? Can't we just arrest our man as he arrives, take DNA?'

'We need to minimise the risk of his refusing,' said Shepherd. 'An approach to Beverley will tie him in to the site and his lawyer will advise him to play nice.'

Keating drummed his fingers on the table. 'If he arrives on his hog, make sure he's a long way from it when we make the arrest. I don't want a high speed chase up the Snake Pass.'

'It's not a Harley,' said Shepherd. "Hog" is slang for a Harley-Davidson. Not a generic term for a motorcycle.'

'Fascinating,' said Keating. 'In other news, our man has been in touch. He's obviously read the *Derbyshire Times* website piece. He says that unless he gets his Bitcoin payment in full by 10pm tonight, then he'll prove to us that we're wrong to treat him as a hoaxer.'

'I take it we're not contemplating the payment?' said Whittaker.

'He's not the killer,' said Sawyer. His phone vibrated in his pocket. A call.

'You know what worries me, DI Sawyer?' said Farrell. 'This is starting to feel a bit like a new twist on the Ripper enquiry. Back then, the SIO was convinced that the caller was the real killer, and the action, or inaction, ended up costing three more women their lives. Here, a senior officer is arrogantly assuming that the contactor *isn't* the killer. Equally without base.'

Shepherd nodded. 'And in the Ripper enquiry, the contactor referred to a senior officer by name, as a challenge.'

Sawyer got to his feet. 'It's not personal. Whoever Mr Bitcoin is, he's not a killer. This is plain old blackmail.' He opened the door. 'And you don't pay blackmailers. You call their bluff. Hopefully, by 10pm this will all be irrelevant, as we may well have a prime suspect in custody.'

Sawyer checked his phone screen—*Unknown*—and headed into his office. He closed the door behind him and took the call.

'Mr Sawyer?' A woman's voice: tentative, tremulous.

'Yes. Who's this?'

'My name is Samantha Coleman. I've been... reading about you.'

He perched on his desk. 'You're not the only one. How can I help?'

'I'm sorry to call you on your personal number. I spoke to Mr Logan. The man who wrote the article on you. He said he thought you'd be interested.'

Sawyer sighed. 'I'm sure he did.'

'My son!' Samantha raised her voice, then calmed herself. 'My son, Darren. He's been missing now for seven years. We live in Matlock Bath, Mr Sawyer. He was only fifteen. He went to a party and didn't come home.'

Sawyer ran his fingers through his hair. 'I'm so sorry to hear that, Mrs Coleman.'

'Miss.'

'Sorry. I'm not sure why you think I might be able to help. I do deal with serious crime, but your son's case... I assume the leads have been exhausted and no new information has—'

'Please!' She raised her voice again, lowered it. 'Please don't say it will be reassessed as a cold case. I'm not calling you to ask for a referral or an expedition. I've jumped through so many legal hoops, Mr Sawyer. The police have been sympathetic, but unhelpful. I've called you because of who you are, because of what you've achieved.' She hesitated. 'Because of what you've been through personally. You know the pain of someone you love suddenly being removed from your life. The pain of not being able to express your love any more. It's not just the missing person processes. You know how it *feels*. How it's like to have the floor pulled away from underneath you. The emptiness below.'

Sawyer closed his eyes.

Stomach lurch.

His mother, smiling at a sandcastle, pushing a plastic flag into the top.

'Miss Coleman...'

Her fingers, smoothing out the red and white beach towel.

'I'm currently working a highly complex case...'

Her fingers, reaching out, dripping with blood. Beads of it around her fingertips, shining in the sunlight.

The office around him grew constricted, folding in at the edges. A suffocating shadow.

A voice down the phone, faraway now. 'My son's case is not "cold", Mr Sawyer. My son is not "cold". He is alive. I am sure of it. Please will you help me to find him?'

Sawyer stumbled off the desk and sank into his chair, breathing heavily. He leaned forward; a drip of sweat splashed off his knee.

Keating's face. Outside the office, looking in.

'It is still a missing persons case, Mr Sawyer. Please will you meet me and hear me out? I'm losing faith in the authorities—'

Sawyer waved a hand. 'Yes. I'm just... busy at the moment. I have your number now. I'll call you when my current case is complete.'

The heavy hammer head.

He caught his breath: ragged, juddering.

Metal on bone. Again and again, into his mother's face, into her forehead.

Keating was in the office now, looking down at him, frowning.

Inhale, exhale.

Inhale, exhale.

Inhale, exhale.

Too many breaths, but not enough oxygen.

A swell of nausea, rising through his core.

Sawyer's phone slipped from his hand and tumbled across the desk.

He just had time to see Keating hurrying around to him, before the shadow sealed over his vision and he slumped to the floor.

22

Water at his lips. The office, unnaturally dark.

'Jake. Are you still with us?' Keating's voice.

Sawyer was on the floor, back pushed up against the far wall, Keating crouched beside him, holding a white plastic cup of chilled water.

He sprang to his feet, shook his head. 'I think so. This is a pretty shitty heaven, if I'm not.'

Keating rose and faced him. 'I'm going to ask you a delicate question.'

Sawyer grabbed the cup of water and guzzled it down. 'No.'

'No?'

'I haven't been drinking. No drugs, either. I had a cup of tea and some artisanal granola for breakfast. It's just... A virus or something. Been feeling a bit off.'

Keating squinted at him. 'A bit off?'

Sawyer looked around; Keating had drawn the blinds. 'I'm going to get outside for an hour or two. Move my legs. Get sweaty. I'll be back in good time for the op later.' He opened the blinds, smoothed down his hair and smiled at Keating. 'Sir.'

As Sawyer moved for the door, Keating shifted across and stood in his way. 'You told me you were fine.'

'No. I told you I was okay.'

At the Dovedale car park, Sawyer had to flash his warrant card to the attendant to secure an unofficial staff space for the Mini. He screwed in his earphones and walked past the visitor centre, weaving through the tourist scrum along the western shore of the River Dove. Pushchairs and wheelchairs, hiking groups, mini armies of extended families. Children in swimwear swarmed around, dogs romped through the shallow stream. He screened it all out with his Rock Favourites playlist: Manics, Ride, Suede, Nirvana.

He bought a 99 ice cream from a van at the end of the path, and crossed the stepping stones, from Staffordshire into Derbyshire, joining a walking route that took him past the busy hiking trail to the top of Thorpe Cloud, across the fields to the woodland where they had discovered Angela Holt's body.

'Hey!'

A shout from ahead. Angry voices in response. A barking dog. The bleating of a distressed sheep.

He rounded the hill. A middle-aged man and woman in full hiking gear waved and pointed at another couple, younger, in T-shirts and jeans. A sheep had stumbled down into the river and cowered beneath an overhang of rock, cornered by a black-and-white mongrel dog.

The hiking man was red-faced and raging. He tore off his floppy white summer hat and waved it in the direction of the younger couple. 'If you can't control your dog, you should keep it on the lead. That sheep is livestock. It's part of a farmer's livelihood. If he were here now, he would have every right to shoot your dog.'

The younger woman laughed. 'Yeah, but he isn't, is he?'

Sawyer threw his ice cream aside. He climbed down into the water and waded out to the sheep. The dog snarled at him, but he waved it away, and it retreated to the shore, where the younger man grabbed its collar and held it back.

He jabbed a finger at Sawyer. 'Don't be stressing my dog, mate!'

Sawyer edged towards the sheep and, in a swift, sharp movement, bent down and hitched his arms underneath its body, trapping its legs. It trembled as he lifted it out of the water and set it down in the field, where it trotted away.

The older woman called to Sawyer. 'Thank you. That's very kind.'

By the time he had climbed out of the river, the younger couple had settled the dog. The woman kept her distance, while the man made his way along the shore towards them.

The older man approached Sawyer and gave him an awkward pat on the shoulder. Up close, his features were gnome-like, with trimmed grey stubble and a bulbous nose, reddened at the tip. 'Thank you for the help. It's always a nightmare round here during summer. People lighting barbecues and showing total disregard for others.'

The woman joined them. 'Bloody townies. Ruining the parks.'

'Oi!' The younger man called over as he approached, pointing at Sawyer.

'Us and them, though,' said Sawyer. 'That's not going to help, is it?'

The man frowned. 'Sorry?'

'Dividing people into categories. Country folk and

townies. Setting them apart, stereotyping values, pitching them against each other.'

'Ah. But the non-local people *do* all behave this way,' said the man, replacing his floppy hat. 'It's not a stereotype if it's true.'

'Who the fuck do you think you are?' The younger man stopped, a few feet away.

Sawyer ignored him. 'Well. It's a generalisation, at best. I'm just saying it's not helpful to make neat little divisions. This place became a national park in the first place because of walkers demanding their right to enjoy the open countryside. Right to roam. Nature for all.' He smiled. 'I'm just preaching for a bit more tolerance.'

'I see what you're saying,' said the woman. 'But it's these people with dogs. They are always—'

'I'm talking to you!' The younger man moved closer, within striking distance of Sawyer. He was shorter, but well built. Sawyer caught a whiff of marijuana on his breath.

Sawyer turned to face him, smiled. 'I know where you live.'

The man frowned. 'Eh?'

'Lindale village. Yes? You don't seem like tourists to me. It's a guess, but the accent helps. And Lindale is nearest. You're probably a farm labourer or something. Maybe a trade. Although that would be skilled and specialist, and I don't get the impression you have the intelligence for it.' He paused, pointed at the man. 'Tell you what. I'll go with silage technician.'

'You what?'

'Muckraker. Shit clearer. You clear the effluent from the pig pens.' He smiled. 'You've found your level.'

The man shook his head. 'Ah! You think you're clever. Well. I work at a bike shop in Lindale, mate.' He stepped closer. 'In fact, I own the fucking place. I founded the business. One out of two ain't bad, though. We are local.'

Sawyer stared him out. 'Well, then you should know that you need to keep your dog on a lead when there are livestock nearby.'

The man sniffed, looked across the stream. 'And you need to be careful with that mouth. Keep it shut sometimes, before someone shuts it for you.'

Sawyer grinned, nodded. 'That's almost a sentence.'

The man shook his head, turned, and walked back to the woman and dog.

'See?' said Sawyer to the older couple. 'People are rarely what they seem. But the real version is never far from the surface. All it takes is a little scratch.'

Sawyer moved off and continued to the deposition scene, long since cleared. He crouched, running his fingertips through the arid soil. Farrell's words nagged at him. Perhaps he was assuming too much. Perhaps the killer and the blackmailer *were* one and the same, and they were drifting off course, following their noses, following a desired outcome rather than the most likely. The messenger's reference to biting, and the bracelet... He may just be an arrogant psychopath, taunting them with detail, wallowing in the terrible intimacy of the shared knowledge.

He scrolled through the various crime scene photos on his phone, pondered the victims' journeys: from their violent deaths to their discarding, in lonely woodland. The killer had shown his victims no mercy in life, but had adorned them in death. The make-up, the covering, the flowers. This disconnect was the key to catching him. Was his hatred only reserved for living women? Why did it transform into something softer after their death?

He paused at the full-screen image of Angela Holt's body. Who was he? *What* was he? The deadly triad—domination, manipulation, control—were all present in the killing. But who were these women? What did they represent to him? He would have a triggering moment, a stressor. Something in his past. There would have been odd behaviour, misdemeanours, all showing a lack of empathy, or at least a limited understanding of the suffering of others. The behaviour would escalate, refine itself.

The killer had organised himself and perfected his MO since the messy, almost impulsive killing of Laura Bertrand. But it seemed that his signature—what he was getting out of the murders personally—wasn't changing. Did he need the pre-death violence to fulfil something in himself? Was it to force the women to beg for their lives? To dominate, manipulate, control?

And was the post-death presentation a fetish, or some twisted expression of guilt? Many killers who showed a hatred for women would present their victims in humiliating, sexualised poses. Was this posing? That is, was it part of his fulfilment? Or was it staging? A subterfuge. An attempt to send police scurrying down a rabbit hole, rooting around for phantom psychological interpretations.

Sawyer turned his phone around, viewing the picture from several angles. He had a well-worn line for junior detectives baffled by cases. Step away from your emotional involvement, from your outrage. Interpret the killer as he sees himself: as an artist, expressing something. If you want to understand an artist, you study his work.

And for the first time, he saw it. He allowed himself to see it, in the image of a naked young woman: brutalised and murdered, then dressed, embellished, decorated, and laid out before the elements.

He saw a work of art.

23

Luka Strickland pulled the front door wide open. 'I did it!'

Sawyer reeled. 'Did what?'

'The lock. The technique you showed me. I picked it. I used the grips. The hairpins.'

'*My* hairpins!' A voice from behind, in the hall.

'Come through,' said Luka. 'I'll show you!'

Luka ran through to the kitchen at the back of the hall. Sawyer followed and closed the door behind him.

As Luka rummaged in a drawer, Eva ambushed Sawyer, pulling him into the sitting room by his collar. He kissed her; she lingered, but he pulled away.

'Darling,' he said. 'Not in front of the children.'

Eva took a step back. She had tied her black hair into a high ponytail and wore a light blue Adidas T-shirt and black Lycra running shorts. She propped her hands on her hips and looked at him over the top of her Tom Fords. '"Darling" is good. Even when you're not being serious.'

Sawyer nodded and licked his lips, tasting her cherry balm. 'We don't do pet names.'

She gave him a shove. 'We don't do seeing each other.'

'We went to the zoo.'

She picked up a purple plastic water bottle from a bookshelf. 'Yes. And didn't that go well?'

'I'm on this case. It's grim.'

'I know.' She studied him, smiled, pushed past and walked through to the kitchen.

Sawyer followed. 'We'll do something special.'

Eva sighed, and filled her bottle from the kitchen sink tap. 'When it's over.'

'Yes.'

Luka had hitched himself up onto a chair and placed a padlock and two kirby grips in the centre of the kitchen table. He leaned forward and ran the fingers of both hands through his blond mane. He took off his red glasses and cleaned the lenses on his white Liverpool FC shirt.

'It's okay,' said Eva. 'Really. I'm used to secretive men.'

'No choice,' said Sawyer.

'I don't suppose you can stay?'

'Working.'

Eva stole another kiss as she squeezed past, heading for the front door. 'After your stunt at the zoo—'

'That was so cool!' Luka raised his head.

Eva sighed. 'After your stunt at the zoo, you are seriously in the red.'

Sawyer pondered. 'Rowley's?'

She shook her head. 'Fischer's. And we're talking tasting menu.' She whispered in his ear. 'I love you.'

Sawyer smiled, but said nothing.

Eva wheeled away, cheerful. 'It's okay. You can text me a reply later.'

She hurried to the front door and jogged out into the lane, heading for the river path that led away from Bakewell town centre.

Sawyer sat at the table and smiled at Luka. 'Okay, Houdini. Show me.'

Luka bent one of the pins into a ninety-degree angle and slotted it into the padlock keyhole, creating a makeshift handle by twisting it to the side. He pushed in the other pin above the first and worked it around, staring at Sawyer and smiling.

'That's good,' said Sawyer. 'You're feeling out the tension.'

'I know that!' Luka continued to work the handle and pick. His smile cracked as he struggled to find his way through the pins to feel the holding plug.

'Nice kit,' said Sawyer.

'I like the away best. Red looks weird with my glasses.'

'I thought you supported Man Utd, like your dad.'

'Liverpool are better. Dale doesn't take me to Old Trafford any more, anyway.'

Sawyer frowned. 'You call your dad Dale now?'

Luka shrugged. 'That's his name.' He continued his struggle with the pins, scowling, staring down by the side of the keyhole.

'Nice and easy,' said Sawyer. 'Don't try to force it. Just feel for the tiny pins, like jaws. You'll get the one that holds the pins soon. Just be patient.'

But Luka's cheeks were reddening, and he jerked and yanked at the grips.

'Still playing FIFA?' said Sawyer.

Luka shook his head. 'Playing a thing called *For Honour*. Knights, samurai. Waiting for the new *Call Of Duty*.'

'You're seven years too young for it.'

He scoffed. 'I used to play the old one with Dale. *Did it*!' The padlock clicked and Luka opened the clasp. He held his arms aloft.

Sawyer beamed and shook his hand. 'Nice work. Now you just have to do it without the grips.'

'What? How? It's hard enough with them.'

'The grips are just to get you used to the principle. You can do it with a couple of bits of wire, paperclips. If you get captured by the enemy, they're not going to give you two nice fresh kirby grips, are they?'

'So you keep some secret wire in your shoe or something?'

'You might have to hide it somewhere more... intimate.'

Luka thought for a second, then screwed up his face. 'No way.'

Sawyer got up and opened the fridge. He took out two cold cans of Diet Coke, handed one to Luka and opened one himself. 'Luka. I can't stay too long. I have to leave soon, after your mum is back. Busy on a case.'

Luka opened his can. 'The Ripper.'

'That's just what the papers are calling him.'

Luka slurped his drink. 'The papers?'

'The media, I mean. The news. Look. Before I go. I wanted to ask you something. But you must promise not to mention it to your mum. It's nothing to worry about.'

'She can't worry if I don't tell her.'

'Exactly.' He took out his phone and showed Luka a photograph of Austin Fletcher, in a black baseball cap, taken in secret a few months earlier by his friend Richard Jensen. 'Have you seen this guy anywhere? In town? Near here? Your school?'

Luka studied the picture. 'I've seen him, yeah. With Dad. *Dale*. It was ages ago, though. He came here. But it was before Dale went to prison the first time. When he was still married to Mum.' Luka tapped the phone screen twice, enlarging Fletcher's head. 'I haven't seen him for a long time. He's weird.'

Sawyer put the phone away. 'A bit. But nothing to be scared of.'

Luka gathered away the padlock and grips. He smiled. 'I'm not scared.'

24

Sawyer took a seat at a wooden picnic table in the beer garden of the Yorkshire Bridge Inn, a vast, stone-built pub hotel located off the southern lip of Ladybower Reservoir. It had just gone 6:30pm, but the wood of the table was still hot to the touch. He looked up at the pristine blue sky, speckled with faint patches of fuzzy cloud.

Shepherd backed into the door of the conservatory and sidestepped out, hands occupied by two pint pots of iced lemonade. He shuffled over, taking short, careful steps, set down the glasses and gave a grunt as he flopped down on the seat.

'Old man noises,' said Sawyer. 'Again.'

Shepherd smiled. 'We can't all be agile young ectomorphs. And I don't care, anyway. I'm happy with my old man noises. I'm owning them.'

Sawyer nodded. 'What were you thinking?'

Shepherd frowned. 'Oh! Yes. There's a bunch of older fellas in there, and I was thinking, as you get older, do you start to see each new day as a victory? Wake up, bedroom, bedside clock, made it through another night. And at what point do you start to get sick of it all and look forward to it being over?'

Sawyer took a tentative sip of his drink. 'You really are the ideal companion on a life-affirming summer's day.'

He shrugged. 'Interesting, though. The things that sneak into your head.'

'How are we doing?'

'Beverley is in there with her Kindle. Booth seat in the near corner, by the door. Two DCs inside, two more over there.' He nodded at a table set on a raised verge near the roadside, where a twentysomething man and woman sat facing each other, in matching light summer hoodies and shorts. The woman offered a subtle nod in return. 'There's one way in and one way out, apart from the tradesmen's near the kitchen out back. Moran wanted to come, so I've stuck him in a booth with a good view of the kitchen and back door. If our friend shows, it should be a simple enough arrest. Sound like a plan?'

'Everyone has a plan until they get punched in the mouth.'

Shepherd slurped his pint. 'Is this your man Sun-Tzu again?'

Sawyer smiled. 'Mike Tyson.'

At 7:30, a gleaming motorcycle roared into the car park, ridden by a man in a black jacket with red and white stripes across the shoulder pads. He parked the bike, took off his helmet, and flattened down his hair.

'Easy rider,' said Shepherd.

Sawyer caught his eye. 'That's him.'

The biker broke into a confident stride and entered the pub through the conservatory double doors.

Sawyer stood up. 'You stay.'

'Can we do it the other way round?'

Sawyer moved off. 'No. I did the seduction, remember? Technically, he's here for a date with me.'

He headed inside and lingered by the bar, catching Beverley's eye in the booth as she looked up from her Kindle. The man had also taken a spot at the bar, and Sawyer stood close enough to hear him order 'Stella, in a bottle'. While the man waited, he took out his phone and pretended to be distracted by something, then looked up, clearly spotting Beverley. He paid for his drink and approached her.

Shepherd laid a hand on Sawyer's shoulder. 'Sorry, sir. Couldn't resist. The other two are still out front. We ran the bike plate. Tommie Nash. "Tommie" with an "ie", not a "y".'

'That's grounds for arrest alone.'

Nash said something to Beverley, then slid into the booth seat opposite, smiling.

'Pretty slick,' said Shepherd.

He got up and headed back towards the bar. Beverley nodded at Sawyer, who stepped forward.

'Thomas Nash?'

Nash startled at the sound of his name. He squinted at Sawyer. 'Sort of. Only my mum calls me Thomas, though.'

'I'm afraid I'm not your mum.' Sawyer showed his warrant card. 'I'm arresting you on suspicion of the murder of Angela Holt. You do not have to say anything, but it may harm your defence if you do not mention when questioned something which you later rely on in court. Anything you do say may be given in evidence.'

The colour drained from Nash's face. He looked to Beverley, back at Sawyer. Moran moved in behind him, along with the two other DCs.

He gaped at Sawyer. 'This isn't illegal, is it? Just a bit of fun. We met online.'

Sawyer took out his handcuffs. 'Given the nature of the alleged offence, I'll need to put these on.'

Nash pushed his wrists together and held them out. Sawyer slipped on the cuffs and ratcheted them tight.

He looked around again, as if expecting the façade to fall away and the joke to be revealed. 'What about—'

'The bike will be impounded for evidence,' said Sawyer.

Sawyer nodded at Moran, and he guided Nash out through the front door, followed by the two DCs. The arrest had been so smooth, only a few drinkers had bothered to look up.

Beverley joined them. 'Is that it, then?'

'You know in films,' said Shepherd, 'when they say it's too quiet? That was too easy.'

25

They took a mouth swab from Nash and held him in one of the cells on the ground floor at Buxton, while Myers and Shepherd worked up the background and Sawyer devised an interview plan. The duty solicitor, Graham Whittingham, arrived soon after Nash's detention, and they spent half an hour or so in private discussion before Sawyer and Shepherd faced them across the interview room desk.

A beefy man in a short-sleeved uniform shirt entered, and set a large desktop fan on a desk in the corner. 'Thanks, Gerry,' said Sawyer. 'Full blast, please. On rotate.'

Sergeant Gerry Sherman shook his head. 'Rotate doesn't work.'

Shepherd sat back in his chair and gave a fake diva sigh. 'I can't work in these conditions.'

Sherman set the fan running and left.

Sawyer looked up at Nash and Whittingham. 'Sorry about the heat. This is the best we can do.'

Whittingham gave a stiff nod and consulted his notes as Sawyer activated the voice recorder and ran through the initial formalities. Beside him, Nash kept his eyes down, giving the detectives a full view of the top of his head:

balding, sunburnt. He smelt of an exotic cologne, not unpleasant. Sawyer watched as he rested his hands on the table, then moved them to his knee, clasping them together, fingers writhing.

'Tommie,' said Sawyer. 'Thomas? Or would you prefer Mr Nash?' Nash shrugged, shook his head, kept his eyes down. 'Or maybe we could go with Bikerboy. That's your profile name on *Secret Encounters*, isn't it?'

A pause: long and painful. At last, Nash raised his reddened eyes to Sawyer. 'No comment.'

Sawyer smiled. 'Yes. Your profile states you like women who eat ice cream in bed. Does Miranda eat ice cream in bed, Tommie? Miranda, your wife.'

'No comment.'

'I'm not here to judge you. That's not the purpose of this interview. Whatever's going on, or not going on, in your marriage, is none of my concern.'

Nash raised his head. 'No, it fucking isn't.'

'Thomas.' Whittingham rested a hand on Nash's forearm and spoke in a low voice with a hint of warning.

Sawyer took a breath. 'I'm more interested in the women you've been contacting on *Secret Encounters*, and maybe other sites, under other nicknames.'

Another pause. Nash glanced at Whittingham, who angled his head. 'Is there a question, detective?'

'I've got one,' said Shepherd. 'Did you contact a profile called "Miss Chievous"? A couple of weeks ago?'

Nash sniffed. 'No comment.'

'You see,' said Sawyer. 'Miss Chievous is the alias of a young woman named Angela Holt. She was found dead a few days ago. So, now can you see why I'm interested in you and your activities on *Secret Encounters*?'

'No comment.'

'Did you meet Angela Holt?'

'No comment.'

'Did you contact her online?'

'No comment.'

'Did you eat ice cream in bed with her?'

'No comment.'

'Did you have sex with her?'

'No comment.'

'Did you kill her?'

'No comment.'

Sawyer sat back, took a long drink from a bottle of lukewarm water.

The fan whirred in the corner, the elderly blades catching on the frame.

Sawyer opened a folder and took out a screen grab image of Nash's *Secret Encounters* photograph. He pushed it across the desk. 'This is you, right? Next to your bike.'

Nash glanced at the picture. 'No comment.'

'If that's not you, then I can only assume you have an identical twin brother. Do you have an identical twin brother, Tommie?'

'No c—'

'Sorry. That one was rhetorical. I can confirm that you don't. *Ergo*, this person here who looks exactly like you, who is wearing the same style biker jacket as the one you were wearing when you were arrested, and who is pictured next to a motorcycle that looks exactly like the one you rode into the Yorkshire Bridge Inn car park two hours ago... I'm going to stick my neck out here, and say that it's you. Now, we have proof that you made contact with Angela Holt, aka Miss Chievous, on the second and third of the month. Two weeks ago. I'm suggesting that you maybe talked to her for a while in the site's private chat area, and you arranged to meet. Did you do that, Tommie?'

'No comment.'

'And then, you took her somewhere private.' Sawyer brought out two full-colour photographs of Angela Holt's body on Drummond's autopsy table. The first showed her face and neck in close-up, the second showed her full-length body: bloodless white beneath the overhead lighting. He laid them out on the table. 'And then, when you'd got her somewhere private, you punched her, didn't you, Tommie? You punched her so hard that you broke her jaw.'

Sawyer paused. Nash shook his head. 'For the benefit of the tape, Mr Nash is shaking his head. And then, after you broke her jaw, you beat her unconscious, and you strangled her. And you used your thumbs to do that, didn't you, Tommie? Your bare hands. Because what kind of a weakling needs rope to strangle a woman? And when you'd strangled her, you—'

'We never even met!' Nash snapped his head up. His shoulders heaved as he suppressed the sobs. He looked up to the ceiling. Two tears trickled down his cheeks, in almost comic synchronicity. They pooled at his jawline and he wiped them away. He shook his head, rubbed his eyes. 'We exchanged a couple of messages. But we never met. Look. I'm sorry that she died, but it was nothing to do with me.'

Whittingham leaned forward and turned to face Nash, as if the physical barrier might silence him.

A knock on the door. Myers peeked his head into the room and raised his eyebrows at Sawyer.

'And why didn't you meet Angela, Tommie?' Sawyer lowered his voice. 'Was she not to your liking?'

Nash caught his breath. 'Yeah. I liked her. Physically. But she kept going on about her bloody husband and kid. To be honest, that put me off. I joined the site to... to get away from that.' He leaned forward. 'Look. I'm not perfect, right? But I didn't hurt anybody. I didn't kill anybody.'

Sawyer studied him. 'Let's take a break.'

Outside, Myers pulled Sawyer and Shepherd into the empty interview room across the corridor. Shepherd closed the door behind them.

'Sally fast-tracked the DNA,' said Myers.

Sawyer nodded. 'No match.'

'No match. His DNA isn't in the database, and it doesn't match either the blood from Laura Bertrand's dog bite or the cigarette end we found at the Holt scene. We have literally nothing.'

'There's the online contact,' said Shepherd.

Myers eyed him. 'That's as good as nothing, sir. We can't charge someone with murder on the evidence of contact via an online dating site. The CPS will laugh me off the phone.'

Sawyer closed his eyes. 'What else?'

'Sorry?' said Myers.

'There's something else.'

Myers sighed. 'Whether Nash is the killer or not, he isn't the person who's been trying to blackmail us.'

'We had another message,' said Sawyer.

Myers nodded. 'Five minutes ago.'

26

They marched up to the first floor, into Keating's office. The DSI sat at his desk, turned away towards his screen. He nodded to Rhodes, installed at the corner desk with his laptop.

'We received another encrypted email,' said Rhodes. 'With a twist.'

'Read it,' said Sawyer.

Rhodes peered into the screen. 'Police,' he read aloud. 'You asked for this. You've tried my patience and now you're going to pay the price. Take a good look at the attached picture. Unless I get a Bitcoin transfer of fifteen thousand pounds within the hour, then I will make this image public, and I'll be killing another very soon.'

Rhodes flipped the laptop around.

The screen showed an image of Angela Holt's body, as they had found her in the woodland: hair splayed out, covered by the fabric, garlanded with flowers.

'Could it be an official crime scene photo he's somehow got access to?' said Shepherd. 'A hack?'

Myers shook his head. 'I've seen all the photos. It's different.'

'Wherever he got the picture,' said Sawyer, 'he's getting desperate. As I've said, the killer would kill. He wouldn't keep asking for more money and—'

'We paid it,' said Keating, turning to face them.

Sawyer frowned. 'What?'

Keating leaned forward and rested his forearms on the desk. 'We made the transfer. Fifteen thousand pounds.' He set his phone on speaker and placed it on the desk. 'Robert. You're on with DI Sawyer, DS Shepherd, DC Myers and DC Rhodes.'

'Gentlemen. DCI Robert Payne.' The voice from Keating's phone was clipped, high-born. A politician? 'I oversee the City of London Police fraud teams in Wood Street. DI Sawyer, we briefly crossed paths on a case during your time in the Met, several years ago. The banker chap and the parties?'

Sawyer leaned on Keating's desk and spoke at the phone. 'Yes. With Max Reeves.'

'Indeed. DSI Keating has called me in to help in your current case. I hope the need-to-know aspect doesn't put any noses out of joint. But the digital infrastructure is notoriously porous, and so intelligence hygiene has to be scrupulous.'

Sawyer glanced at Keating. 'Understood, sir.'

'My work deals with the expanding range of crimes increasingly facilitated by cyber technology. Boiler room fraud, organised crime gangs operating schemes involving shares, land, diamonds, gold and oil, carbon credits. We also handle mortgage fraud, insider and illegal trading, ticketing and identity crime. It's colourful stuff, and, as I'm sure you appreciate, amorphous. Ever changing. Now, in recent years, we've seen increasing instances of blackmailers using crypto currency because it has a reputation for being untraceable. But that isn't necessarily the truth. The individual who has been contacting you, demanding Bitcoin payment, would need to be extremely clever to circumvent our tracing techniques. I'm happy to inform you that he's done well with the basic IP masking, but extremely clever he is not. We have access to high-end software that can perform a deep blockchain analysis. It examines the transactions from a unique Bitcoin wallet, and it can link Bitcoin transactions to real identities.'

'This is why we paid up,' said Keating. 'Now Robert's team have some data on the transaction.'

Payne continued. 'Precisely. We facilitated the transfer using the Tor browser, and applied various protocols to hide things at our end. I can now get to work analysing the blockchain and wallet, and see if we can find a way to de-anonymise this guy. It's tricky, but it's been done before. The FBI caught a couple of rogue agents this way recently. We just have to hope that your man has been sloppy with the privacy options in his unique Bitcoin wallet. The good news is that most people are.'

'Sorry to interrupt, sir, but we've just received another email,' said Rhodes.

Keating's eyes widened. 'Robert,' he said, 'this is DC Rhodes from our digital media department. Read it out.'

'Police,' Rhodes read, 'I thank you for the speedy payment. I'm sorry, but I'm afraid I can't provide a receipt. And, since you have fucked me around, then I'm going to fuck you around.' Rhodes looked up. 'There's a link, sir. Looks like YouTube. We should probably screen it—'

'Follow it,' said Keating. He got up from his desk and joined Sawyer, Shepherd and Myers as they watched Rhodes's screen over his shoulder.

Rhodes clicked the link. It led to a YouTube page with no title or caption. The play screen showed a static image of

Angela Holt's body, clearly embedded into the video track, on a one-hour timeline.

'Jesus wept,' said Keating. 'Robert. He's posted a crime-scene picture of the latest victim's body on YouTube.'

'That's regrettable. He's likely to ask for more money. Is there an option to release the imagery officially? Rob him of his leverage?'

'Out of the question,' said Sawyer. 'Risk of copycat crime, and the presentation is so unique we have to keep it internal. And, anyway. It's far too graphic.'

'Another email,' said Rhodes, reading. 'He says he's "happy" to take the video down if we make another immediate payment.' He looked up. 'Of ten thousand pounds.'

'No chance,' said Keating. 'It's already out there, anyway. Could we appeal to YouTube to remove it?'

Rhodes barked a laugh. 'Good luck with that.'

Sawyer's phone buzzed with a text. Dean Logan.

CALL ME. HE'S POSTED THE LINK ON OUR SITE.

Sawyer nodded at Keating. '*Derbyshire Times*.' He called; Logan answered immediately.

'Sawyer. There's a YouTube link to the crime scene photo in the Comments thread of my *Derbyshire Times* article.'

'The "pay up or I'll kill again" piece?'

Commotion in the background. Logan talking to someone else.

'Looks like he's just deleted the comment with the link. Slippery fucker. But anyone following the thread will have received a notification of the update, and they might have already seen the image on YouTube. There are a couple of replies coming through now, asking if it's legit. I'm closing the thread for comments now. Hopefully we won't get anyone sharing the link.'

'Thanks,' said Sawyer, disconnecting.

'The YouTube page has already gone,' said Rhodes. He looked up from his screen. 'He's already taken it down. Hold on. *Another* email. I'll read it: "As I said, police. Just fucking with you. I hope I haven't caused you too much inconvenience. I'll leave you alone for a while now. Spend my hard-earned public money. Maybe take a holiday."'

'He posted the link in the comments on the *Derbyshire Times* website piece,' said Sawyer. 'Then took it down straight away. It might still have been seen, though.'

Keating walked back to his desk and sat down. 'Robert.'

'My team are already working on the transaction. I'll hopefully have something for you soon.'

Keating disconnected the call. 'So, we know that Nash isn't the blackmailer.' He looked at Sawyer. 'Could he be the killer?'

'I don't think so. Even if he was, we don't have anything to connect him to any of the scenes.'

'Aren't we getting a bit tangled here?' said Myers. 'The blackmailer *could* be the killer, right?'

Sawyer caught Keating's eye and offered a reluctant nod.

'Release Nash,' said Keating. 'Tell him to keep his phone on. He's probably terrified that we'll tell his wife, anyway. I'll brief Farrell and the others. Full conference tomorrow, 9am.'

27

Austin Fletcher dampened down the fire and rose to his feet. He pulled on a pair of walking boots and shouldered a small grey backpack containing water, a black baseball cap, a hunting knife, a pair of binoculars, and, stuffed into a side pocket, a bottle of pills marked with a green logo: three overlaid C-symbols, inverted and concentric.

He wriggled his short, thick fingers into a pair of fitted leather gloves and stretched himself to his full height, his scalp grazing the dislodged wooden beam that propped up the outbuilding. It was little more than a shed: a floor of rancid mulch, half-open roof of rotted planks, back wall with a splintered fissure overlooking the grazing fields over Edale, and a distant farmhouse where, presumably, the shed's owner lived.

Fletcher gathered the thin blanket from the floor, rolled it up, and stuffed it into the inside pocket of his black bomber jacket. He stepped outside and looked back to the farmhouse, where a single interior light twinkled in the muted gloom. He checked his watch—10:30pm—and began his familiar trudge through the dense grass, down to the lane. The air was close and clammy, and, as he reached the tea-coloured Fiesta, he swiped at his brow with the back of his glove.

He made the five-minute drive to the lay-by, and positioned the car side on, keeping the headlights away from the road and possible reflections. To an observer in the house across the ditch, a few hundred yards away, the vehicle would be shadowed by the tall bushes spilling out from the edge of the field.

Fletcher rolled down the Fiesta's window and lit an unfiltered cigarette. He settled his eyes into the viewing cups of the binoculars and adjusted for focus. He swung his view from the dim porch light and Mini towards Sawyer's bedroom window. Open a few inches. A sure sign that he was home and probably asleep.

He unzipped the backpack and slid out the knife. Scubapro. Both straight and serrated edges. Grey and black inlay handle with rubber grip.

A car approached from the front, and he lowered his head as the lights passed over the road and the engine noise receded behind him. He opened the other window and listened as the car slowed for the turn-off to Hayfield.

He held the knife loosely and eased his grip as he flicked his thumb across the handle, spinning it around. The time for caution had passed. He was tired of being managed and muted. He had been patient: amassed the research, cross-referenced his findings, considered all the options. He had been assigned a mission, then stood down, cast into limbo.

Unfinished business.

But Fletcher was not a sleeper; he was a hunter. And no true hunter would centre his quarry in the cross-hairs and delay the dispatch, whatever the consequences. And he was tired of considering the consequences.

He took out the bottle of pills, threw two into his mouth, and washed them down with water.

He rolled his head from side to side, cracking his neck muscles. In their last encounter, Sawyer had been an astute, effective fighter, clearly trained in a non-classical discipline. Possibly *krav maga*. Or some form of MMR. But now he was braced for the moves. And he had freed himself of the most constrictive element: someone else's agenda.

He paused, listening for the car behind. It still hadn't revved its engine and pulled out into the Hayfield road. And it was too late for it to have stopped for passing traffic.

A fist drove through the open window and connected with the side of Fletcher's head, bouncing it off the steering wheel. He twisted himself around and shouldered through the door, out onto the roadside. His assailant was large, bigger than Fletcher, but he had made the mistake of not downing him when he still had the element of surprise. Head ringing from the punch, Fletcher rounded on the figure. He held out the knife and slipped into a front fighting stance.

His eyes adjusted to the light and he caught the man's features: square jaw, shaven head, deep-set eyes. Hector.

'Freeze!' Another voice off the side.

Fletcher turned to see Marco, aiming a handgun.

Marco smiled. 'I've always wanted to say that.'

Fletcher crouched low, breathing hard, looking from Marco to Hector and back again. He spat, and winced at the flash of pain across his cheekbone.

'I'll take the weapon,' said Hector.

Fletcher sucked in a breath, steeling himself to pounce.

Marco smiled. 'You've literally brought a knife to a gun fight.' Fletcher kept his gaze low, staring at the ground between Marco and Hector. 'We're not here to kill you. But we are licensed to kill, if you insist.'

Hector held out his hand. Fletcher gave him the knife and turned towards the car.

'Easy now,' said Marco, holding the gun higher.

Fletcher looked over his shoulder. 'Smoke.' He reached into the car footwell and took out the dropped cigarette. He turned back to them and took a slow drag, puffing the smoke up into the air.

Marco reached into an inside pocket and threw a weighty envelope onto the grass at Fletcher's feet. 'Check out of your little kennel. Find a homely B&B somewhere with a view. Get yourself something nice.' He took a step closer, keeping the gun raised but withdrawn. 'Most of all, though, hear this. You need to swallow your pride. The calculus has changed. You will get to finish the job. But not yet. Not until *we* say so. In football terms, you just got a yellow card.'

28

Sawyer rose with the early morning light and worked out on the wooden man dummy: thrusting and blocking, forearm jabs, elbow strikes. He settled in front of the mirror and carried out the first form of Wing Chun Kung Fu: *Sil Lim Tao* ('Little Idea'). The form was a rigid series of precise, disciplined movements that reflected the principles: economy and efficiency, nothing extraneous, nothing for show.

He dug out a Nutribullet and made a smoothie with strawberry, mango, banana and natural yoghurt, and browsed his laptop as he sipped. He signed in to *Secret Encounters* and opened the browser tab with the profile page of PlayWithFire99. He leaned in to the photograph, sent in response to a message from their fake blonde. The man had cropped the image at the neck, and the anonymity emphasised his powerful, hairless physique. The musculature was almost cartoonish in its extremity: taut, breast-like pectorals; three neat rows of sculpted abdominals packed between knotted obliques.

Sawyer dragged the picture onto his desktop and opened it in his image software. He played with the brightness and contrast settings, but picked out little detail from the darkened surroundings. The man wore black tracksuit trousers with red stripes, and the rest of the room was bare, apart from a neatly made double bed with white sheets and dark pillows.

He toyed with the colour scale options and picked out a sliver of blue somewhere in the drawn vertical blinds. He zoomed in and saw that one of the slats was kinked slightly, and the blue was part of something in the background, outside the window. He zoomed in a little more, and although the resolution deteriorated, Sawyer could just make out a curl of white at the bottom of the blue. A number six. Part of the bottom of a clock face.

He fed Bruce, and stepped outside, looking up across the sloping farmland opposite. The rising sun had formed an amber aura just behind the summit of Kinder Scout, and the rays shimmered on the fringes, eager to conquer the mountain and begin yet another day of roasting the withered land.

Sawyer paused at the Mini and sniffed the air: dewy grass; the synthetic tang of metal and plastic; a distant sweetness delivered by the tepid breeze. No smoke.

He drove to Edale station and took a seat in the Penny Pot Café, a converted barn that offered breakfast for the Sheffield commuters and portable lunches for the Kinder walkers. It was quiet, and he took a corner sofa and ate scrambled eggs with spinach, while browsing an old copy of *GQ Watch*.

At 8am, a squat, top-heavy man entered and pushed his mirrored sunglasses up onto his balding head. He looked like a misplaced tourist, in a loose yellow T-shirt, new-looking Converse trainers, and a pair of unwise cargo shorts: white with a pattern of blue flowers.

The man spotted Sawyer and walked over, blinding him with a toothy grin. He slapped a hand into Sawyer's and squeezed. 'Good to see you, my friend. You're looking... lean.'

Sawyer smiled. 'Tony. You're looking...' Cross raised an eyebrow. 'Colourful.'

He laughed. 'Diplomatic.'

Cross brought over two lattes and crashed down into the sofa opposite. 'So, how are you getting on? Saw you on telly. Progress in the case?'

Sawyer winced. 'Yes, but it's a slow one.'

'Press not helping, I imagine.' He set down his sunglasses and sipped his drink, holding the latte glass around the rim. For a stocky man, he had long, slender fingers. 'Well. Now you know what it's like to get your own little epithet. I'm "Disgraced Marksman"; you're "Hero Cop". At least you're on the streets, though. I'm doing the freelance gigs, bit of training and security. Might try and start my own firm.'

'No chance of getting back on the inside?'

Cross waved a hand. 'You're having a laugh. I'd be on armoury admin, at best. Me and Steve Fulcher, Jake. We're the poster boys. Doing the wrong thing for the right reason.'

'Would Martin Freeman play you on TV, though?'

Cross laughed: full throated, loud enough to draw a sharp look from the man at the counter. 'They won't be making any films about me, mate. I'm an embarrassment. I did some work in the States last year. Their guys can't believe the shit we have to go through when someone discharges a weapon. Full-blown enquiry for every fucking bullet.' He leaned forward, lowered his voice. 'The way I saw it, there was a career scumbag toting a MAC-10. That wasn't going to end well for someone. I just made sure that someone was the bad guy.' He sat back, took another slurp of coffee. 'Why d'you come back up here, then? You had it made in the Met.'

Sawyer tipped a sachet of brown sugar into his coffee and watched it sink into the foam. 'Mother. Had to work that out.'

Cross frowned. 'Sorry about your dad, mate. You got the bloke who did it, though.'

Sawyer stirred his coffee. 'I was never keen on guns.'

'No. I read a thing by your gaffer, Keating, a couple of years ago. He wasn't too keen, either. Neither was your hero, Bruce Lee.'

Sawyer nodded, raised his eyes to Cross. 'Remember the marathon at the Prince Charles? I didn't know you were even going.'

'Yeah! It was our secret shame. A shared love of a dead martial arts movie star who was mainly all choreography, anyway.' Sawyer eyed him. 'Strange,' said Cross, 'that Bruce Lee wasn't a fan of guns. They're efficient, direct. No excess. You aim, you fire, you're done. Hey. You still with that posh bird?'

'Sheena? Not a fan of long-distance relationships.'

Cross toyed with his sunglasses. 'Shame. She was tidy.'

Sawyer held the moment, looked across at the counter queue, growing now. 'I wanted to ask you how you dealt with the media attention, after your case. I know it was different, but—'

'I was lucky. I had the attention, got my acquittal. Now I can apply my expertise in different areas. Your story is harder to shake off.'

Sawyer took a drink and looked over at the lengthening queue. 'Would you consider a bit of surveillance work?'

'Who am I watching?'

'Me. Maybe long-distance observation on my place, just down the road. Let me know if you see anything unusual. Maybe for a couple of weeks.'

Cross sniffed. 'It's done. Send me the deets.' He lowered his voice again. 'What are you expecting me to see, anyway?'

'It's messy. Just something I need to get off my desk.'

'Sounds like fun. Beats corporate security. Or this training gig I'm on. Wannabe AFOs. A couple of them are fucking teenagers, Jake.'

Sawyer narrowed his eyes. 'You say you're thinking of starting your own security firm. Is that applying your expertise, or is it something personal?'

'How do you mean?'

'Are you staying out of the limelight, or are you hiding? You must have made enemies. The families of takedowns.'

Cross forced a laugh. 'Yeah. I've had death threats. But you can't live your life forever looking over your shoulder. I always had to be careful about the company I kept. I was a marksman. The longest arm of the law. And that's my expertise. Distance. I stay alive by keeping my friends close, and my enemies far away. You should do likewise.'

On the way in to Buxton, Sawyer's music was interrupted by a call from Shepherd. He set his phone in the dock and answered.

'Sir.'

'This isn't good news, is it?'

'There is some good. But I'll give you the bad first. Misper. Flagged up by Walker. Stephanie Burns. Blonde. Thirty-two. Owns her own rental business. Her partner says she went out to meet a potential client at midday on Saturday. Hasn't been home since.'

'Fits. But might not be related.' Sawyer stopped at a temporary traffic light and gazed across the flat plain of Sterndale Moor. 'And the good news?'

'Keating says we might have some traction on our blackmailer.'

29

Keating convened the briefing. The detectives from the other forces joined remotely, while Sawyer, Shepherd, Walker, Myers, Rhodes and Moran sat around the conference room table. Keating used his console to dial in a new participant, and an extra feed box appeared, showing the lean face of a fiftysomething man with a side-combed mop of white hair and silver-rimmed glasses.

'Good morning, everyone. Joining us today is DCI Robert Payne from the City of London Police fraud team.' Payne gave a brief wave from his box. 'DCI Payne has been working with us to try and establish the identity of the individual who is claiming to be our killer and who has been demanding payment. Before we get to that, though, I wanted to quickly update everyone on a couple of other matters. We arrested and released a man named Tommie Nash, who had been in contact with Angela Holt on the *Secret Encounters* site. As you can see from the information on HOLMES, Nash's DNA didn't match the Laura Bertrand dog-bite blood or the cigarette end found at the Angela Holt scene, and I'm not convinced of his connection to the main enquiry.'

Keating nodded at Shepherd, whose feed box filled the screen as he spoke. 'We're concerned about a local woman who's been missing for almost two days now.' He shared a washed-out photograph of a young woman, smiling into the camera. Shoulder-length blonde hair; mouth closed but smiling; curious, challenging eyes. 'Stephanie Burns, aged thirty-two. She owns a local holiday rental business, Quality Cottages. It's a lucrative niche. Only the high-end places, usually for big parties.'

'She fits the type,' said Whittaker.

Shepherd glanced at Sawyer. 'Indeed. DS Walker has been tasked with speaking to Stephanie's partner and retrieving her computer and devices.'

'According to HOLMES,' said Farrell, 'the blackmailer said he was thinking of "taking a holiday".'

'So,' said Sawyer. 'Channelling my inner Sherlock Holmes for a second, either he isn't our man, or he's not being entirely honest with us. If he is our man, then we know he tends to hold on to his captives for a couple of days before killing them. So, given Stephanie's look, age, and status, we have to assume that she's part of this enquiry and channel resource into finding her.'

'DCI Payne,' said Keating.

'Sir.' Payne's wizardly face filled the screen. 'I'm afraid my teams in Wood Street have had no luck in de-anonymising the blackmailer from the Bitcoin transaction. But I've been working with your Digital Media Advisor, DC Karl Rhodes, and we may have another way in.'

Rhodes grinned. 'Basically, he fucked up. He got sloppy with his VPN hygiene on the last set of emails, and I managed to link an IP address to an actual address.'

'Real address?' said Barlow. 'Or virtual?'

'Real. As in bricks, windows.'

'He's been clever,' said Payne. 'It looks like he stole the

ID of a missing person to do the emails. Joel Bailey, a fifty-two-year-old from Youlgreave. He also used this ID with the Bitcoin interactions, which is why we struggled to de-anonymise. This isn't easy to just Google. He knows his stuff.'

'The headline,' said Keating, 'is that we know the location of the computer used to send the emails.' He paused, to catch a little effect. 'A detached house, a cottage, in Mottram, Longdendale.'

Farrell's face filled the screen. 'In Greater Manchester.'

Keating nodded. '*Just* over the Derbyshire border.'

'But still,' said Farrell, smiling. 'In Greater Manchester. My jurisdiction, DSI Keating.'

'This is still the base of operations,' said Sawyer.

Farrell held his smile. 'Of course, of course. But—'

'We go in straight away,' said Keating. 'I'm the SIO of this task force, but I'm assigning you the role of lead officer in the field, DCI Farrell. We need to assume that our blackmailer is also our killer. Section 17 applies, as there's also the possibility that he's holding Stephanie Burns at the address. I want visual and audio contact with the AFO team, and full monitoring from here. Set it up, go within the hour.'

'Joint resources, sir?' said Sawyer.

DCI Farrell's face filled the screen again. 'I appreciate the offer, DI Sawyer. But we can handle it from my side. You can talk to the suspect once we've done the hard bit. It'll be a new experience for you. Staying out of the limelight.'

30

Sawyer gazed out of Keating's window, down at the Tarmac Silverlands Stadium. A small-sided game was in progress on the Astro pitch; a group of teenagers in fluorescent training bibs jabbed the ball to each other, using short, sharp passes.

Keating had his back turned, typing at his computer. 'Farrell's team is in place. Fifteen minutes to entry.'

'And you're good with him running the show?'

Keating glanced over his shoulder. 'Of course not. As I said, Farrell can be a prick, but he'll be fine. And we don't really have a choice. We have to assume it's time critical, and it'd be too relaxed to send the cavalry from here.'

Out on the pitch, a misplaced tackle led to an ugly sprawl of pointing and arm waving. The players' shouts slipped in through the open window. A tubby man in a tracksuit bounded into the fray, separating the players.

'How did he get the crime scene photo?' said Sawyer.

'You heard Payne. The digital skills are strong. IP masking, crypto-currency, dark web. Easy to imagine him hacking our servers. I'll get Rhodes to look into security.'

Sawyer turned to face him. 'No. Myers said it wasn't an image he recognised from the official batch.'

Keating nodded. 'You thinking Mr Bitcoin might be the killer, after all? And he took a picture with the extortion in mind?'

'It makes sense logically,' said Sawyer, turning back to the game. 'But it just doesn't connect for me. He likes to dominate, manipulate, exercise control. That's what he's getting out of the killings.'

Keating turned. 'Yes. And that's also what he's getting out of fucking us around, extorting money, demanding to release confidential intelligence. We know for sure that the house we're raiding today contains the computer that's the source of the contact. If he's the killer, then we might get lucky and find Stephanie Burns there, too. If he's not the killer, then we remove a complication from the main enquiry, which means we can focus on looking for Stephanie, and catching our real killer.'

Sawyer kept his eyes on the game. 'Good ball!'

Keating got to his feet. 'Right. Let's get in there. We're here to support the operation, remember, not exchange barbs.' Sawyer headed for the door, but Keating stepped into his path. 'And you? Please don't say you're "okay".'

'Don't worry. I'm still in the tent.'

The senior detectives gathered around the central screen in the conference room. Farrell had patched through video and audio feeds from his own bodycam, and a separate video connection from the lead AFO ran in a smaller inlay screen.

Keating parked himself nearest to the main screen, while Sawyer took the head seat, where he used the individual touchscreen to swipe through the logged HOLMES data.

The central image on the main screen showed a detached, two-storey stone-built cottage set at the edge of sparse woodland.

Farrell's voice came through, low. 'We have a light on upstairs. Strange, as it's daylight, and bright.' The image swung round to show a black-and-white Land Rover Discovery, parked on open ground near the front of the house. 'Car is here, though.'

'Are the teams in place?' said Keating.

Farrell's connection crackled. 'Yes. Three back, three front, plus myself, DS Whittaker. No sound or movement from inside the property.'

Sawyer continued to swipe at his screen. He caught Keating's eye.

'Go,' said Keating.

The images lurched and jolted as the teams approached the house.

Sawyer opened the PlayWithFire99 photo again, angling his head and zooming in to the gap in the blind, and the blue clock face.

On-screen, the front side AFO team halted at a bottle-green front door with a low letterbox and a small, patterned window in the top centre.

'Looks clear through ground-floor windows,' said Farrell.

Keating nodded, studied the video feeds. 'No lights on downstairs?'

'Negative,' said Farrell.

Sawyer scrolled through the Angela Holt crime scene photos. None of them resembled the image the blackmailer had threatened to release; the official pictures were all taken with flash, but the blackmailer's shot was illuminated by natural light only, and captured from a lower angle.

'Rhodes,' said Sawyer.

Farrell's voice crackled through the conference room. 'Awaiting your order, sir.'

Rhodes walked over to Sawyer's seat and looked at his screen.

Sawyer glanced up at him, keeping his voice low. 'I don't suppose you could get any metadata from the crime scene image sent by the blackmailer?'

Rhodes scoffed. 'He rinsed it. Probably screenshotted the original and saved out of different image software.'

'Farrell,' said Keating. 'Check the rooms for signs of captivity, female presence. Are there any outbuildings?'

Farrell gave a command to the teams, then spoke to Keating. 'No outbuildings, sir. Just the house.'

'So,' said Sawyer to Rhodes, 'if he didn't hack an official crime scene photo from us, then he must have taken the picture himself.'

Rhodes frowned. 'Uhuh. Meaning he's the killer.'

'No sign of anyone or evidence of captivity, sir,' said Farrell.

Sawyer looked up at Rhodes. 'Or...'

'Go loud,' said Keating to Farrell.

There was a splintered crash as a member of the front side team used an Enforcer battering ram to break through the green door.

'Armed police!' A shout, from the front and back teams, almost in unison.

Chaos on-screen as the teams pushed into the house.

Farrell's bodycam followed them in, down a narrow entrance hall, through to the kitchen. The images moved to the sitting room, as the AFO team declared the ground floor secure, room by room.

'Sir,' said Sawyer. 'It's not the killer.'

Keating glanced at him, then turned his eyes back to the screen. The AFO team climbed the stairs ahead of Farrell, their barrel-mounted lights flashing across the chintzy fittings.

'It's Damien Mount.'

'What?' said Shepherd.

'The guy who called it in.'

Another shout from the screen, as the AFOs neared the top of the stairs. 'Armed police!'

'The guy who works for the National Trust. He found Angela Holt's body. He could have seen the bracelet and the bites, taken the photo, thought he'd make a bit of money out of the police by posing as the killer. What does he do at the NT?'

'Works on their website,' said Walker. 'And the app, I think.'

'It fits. He's techy. He'd be confident with the crypto-currency thing. The VPN. The ID fraud.'

Walker swiped at his console screen.

'Mount said he was visiting his mother down in Thorpe,' said Sawyer. 'But what's his own address?'

Walker looked up, then nodded to the main screen. 'He lives here. This is Mount's place.'

'Fuck!' said Farrell.

The main feed showed a double bed, with a heavily bloodstained duvet gathered over one corner. A naked man lay on the bed, on his side, with his knees pulled up to his chest. He lay in a sunken puddle of crusted red blood, and his torso was disfigured with several deep stab wounds.

Sawyer got up and walked over to the main screen. He leaned in, studying the image. 'That's not a killer. It's a fucking dog walker.'

PART TWO

DREAMS BURN DOWN

31

JULY 2003

David Bowman emerged from the trees and approached the Red Cow Inn, staying low. The pub had been decorated with several copies of a garish banner, announcing, *THROWBACK NITE: RETRO DISCO.* A subtitle beneath, in a barely legible cartoonish font, read, *PARTY LIKE IT'S 1979!*

Bowman was tall and agile, and carried a striking bulk of upper-body muscle; a teenager with the build of a middleweight boxer. He had cut his black hair short, but kept a protruding patch at the front-centre of his scalp, like a mini Mohican. He wore a sleeveless maroon vest, training shorts, running shoes. It had been the hottest July day on record, and the front porch of the pub was rammed with sweltering drinkers: the men in their polyester bell bottoms, comedy wigs and open-neck paisley shirts, and the women in cut-off shorts, low-waisted hot pants, stripy crop tops, flowery wrap dresses.

As Bowman moved along the side wall of the pub, he winced at the libidinous thrum of the music: surging strings, sensual female vocal, a relentless four-four beat. He caught the lyrical refrains, the sexual metaphors: 'all night long', 'try me once, you'll beg for more'.

He stopped at a window and peered inside. The seating in the main bar area had been shifted to the edge of the room, and a temporary touch-sensitive dance floor had been installed in the centre. Above, a spinning mirrorball showered the dancers in shards of white as their steps switched the floor tiles to red, green and blue.

In the centre, a young blonde woman in a backless orange jumpsuit jerked and gyrated. Her eyelids were painted with heavy purple shadow, and she was long and lithe: a beacon for the male dancers who circled her, trying to catch her attention. Some dared to place their hands on her hips, and she obliged by resting her multi-braceleted wrists on their shoulders for a few seconds, before wriggling free and sashaying to another part of the dancefloor.

'Is that your mum?'

Bowman spun. A teenager, around the same age, stood a few feet away. He wore a tight white T-shirt, fitted blue shorts and Dunlop Green Flash tennis shoes. His head was shaved, and he had cultivated uneven patches of stubble around his chin and cheeks.

Bowman glared at him. 'What the fuck are you doing here?'

'That's your mum, isn't it?'

'Fuck off.' Bowman shoved past, and walked out onto the pub driveway. The second boy followed, as he crossed the main road and joined the curving side lane that rose up out of town and back into the western suburbs of Sheffield. He hung back, watching Bowman as he strode into the dusk.

At the entrance to Stannington Park, Bowman tried the gate, but found it padlocked. He cursed and turned away, following the perimeter towards the brutalist cluster of flat-blocks on the northern side.

The second boy caught up and fell in alongside him. 'Were you supposed to be there? At the party?'

Bowman kept walking. 'Just having a look.'

'Isn't it a beautiful evening?'

Bowman glared at him, and turned the corner towards the flats. 'No. It's too hot.'

'I love it like this. Well, when the sun's out. Everything looks much better when the sun's out, don't you think? The world looks more beautiful. Everything is beautiful, really. It's just a question of how you look at it. You know *you're* beautiful, don't you?'

Bowman stopped, and turned to face the boy. 'I always knew you were a fucking queer.'

The boy held out a packet. 'Do you want a cigarette? They're menthol. It's okay. You're allowed to smoke now. You were sixteen last week. There's loads of things you can do now you're sixteen.'

Bowman took a step towards him. 'I do what I want.' He moved off again; the boy followed. 'And, no. I don't want one of your dirty cigarettes.'

They walked for a minute in silence. As they reached the edge of the estate, the boy picked up speed and walked just ahead of Bowman, half-turned towards him. 'I'm working on a new picture for you.'

'No more pictures.'

'What?'

Bowman stopped again. 'I don't need your pictures any more, okay? I can look after myself.' He raised his arm and bulged his bicep. 'Now, leave me the fuck alone.' He jogged away, looking behind to check the boy wasn't following.

Bowman sat on the dilapidated steps that joined the street at the bottom of the flat block. He had forgotten his key, and knew his auntie and her new man wouldn't be back for a while.

A young girl passed along the pavement below the steps. She wore a smart blue-and-white summer dress with pink trainers, and her blonde hair had been pinned up into a tidy bun. She carried a small posy of multicoloured flowers.

'Where y'going?' said Bowman.

The girl slowed. 'Party.'

'It's late.'

The girl stopped, and held up her yellow-strap watch. 'Half past eight. I can tell the time.'

Bowman got up and walked over. The flats were set back from an underlit side street that connected to the main road of shops and restaurants a few hundred yards away.

He smiled at her. 'How old are you?'

She held up her head. 'Nearly ten.'

Bowman laughed. 'No way. You taking your flowers to the party?'

'Yes. But they're not a present.'

He nodded. 'Listen. Can you get me something? From the corner shop up there.'

The girl sighed. 'But I'm very busy.' Her accent wasn't quite posh, but her vowels weren't so languid or local. Bowman guessed that she was probably from Fulwood and had been dropped off by the southern entrance to the park.

'Where's your party?' said Bowman.

She shrugged and pointed to the steep road beyond the shops. 'Up there.'

'What's your name?'

'Caron. With a "C". It means kind-hearted.'

Bowman took out a five-pound note. 'Look, Caron. I've got to watch my house. It's on the top floor of these flats. Can you get me some chocolate? Dairy Milk. A big bar. If you get it, you can have something yourself.' Caron looked around, doubtful. 'Please. I've had no tea, and I can't go myself. Just come up these steps. It's the yellow door. Number twenty-five.'

Caron smiled. 'But I might run off with your money.'

'No, you won't. You're kind-hearted, remember?'

Caron took the note and hurried off towards the shops. Bowman turned, and walked up the five flights of narrow concrete steps to the top floor. His auntie's flat was the only one in the block with its own enclosed landing, and he crouched by the yellow door, looking out over the low wall, to the distant lights of the simmering city.

After a few minutes, he heard light footfalls on the steps below. He stayed crouched, and, as Caron huffed her way to the top of the final flight, rose up to greet her.

She reached the top step. 'I got your chocolate. I bought a Fanta, too. There's one-eighty change.' She caught her breath, and set the chocolate and change down on the floor, along with the empty glass Fanta bottle. 'Your house is high up.'

Bowman smiled. 'Have you seen my trick?'

She caught his eye. 'No. What is it?'

He jerked out a hand and gripped her by the wrist, pulling her close. She felt weightless, doll-like in his grip. Bowman pressed his other hand over Caron's mouth and rasped in her ear. 'If you make a noise, I'll kill you.'

Her eyes widened, and Bowman shushed her. They stood there for a few seconds, and he tuned in to her conflict, the purity of her panic: the urge to break free and escape, but also the terror at his threat. He closed his eyes, and listened to her snatched breaths, savoured her trembling.

The boy with the cigarettes scaled the steps slowly. He had waited, in the shadows across the street, and seen Bowman talk to the girl, then watched her return. He reached the second to last landing and inched his head around the corner.

Bowman lifted his hand away from Caron's mouth and eased the dress strap down from her right shoulder. 'I just want to show you my trick. Then I'll let you go.' He leaned in to her neck, paused, then twisted his head and clamped his teeth around her bare shoulder, biting down hard.

Caron squealed. Bowman hit her with a hooked punch, silencing her, knocking her out cold.

He leaned over her body and encircled her slender neck with both hands.

Below, the boy watched as Bowman worked.

He watched, as the final drops of life squeezed from the girl.

He saw Bowman tear off and pocket her underwear; he saw him smash the glass bottle, but dropped his gaze as Bowman lifted her dress.

He turned and lurched down the steps, crossed the road, and, as he was about to make a run for the west of the park, away from the flats, he slowed, and sunk into the shadows again, watching.

Within minutes, he saw Bowman walk to the bottom of the steps, stuff something into a waste bin and head off towards the shops, in no hurry.

He waited until Bowman was out of sight, then climbed back up the steps.

He found the girl's body sprawled across the landing where he had waited. It looked like Bowman had pushed her down the steps, and her dress had billowed out in the fall, exposing her naked lower body.

He gazed at her: a fledgling life, cruelly cancelled.

He reached down, covered the girl with her dress, brushed the blood-matted hair from her face.

Her posy of flowers lay in the corner of the landing wall, still tightly packed. He picked it up, and turned to face her.

The tremors rose in him, and he averted his eyes as he pulled out the flowers and scattered them around the body.

32

DCI Farrell hustled down the hall, shoving his way through two FSIs in Tyvek suits. He stopped at the kitchen door and faced Keating, standing by the table with Sawyer and Shepherd. 'I have my own forensics team. There really is no cause for—'

'I disagree,' said Keating. 'We know now that the man upstairs was the individual who contacted us. He's a key aspect of our joint enquiry. As SIO of said enquiry, I'm making the call, regardless of geography. Sally O'Callaghan and her team will work this scene, we'll collate our findings into HOLMES, as usual, and we'll discuss at a briefing this afternoon.'

Farrell stepped into the room, jostling one of the FSIs.

'DCI Farrell,' said Keating. 'I could also have insisted on using my Buxton team for this raid, but I erred towards pragmatism. A man is dead, motive unknown, and the missing woman means we have a potential related crime in action.' He lowered his voice, for effect. 'This is the part where we all pull together.'

Sawyer caught Farrell's eye. 'What's been found so far?'

Farrell made a point of turning towards Keating,

placing Sawyer behind his right shoulder. 'Victim is Damien Mount, thirty-eight. Early analysis of computers and digital devices confirm that he was the one sending the messages to us, and for the postings on the *Derbyshire Times* website. We were on the right track, for the wrong reason. Someone got to him before we did.'

'You think?' said Sawyer. 'So, we're definitely discounting suicide by multiple stab wound?' Shaking his head, he exited the kitchen and climbed the stairs, side-stepping past two more FSIs. The bedroom was an overheated soup, seasoned by the familiar spices of death: copper from the blood, hanging on the air like static; a miasma of faeces and urine; the indomitable reek of cellular necrosis, accelerated by the temperature.

Sally O'Callaghan stood by the open window in her usual turquoise Tyvek suit. She scribbled something onto a clipboard and handed it back to one of the FSIs. Sawyer nodded at her and walked around the side of the bed.

He let his eyes glide over the body. Along with the stab wounds, Mount had a deep laceration on the side of his head. Blood from the wound had seeped onto the closed eyelid of his left eye, forming a gelatinous seal over the socket.

'Someone forced the back door lock,' said Sally. 'I'd put ETD at around 4am, but Drummond will clarify.'

Shepherd entered, flinching at the smell.

'They hit him with something,' said Sawyer. 'Hard enough to kill him, I'd say. Nobody dies like that. With no objection.' He looked at Sally. 'Did the killer leave us anything?'

'Every contact leaves a trace.'

'Locard's exchange principle,' said Shepherd.

Sally shook her head. 'You're such a murder nerd, Shepherd. Well. Dr Locard would certainly be happy here.

Fresh boot prints and tyre tracks. A couple of hairs. I'm surprised he hasn't left us his fucking library card.'

'Is that enough?' said Sawyer.

'Too early to say. Depends on the matches, what's in the hair.'

'Could this be unrelated?' said Shepherd. 'Just lousy timing?'

Sawyer eyed him. 'No. It couldn't.'

'You think our killer did this?'

Sawyer turned to Sally. 'Anything missing?'

'Doesn't look like it. His wallet was on the shelf downstairs. Money and cards still in it. Pretty impressive office out back, with a high-end Mac that would easily fit under your arm. Still there.'

Sawyer leaned in close and studied Mount's neck and face. 'No bite marks. Any sexual assault?'

'No,' said Sally. 'And no strangulation.'

Sawyer sniffed. 'Different method. No care in the presentation. Theft not a motive.'

'Not a young blonde,' said Sally.

'Well spotted.'

'So,' said Shepherd. 'Why, then? Relative of Angela Holt, angered by the release of the scene photo?'

'It wasn't publicly available for long enough,' said Sawyer.

Sally shrugged. 'Anyone following the thread could have got a notification and seen it early, before he took it down.'

Sawyer walked to the door. 'Maybe the killer himself saw it. Got mad about someone profiting from his work.'

'But how would he know to target Mount?' said Shepherd. '*We* only realised a couple of hours ago.'

'We?' said Sawyer.

Shepherd sighed. 'You.'

'Fast-track the forensics,' said Sawyer.

Sally scoffed. 'Fast-track is pretty much the new normal, you know.'

'If our killer did find out about Damien Mount and, for whatever reason, decided to kill him, then our focus has to shift to Stephanie Burns.'

33

The door clunked open, and a dusty beam of daylight spilled over the cellar floor. The man took his sweet time descending the uneven stone steps, and Stephanie Burns pulled herself out of the corner. She was dressed only in her underwear, and the chain around her neck made it impossible to stand upright, but she faced him in a crouch, as if ready to pounce.

He sat on the bottom step and stared at her. 'I've brought you a drink. I know it's warm down here. There's a fan upstairs, but... You know. I need it.'

He leaned forward and placed a saucer of water on the stone floor, then sat back on the step.

Stephanie pulled herself towards it, but the chain pulled tight, keeping her a few feet away. She reached out her hand, but the dish remained several inches from her fingers.

She raised her head, but kept her eyes on the cracked plaster of the wall opposite the stairs. Her blonde hair was congealed with dust and sweat, and her arms and face smeared with grime from the cellar floor. 'I need to drink.' With a vast force of effort, Stephanie turned to look at the man; he was slumped to the side, elbow resting on knee, cast in silhouette from the light above.

The man sighed, and shuffled in place. 'Yes. You do. But you'll do it when I want you to do it. I realise that I might be overcompensating here. I never had a pet, see. I killed the others quite early on. But I want to see what that feels like. Caring for something. So sorry, but I won't be taking you for a walk, though.'

He stretched out a leg and nudged the saucer closer to Stephanie. A little of the water spilled out and soaked into the floor. She pulled hard at the chain, but her fingertips still fell short. She gasped and grunted as she tried to pull further forward, then slumped on the floor, breathing hard.

The man got up and walked over to her. He picked up the saucer and shifted it a few feet forward, easily within her reach. He stepped back and watched from the bottom of the steps.

Stephanie raised her head and glared at him, her bloodshot eyes burning with hatred. 'Fuck. You.'

He laughed, nodded. 'You're probably wondering what's going to happen to you. I'm sorry to tell you that you are soon going to die. It's clear that you're already quite seriously dehydrated.' He gestured towards an iron bucket in the far corner, near the thick water pipe which held Stephanie's chain in place. 'So, you can either drink this and die later, or enjoy a hollow little victory against me, and die sooner.' He paused for a few seconds; no response from Stephanie. 'Okay.' He walked towards her again. 'That's a shame. I'll need to take the dish back. Don't want you getting ideas about smashing it and making a weapon.'

Stephanie scrambled towards the saucer, grabbed it with both hands and tipped the tepid water into her mouth.

The man nodded. 'Good dog. Or, to be more accurate,

bitch.' He watched as she licked the saucer dry, then walked to the bottom of the stairs. He reached down and rolled a large plastic bottle of mineral water along the floor to Stephanie. She grabbed it, unscrewed the lid and gulped down the water.

The man climbed the stairs and pulled the door shut behind him, dropping the cellar back into absolute darkness.

34

Keating tapped at the climate control panel on the wall, and took his place at the head of the MIT conference table. All the key players were in attendance—twelve in total—and the atmosphere was mulchy and enervating, even with the air con chilled to maximum.

'So...' said Keating. 'Thoughts? Questions?'

Sawyer stared down at his palm, ran his fingernails down the centre. 'Why?'

'Why what?' said Keating.

'Why kill Mount? If it's related to the blackmail or threats to release the Angela Holt pictures, how did he even know? Why would he care enough to kill Mount?'

'Relative of Angela Holt?' said Walker. 'Desperate to keep her dignity?'

Farrell had stayed on his feet. He tapped out a breath mint and hung his grey suit over the back of his chair. His thick, unnaturally coloured hair sagged over his forehead as he paced, and he swiped it back into place. 'If our killer is responsible for Mount's death, then he changed his MO. No bite marks. No fancy presentation.'

Rhodes drummed his scrawny fingers on the table.

'There's also the "not a woman" thing.'

Farrell ignored him. 'I have officers interviewing locals near Mount's home, but nobody saw anyone going in or out.'

'Sally said there were fresh boot prints and tyre tracks,' said Sawyer. 'Also some hair. We should have something on that in an hour or two.'

Keating looked up at Farrell. 'I want your team to focus on the Mount murder. We don't yet know the significance to the main enquiry, but I'd like to know who did it and why, as soon as possible. DS Walker. What more do we know about Stephanie Burns?'

'I spoke to her husband, Jordan,' said Walker. 'They married quite young. Been together for around ten years. He was adamant that they're happy and settled. Looks like their business, Quality Cottages, is doing well. Expanding into Yorkshire and the Lakes. She employs her husband. He manages the acquisition of the properties. On the night of her disappearance, she told him she was meeting a friend from work. Took a cab from their house in Baslow to Hathersage, where she was dropped off around seven.'

'We have her on CCTV at that moment,' said Rhodes. 'But then she goes into a local park. Looks like she might have been making her way out of town somewhere. Impossible to say for sure.'

'What about her phone?' said DI McBride.

Rhodes checked something on his laptop. 'Bounced off the Padley mast just after 10pm, then nothing. I've been through her computers and devices.' He looked up. 'Jordan Burns might have been happy, but not Stephanie. She was a *Secret Encounters* user, and she's been active in the last few weeks. Sadly, though, she's a lot more hygienic than Angela Holt. Email trash was empty. No contact trace. Tried a few login options, but no joy.'

'Her partner doesn't need to know,' said Shepherd. 'That she was on the site.'

'Does he check out?' said Sawyer.

Walker nodded. 'He played football at Goals in Sheffield, had dinner with a couple of the players after, in the city centre. CCTV at Goals tallies. ANPR shows he left the restaurant at 10.30 and got back home at around 11.15.'

'Get more CCTV,' said Sawyer. 'Check shops and businesses in Hathersage between seven and ten. If she did meet someone from *Secret Encounters*, let's at least find out where. Or get some options. Then trawl the CCTV at the options. Use the civvie team.' He turned to Stephen Bloom, who sat next to Keating, typing into a tablet. 'Circulate a call for sightings on social media.' Sawyer swiped through the HOLMES data on his screen. He brought up the photo of the muscled man in the bedroom. 'Any response to our dummy profile's message to Mr Universe?'

Rhodes shook his head. 'Not yet.'

'We need to find out about his contact with Angela Holt,' said Shepherd.

'We can't do that,' said Barlow, 'until we know who he is.'

Farrell slid into his seat. 'Anything from the court order? To force the release of profile details?'

Keating shook his head. 'Let's focus on what we can control. Continue with the forensics from the Mount scene, but prioritise the Stephanie Burns CCTV. Given the parallels between Stephanie and the previous killings, we have to assume that he's lined her up as his next victim.'

'Three days,' said Sawyer.

Farrell folded his arms. 'Three days?'

Sawyer nodded. 'He's never held on to any of them for more than three days. And we've already lost two.'

35

Austin Fletcher eased the Fiesta into a dried-up lay-by on the edge of an immense plain of verdant farm fields. He switched off the engine and sat there for a few seconds, taking slow, uniform breaths, then swallowed two pills with water and stepped outside. He shouldered his way around the side of the car, past a tall border hedge, its leaves gnarled by the sun. He retrieved his backpack from the boot of the Fiesta and checked the contents: water, small vial of colourless liquid, a ring of ten small keys, gloves, hunting knife, matches, cigarette, and a white five-litre jerry can.

He locked the car and pushed through a gap in the hedge. After a few minutes' walking along the fringe, he crossed into a field of vivid red poppies, defiant and primary in the merciless heat. It was an Instagram hotspot, and a middle-aged couple with a scruffy white dog posed for each other as they took pictures on their phones.

Fletcher kept his head down and passed through the poppies, onto an arid walking track that led to a row of three-storey houses on the edge of Baslow village. The houses had been converted into flats, and he crouched in a patch of high grass for a few minutes, watching the ground-floor windows of the building at the near end.

He approached the back door and gave a short, loud knock. He waited, repeated, then pulled on the gloves and dug the keys out of the backpack. The first fit the lock, but he couldn't get it to connect with the lock's key pins. He tried another, which seemed to be a better fit, and, after bumping it with the base of his palm a few times while applying a light rotation, he managed to transmit the force to the driver pins, turn the cylinders, and release the lock.

He eased the door open and slipped inside.

Fletcher lingered at the edge of the tidy galley kitchen and zoned in to the room: the silky maple of the wall units, the black-and-white chequered flooring, the brushed chrome gas oven and extractor fan. The space was polished and uncluttered, with only light evidence of habitation: cereal packets, opened but neatly tucked; knives, spatulas; a magnetic whiteboard dotted with photos and flyers. He opened the lime-green fridge freezer and took out a bottle of mineral water. He tipped the colourless liquid into the bottle and put it back in the fridge, slotting it into the door shelf.

He looked up to the wall-mounted cupboards opposite the fridge and fixed a small black cube, around an inch square, to the black ceiling fitting of a hanging lamp, angling it just above the curved edge to give the lens on the front side a good view of the fridge. He tapped at the side of the cube, and a small light on the side flickered green, then extinguished. Fletcher stepped back and looked up at the fitting; the edge of the cube became vaguely apparent after he'd stared up for a few seconds, but it was effectively hidden to the casual eye.

He took out his phone and navigated to an app which transmitted a live feed from the camera. The image was clear: a hulking blond man with a short ponytail, dressed in a white T-shirt and blue jeans, holding a backpack at his side. Fletcher gazed up to the camera; it was Sawyer who had given him the idea of using this method for covert surveillance, after he had tried the trick himself, underestimating Fletcher's attention to detail.

He left the kitchen, checked the lock showed no sign of damage, and walked back through the fields to his car. He got in, rolled open the windows an inch or two, and bowed his head, resting but not sleeping.

A few hours later, he stirred at the buzz of a notification from the camera app, activated by the device's motion sensor. He opened the app, and watched, as Hector opened his fridge and took out the bottle. He had his back to the camera, and Fletcher leaned in close, squinting for a better view.

Hector unscrewed the cap, paused for a moment, then lifted the bottle to his lips and tipped back his head. After a few seconds, he replaced the bottle, closed the fridge, and moved off into another room, out of the camera's view.

Fletcher put the phone away, dropped his head and waited, listening to the distant drone of a tractor, the keening curlews, the murmur of late afternoon traffic on the Chatsworth perimeter road.

After an hour, he got out and retraced his steps to the back door of the house. Again, he knocked twice. No answer. He used the bump key on the lock and slid back into the kitchen.

He took down the camera and pocketed it, then walked through into the sitting room, half-expecting to find Hector slumped on the floor in front of a chattering TV.

But the room was empty, and he edged open the adjoining door and padded through into the bedroom.

The wall at the head of the bed was almost completely covered by a gigantic black-and-white photograph of Hector on a beach, in a sleeveless black vest, scowling into camera. A slender woman in a white low-cut swimsuit stood at his side, her arms wrapped around his broad neck, facing the camera with an exaggerated pout. She was at least ten years his junior, with a cascade of black hair and haughty, pornographic eyes.

Fletcher paused at the open door and surveyed the room: wide wooden bed with white pillows and a thin yellow sheet; one bedside table with a digital clock and an orange-and-blue plastic water bottle; an open clothes hanger with blazers, shirts, T-shirts. The room, like the kitchen, was almost entirely functional and free of clutter. Apart from the photograph, the only non-essential object sat on a white wooden dresser pushed into the far corner: a marble model of a Siamese cat, sitting upright. It was around a foot tall and heavy looking, with a fake gold finish.

Hector lay on his back, spread out on top of the yellow sheet. He wore only a pair of Diesel briefs, and Fletcher was surprised to see that he carried a thick layer of belly fat which sagged over the side of his frame. He inhaled and exhaled with a steady rhythm, releasing a slight whistle from his nose on each exhale.

Fletcher went back into the sitting room. He took out the jerry can and layered the accelerant evenly across the fabric surfaces: rug, sofa, curtains. He took out the book of matches and prised a space between two layers. His plan was lo-fi, but notoriously difficult for investigators to detect: light a cigarette, wedge it between the match layers and place it near to a coated surface. It would take the cigarette around ten minutes to burn down, spark the matches, and ignite the accelerant; plenty of time to let him stroll back to the car.

As he twisted at the match-book, he caught a slight movement from the bedroom door, reflected in the television screen. He turned, but too late, as Hector crashed into him, head down.

Fletcher just about managed to jink to the side, and Hector's momentum took them into the front of the sofa. Fletcher struggled to stay on his feet, grappling with the larger, heavier man.

He pulled free, but Hector was up first, and hit Fletcher with a thunderous straight punch across the back of his head, pitching him forward through the bedroom door. He scrambled to his feet, but Hector anticipated his recovery, and landed a powerful right hook to Fletcher's jaw, which smashed him into the wooden dresser, sending the model cat clattering across the bedroom floor.

Fletcher lost his footing and tumbled to the carpet at the side of the bed. He turned and, as Hector loomed over him, thrust his hand up and managed to grip the front of Hector's throat, squeezing hard, trying to crush his larynx. Hector swiped away the choking hand and hit Fletcher square in the face with another punch, which knocked him backwards, allowing Hector to throw himself down on Fletcher's chest, knees first.

Fletcher was pinned down now, and Hector wrapped his powerful fingers around his jaw and held him firm as he struck him again in the face.

Hector coughed and spat to the side. 'Going to smoke me to death?' He hit Fletcher again. 'You've already tried that, with those stinking fucking cigarettes.' Another punch. 'You don't like to face me like a man? Sneaking around, using poison. A woman's weapon.' He gripped Fletcher's head with both hands and raised him up. 'You think I'm stupid?' He smashed the back of Fletcher's head into the wall. 'You think I don't know your methods?' Another smash. 'You're not so smart. The water was in the fridge door. I always put it on the bottom shelf.'

Fletcher's head lolled, stupefied from the blows, his face bloodied. Hector watched him for a few seconds, holding on to his chin with one hand, feeling his opponent's waning strength. He reached over, flipped open the dressing table drawer and pulled out the gun he had held on Fletcher near to Sawyer's house.

'You think you're some kind of big alpha man, yes?' said Hector. 'But you're a mad dog.' He released Fletcher's chin and cocked the gun. 'And you need to be put down.'

Fletcher lunged for the marble cat, lying on the floor just behind Hector's peripheral vision. The movement dislodged Hector from Fletcher's chest, and in the second it took to correct himself and raise the gun, Fletcher had swung the heavy ornament into the side of Hector's head. The impact was square and solid, and Hector listed to the side and flopped onto the bed, dropping the gun to the floor. Fletcher ignored it, and swung the cat again, crunching it into Hector's head. He climbed onto Hector, his face red and raging, an unholy fire in his normally vacant eyes.

Hector was dazed, but he made a feeble effort to reach for the cat. Fletcher held it out of his reach, then crashed it down across Hector's forehead, knocking him unconscious. He manoeuvred himself around on the bed and sat behind Hector, lifting him up, holding his head firm between both hands. Hector roused himself and flailed his hefty arms behind him. But Fletcher leaned back, out of range.

He leaned forward and whispered in Hector's ear. 'Ssh.'

He wedged his forearm under Hector's chin and squeezed it up into his throat, starving him of oxygen, crushing his trachea. Hector flailed weakly, but went limp after a few seconds.

Fletcher rolled away and stood at the side of the bed, staring down at Hector. He checked for a pulse. Nothing.

He retrieved his backpack, and stuffed in the gun and ornamental cat.

He washed the blood off his face in the kitchen sink, and revived himself by tipping water over his head. The rage subsided, doused by the washing, but his head throbbed from Hector's attacks.

Back in the sitting room, Fletcher lit a cigarette and took a couple of drags, staring through the bedroom door at Hector's lifeless body.

He wedged the cigarette into the matchbook and set it down on the sofa, in a patch of accelerant.

Back at the car, he swallowed two more pills from the bottle with the green logo, sucked in a deep breath, and drove away.

36

Sawyer settled into his office chair and opened his laptop. He logged in to the HOLMES database and sifted through the case files, photos, evidence logs and action reports. The intelligence had been acquired from multiple streams and from four separate forces, but Moran had done a decent job keeping it sequential and filed into subcategories. He reviewed the freshest entry—Farrell's report on the Mount operation—but struggled to stay focused on the detail, and his eyes drifted to the open window and the sun-bleached world outside.

A flash.

It was the hue of the sunlight: mellow and honeyed in the early evening.

Adult arms, carrying him away from his mother as she lay in the bloodied grass. His six-year-old screams, shrill with disbelief, filled the office around him, rattling the plastic tray on his desk.

He glanced through the partition window at the busy MIT office. Could they not hear?

Nausea in his stomach: hot, volcanic.

His dog, on his side, twitching and growling.

His breathing quickened. He drank from a bottle of water and closed his eyes, trying to tune in to the office activity: phones, voices, keyboard clatter. But the blackness behind his eyes was a canvas, and the images flared across his inner vision: the rise and fall of Caldwell's hammer, the splashing red, the ambulance and the adult arms.

And the voices, around him now.

'Why?'

'Oh my good God.'

'Get help!'

'Run, my darling!'

The dog's impotent snarl; its dying yelps.

Sawyer opened his eyes and placed his hands on the desk. He stared at the ridges between his knuckles. The veins, the contours. He had to wrench his mind back into the present, restrict the space in which the visions could hijack him.

He walked to the window and partially drew the blinds, muffling the intensity of the daylight. Back at his desk, he accessed the *Secret Encounters* profile image sent by PlayWithFire99. He zoomed in on the white number '6' and the blue background.

Shepherd knocked and entered, followed by Keating.

'Loving the Goth styling,' said Shepherd.

Keating scowled at the half-closed blinds. 'It's five-fifteen, Sawyer. If it's a hangover, then you're *really* milking it.' He walked to the window and opened the blinds wide; Sawyer winced at the bright light.

Shepherd studied Sawyer for a second, then pushed on. 'No CCTV of Stephanie yet. No indication of where she might have gone after her phone pinged the Padley mast.'

'Some movement on forensics, though,' said Keating.

Shepherd nodded. 'There's a match on the tyre tracks with the Holt scene.'

'But not the others?' said Sawyer.

'No,' said Shepherd. 'Only the Holt scene. And the hairs Sally found at the Mount house have no roots, so there's no DNA.'

Sawyer breathed, deep and slow. 'The boot prints?'

'Sally took a cast and got a 3D scan,' said Shepherd. 'We have a clear imprint of the outsole, and it's a match for the Dianne Walton scene. Winscar Reservoir in Yorkshire.'

Sawyer lowered his head, pondering. 'Same tyre tracks from the Mount and Holt scenes and same boot prints for Mount and Dianne Walton. The same car and the same boot wearer at two murder scenes. Why not boot print and tyre match for all the scenes?'

'Changes his shoes?' said Keating. 'Different stolen car? It has to be our man. Whoever is responsible for the killings, it looks extremely likely that he also murdered Damien Mount.'

'There's one thing missing,' said Sawyer.

Shepherd nodded. 'A motive for Mount's murder.'

'We have patterns for the women, but why would he kill Mount? And it's odd that he's left us pretty much nothing at the other scenes, but he was sloppy covering his tracks at Mount's place.'

'Outside of his comfort zone?' said Keating. 'He's more used to kidnapping the women and killing them on his terms, then dumping the bodies. With Mount, he would have had to gain entry to a separate property, kill his man, get out.' He stood up. 'I'll set up a press conference. It's about time we updated the media. And now we need as much help as we can with finding Stephanie. We just have to be open and say we have strong reason to believe her disappearance may be connected.'

Sawyer nodded. 'Focus on witnesses around the Mount scene. Entry and exit roads.'

Keating strode out, but Shepherd lingered. He kept his gaze on Sawyer, drawing eye contact. 'Sir. Everything okay?'

Sawyer smiled. 'Not everything.' He walked to the window and half-closed the blinds again. 'I'm fine. Got to make a couple of phone calls.'

Shepherd left, closing the door behind him.

Sawyer dialled a number; the call connected immediately. 'Anything?'

'Not last night,' said Tony Cross. 'I did some long-range surveillance, pretty wide perimeters. Had a look around for potential stakeout spots. There's one or two bothies and blasted old farm sheds near to your place, but nothing any sane person would use. Sorry to bruise your ego, Sawyer, but it doesn't look like anyone is finding you interesting enough to watch right now. I'll go again for the next couple of nights and let you know if anything crops up.'

Sawyer thanked Cross and rang off. He opened his laptop, accessed the Skype app, and dialled a video call.

As the ring tone trilled and burbled, he closed his eyes and tried to settle in the gloom.

The call connected, and the face of a man in his early sixties appeared in the inlay screen, sitting at a desk, in front of a floor-to-ceiling bookshelf. He wore a saggy, short-sleeved white shirt with a loosened green tie, and wire-framed spectacles that only just covered the radius of his eye sockets. He swiped away his flyaway grey hair and leaned forward, peering into the screen.

'Professor Ainsworth,' said Sawyer.

'Oh, Christ. Donald, please, Jake! What a pleasure. I got your message. How are you today?'

'I'm good.'

Ainsworth dropped his head slightly. 'You've been through quite a time, Jake. I'm so sorry about your father. I... say "today" because, well... "How are you?" is just too big a question, don't you think? Where do you begin and end? But, "how are you, today?" That feels answerable. It's something I learned from my therapist, after Lena's death.'

Sawyer nodded. Ainsworth's soft Scottish brogue made his eyelids pleasantly heavy. 'How are things at Strathclyde? Did you finish your book with Jensen?'

'We did. It's due out this Christmas. It's called *Is There Anybody There?* A history of the candidates who took the paranormal challenge, a look at the world of psychology and parapsychology, with elements of memoir. Richard has been a fine collaborator. And I won my reputation damage claim from Beck.'

'Good news.'

Ainsworth took a sip from a glass. 'My work is now more focused on the real world, though. Criminology, psychology. I'm working on a paper about how criminal methods have changed in the digital world. How is your enquiry going? Operation Orca, isn't it?'

'Yes. I wanted to get your opinion on a couple of elements of the case.' Sawyer raised his legs and propped his feet on the desk. 'When you're in the middle of such a complex investigation... Well, that's the problem. You're in the middle. It's difficult to gain perspective, when you're so close to everything and you're following all the processes.'

Ainsworth nodded. 'You have four victims. Am I correct?'

'Yes. Four women, similar type. Blonde, thirtysomething, successful.'

'Not your typical vulnerable types.'

'No. And at first, I thought that could be a factor. The killer's arrogance pushing him to a tougher challenge. But his recent actions lead me to believe there's something more beneath the surface.' Ainsworth said nothing, and Sawyer took a deep breath. 'The killings are extremely brutal, with intimate mutilation, biting. But the bodies are presented in an almost aesthetic way. Garlanded with flowers, body covered, make-up applied.'

'Beautified,' said Ainsworth.

'Yes. As if he feels shame at what he's done, and wants to give them some kind of dignity in death.'

'Biting is interesting,' said Ainsworth. 'It's socially abhorrent behaviour, but the compulsion is powerful. It often speaks to a... hunger for control. It's a stress response. Perhaps he's tried and failed to control in the past.'

'We have reason to believe that he's also murdered a man,' said Sawyer. 'But he didn't leave bite marks or present the body in the same way.'

Ainsworth drummed at his desk. 'Maybe this urge for control only applies to women. Perhaps he's suffered a sense of impotence when faced with relationships in the past.'

'There is misogyny in the violence,' said Sawyer. 'In the choice of victims. It seems that he kidnaps and holds on to the women for two to three days.'

'Savouring the control?' said Ainsworth.

'Maybe. But usually misogyny of this type carries right through to the presentation or method of disposal. If the women are nothing to him, if he despises them for whatever reason, then why does he afford them this final status, with the attractive presentation? It almost feels like a statement in itself.'

'There is something personal there,' said Ainsworth. 'As you suggest, maybe the killings satisfy a certain part of him, but the presentation is the way he expresses remorse. Is there evidence of sexual arousal?'

'No.'

'Well, perhaps the killings are his mission, for whatever reason, but the presentation speaks to his psychopathology, his compulsion?'

Shepherd tapped at the door, but Sawyer held up his hand. 'How do you mean?'

'Have you heard of a thing called Stendahl Syndrome? There's little concrete research and many psychologists refuse to acknowledge it as a genuine condition, but there are people who display an intense hypersensitivity to... beauty. Both natural and man-made. Often to the degree where they feel so overwhelmed that they lose consciousness.'

'So, he could be getting nothing personally from the violence, but the artistic presentation of the bodies gives him a deeper satisfaction?'

Ainsworth wobbled his head. 'It's a bit of a reach, but other than good old-fashioned guilt, I can't really understand why you would depersonalise someone to the point where you can visit extreme violence on them, but then feel the urge to dress them up for their discovery.'

'So,' said Sawyer, 'his final impression, before he walks away, is that he's created something ugly but then reworked it into something beautiful.'

'And the image of your handiwork delivers a visceral thrill. A pleasure. An intense dopamine fix.'

Shepherd entered. 'Sorry to interrupt, sir.'

Sawyer muted the Skype call. 'Stephanie? CCTV?'

Shepherd shook his head. 'Mr Universe has replied.'

37

Sawyer followed Shepherd into Keating's office. As before, Rhodes sat at the corner table, laptop open.

'He's online now,' said Keating, gathering at the table with Shepherd. 'I know Nash didn't pan out, but we do know that the person behind this profile had contact with Angela Holt. Make sure you reel him in like before.'

Sawyer took a seat at the laptop.

'Previously on *Copper Catfish*,' said Rhodes. 'He sent us the torso pic and a message saying "U like?". We replied with, "I certainly do. Tell me more!" Silence since then. He's just replied with another message. Now. I have to warn you, it's not in contention for the Booker Prize.'

Sawyer opened the fake profile inbox and clicked on the new message from PlayWithFire99. The green text next to his profile name confirmed he was online.

The message was short and unpunctuated.

you look like my kind of woman

Sawyer typed.

Chat now?

The reply came back immediately.

ok

Sawyer opened the private chat window. A message was already waiting for him.

lets see more

Sawyer typed.

I love your body. I'd like to see your face.

'He's hardly likely to comply with that,' said Shepherd, 'if he's our killer.'

Sawyer nodded. 'Of course not, but I want to see his reaction.'

After a painful minute of delay, the reply came.

you can see more when we meet

Sawyer replied.

How will I recognise you if you don't show your face?

An immediate response.

you'll know let's just meet

Sawyer held back for a few seconds, then typed.

You've seen my face. Let me see yours.

Another delay. Then the reply.

bitch

The label next to the PlayWithFire99 profile name switched to a red *OFFLINE*.

'Well,' said Rhodes. 'He's certainly a lady-killer.'

Sawyer sat back. 'He's undeniably keen on being the one in control.'

Keating's desk phone rang; he answered.

Shepherd walked to Keating's closed door and looked out at the MIT office. 'He's more wary than Nash. We should pander to him. Apologise. Ask where and when he wants to meet.'

Keating replaced the phone and opened the door, barging past Shepherd. 'Reception. Now.'

On the ground floor, Sawyer was out of the lift first. He hurried to the end of the corridor and faced Sergeant Gerry Sherman at the custody and charge desk.

Sherman ushered Sawyer, Keating, Shepherd and Rhodes to the Perspex privacy barrier at the side of the desk. He leaned forward and spoke in a low voice.

'He's over there.'

As Sawyer turned, a tall, powerfully built man in his early thirties rose from the bench by the door that led to the cells and interview rooms. The man had a polished bald head and a tidy black beard, and he wore a pair of sky-blue knee-length shorts and a tight white T-shirt that flattered his thick biceps.

As he stood, he slid on a pair of thick-framed black glasses.

He took a couple of steps towards the group, then stopped.

'Laura Jayne Bertrand,' he said. 'Dianne Walton.' His voice was flat and colourless, and he shifted his blank eyes from detective to detective. 'Hannah Lane. Angela Holt.' He took another couple of steps forward, stopped. 'Stephanie Burns is still alive.' He turned to Sawyer. 'And the killing must stop now.'

38

‘His name is Julius Newton,’ said Shepherd, in the corridor outside the interview room. Sawyer peered in through the small one-way window at the top of the door. Newton sat on the far side of the desk, beside the duty solicitor, Graham Whittingham. He stared straight ahead, as Whittingham attended to paperwork.

‘And you recognise him?’ said Sawyer, turning to Maggie.

She nodded. ‘He’s a curator at Sheffield’s Institute of Arts Gallery. I was there on Saturday. One of my clients is exhibiting.’

Keating stepped forward and looked in to the room. ‘Maggie. He seems pretty…’

‘Disturbed,’ said Shepherd. ‘Like he’s on drugs.’

‘Was he like that when you saw him?’ said Sawyer.

‘No. The opposite. He was animated, enthusiastic. Almost disturbingly so.’

‘Sit in,’ said Keating. ‘You watch, while Sawyer talks. Just the two of you. He’s handed himself in, but he’s not saying much else, and it’s not clear whether he’s actually confessing to anything. Technically, it’s a voluntary interview, but he's been cautioned, on Whittingham's insistence.' He turned to Sawyer. 'Easy does it. We've switched on the intercom. I'll listen with Shepherd in my office.'

Shepherd followed Keating through the door, back out into reception.

Sawyer stared through the window, at Newton. Maggie touched his shoulder and turned him towards her. 'Is the solicitor aware of my role?'

'Appropriate adult,' said Sawyer. 'It's a fudge, but we've cleared it, given the urgency. Because of Stephanie Burns. We need to question him without delay. Given your qualifications…' He looked at her, smiled. 'Thanks for coming.'

Sawyer switched on the recording and ran through the introductory formalities. Newton kept his hands on his knees and his eyes fixed on the wall behind. In the corner, the desktop fan wafted warm air across the interview desk.

'The women you named, Julius,' said Sawyer. 'Tell me what happened to them.'

Newton looked at Sawyer; he seemed confused. 'He killed them. I let it happen, but now I want it to stop.'

'He?'

Newton nodded. 'He's been doing it for so long now. It has to stop.'

'Where is Stephanie Burns?'

'I don't know. But he does.'

Maggie glanced at Sawyer. 'Is he with us now, Julius?'

Newton took off his glasses and rubbed his eyes. Whittingham touched his arm and whispered something into his ear.

Newton looked back at Sawyer. 'No comment.'

'Ah, we were just getting started,' said Sawyer. 'Here's a side question. Did you kill Damien Mount?'

Newton dropped his gaze to the floor. 'No comment.'

'Did *he* kill Damien Mount, as well as the women?'

'No comment.'

Sawyer tried a few more questions—direct, open-ended, neutral—before giving up and suspending the interview. A duty officer entered to take Newton to one of the cells. Sawyer glared at Whittingham as they left.

Keating and Shepherd entered.

'There seems to be a separation,' said Maggie. 'A depersonalisation. If he is the killer, then he's created a sort of internalised fiction, detaching the version of himself that's doing the killing.'

'Disavowing himself,' said Shepherd.

'I suppose. A coping strategy.'

'If he wants the killing to stop,' said Sawyer, 'then why is he giving us the no comment? How does that help to stop the killing?'

Shepherd massaged his beard. 'Perhaps he feels it's enough to just hand himself in. If he is the killer, at least it gets him off the streets.'

'Doesn't help us find Stephanie Burns, though.' said Sawyer. 'Newton says "he" knows where she is.'

'Second time lucky,' said Keating. 'We didn't get a match with Nash, so let's work on linking him to the forensics. So far, we have nothing, other than the fact that he knows the names of the women. He might be another crank, getting off on wasting our time. Follow the science.'

Sawyer went back to his office and, once again, looked through the collected HOLMES intelligence. He reviewed the passive data, a few relative interviews, and the aborted attempt to build a case against Tommie Nash. But his eye was repeatedly drawn back to the *Secret Encounters* section, and the PlayWithFire99 image. Newton was well built and worked out, and the body in the picture could easily belong to him. But then PlayWithFire99 may well be nothing to do with the killings, and until they had concrete forensic evidence, the same could be said for Newton, despite the theatrics.

His phone rang, and he picked up.

'Newsflash,' said Sally O'Callaghan. 'Your new man, Mr Newton. His boot print is the same as the prints we found at the Mount scene. Even better, his swab is a match for the DNA from the cigarette end at the Holt scene.'

Sawyer sat back, closed his eyes. 'And the blood from the Laura Bertrand dog bite?'

'It's not his.'

'So, we can't connect him to the Laura Bertrand murder, but he was definitely at Mount's place.'

'But there's still no distinct motive for that murder, right?'

'Not that we know of, yet. And he discarded a cigarette at the Holt scene. So, either he murdered Angela Holt...' He opened his eyes. 'Or maybe he found the body before Mount, but didn't call it in.'

'But why would that give him motive to kill Mount? Or, could Mount himself be the killer, after all?'

'Or perhaps Newton *mistakenly* thinks that Mount is the killer. He stumbles on him taking photos of Angela

Holt's body, assumes he's killed her, then tracks him down, kills him...'

He hung up and dashed out, across to the lift and down to the cells.

Sherman unlocked Newton's cell and Sawyer shouldered his way inside. Newton sat up in his bed.

Sawyer took a step towards him. 'Why?' Newton put on his glasses and returned a quizzical look. 'You say you want the killing to stop. So, now is your chance to do the right thing. You can *save a life*. Have you imprisoned her somewhere? Has he imprisoned her somewhere?'

Newton dropped his head.

'Has he already killed her, Julius?'

'No comment.'

39

Dale Strickland disconnected the call, and lowered himself into his seat at the glass-topped desk. He sat for a while, listening to the traffic below.

Marco watched him, waited. At last, Dale looked up and shrugged. 'It was always going to be Hogan. It's between him and the Rochdale guy. Lib Dem.'

Marco nodded at Dale's phone. 'Was that Hogan?'

'He says if he gets it, and he will, he's going to make me the Greater Manchester "drug czar".'

Marco slapped the desk. 'Out-fucking-standing!'

Dale cracked a smile. 'It's a good base. Solid profile to build on. And it's more than I really expected.'

Marco gave a neutral nod. 'Right.'

'Don't worry. We can dial down the charm now. It means we can re-focus on our other issue.'

Marco looked up, searched the ceiling. 'Hector's gone dark. No answer from his phone. Mina is in Split. She says he normally calls or messages once or twice a day. She's heard nothing since late last night.'

Dale took a bottle of Glenfiddich and two glasses from a drawer. 'And that's enough to worry?'

'He might not be on call for her, but he always replies to me, usually within minutes. I've sent him six messages in the last two hours. All unread.'

Dale splashed two measures of whisky into the glasses and handed one to Marco. 'Go to his place. Check on him.' Marco nodded, morose. 'What's your worry? Worst case.'

Marco sipped, winced. 'My worry is that Fletcher might be covering his tracks. Cleaning up anyone who knows about Shaun. Hector, me, maybe even you.'

'And Sawyer.'

'He knows that Sawyer has the leverage, knows he has the gun used on Shaun. So, he saves Sawyer until last. Then if it turns out that Sawyer *has* left something for the police to find, there will be fewer people to speak to who actually know anything.'

'Scorched earth.'

'Sort of. And, my worry is that he's already got to Hector.'

'And he'll hit one of us next?'

Marco screwed up his face. 'I don't know, Dale. I don't know him. He's like... a fucking shark. Or some kind of zombie. Like he's had a transplant. They took out his heart but forgot to put a new one in.'

Dale slugged his whisky. 'Me and Fletcher used to hang out a lot, after college. The usual mischief. There was this Jewish guy in our little group. He once told me he thought that Fletcher was like a golem. Some kind of elemental creature. Made of stone. Incapable of emotion.' Dale locked his glinting blue eyes on Marco's. 'But the truth is, that's all a front. The one-word replies, the blankness. It's like his disguise. It's how he gains an advantage. He wants people to underestimate him. I mean, he really works at that. But underneath it all, he's busy. There's a lot going on in there.'

'Were you close?'

Dale grinned. 'Practically brotherly. Believe it or not, he used to be pretty sharp. Funny, even. But something got to him. Blunted his edges.' He finished the whisky. 'No! Tainted him, more like. I never found out what it was. It was before he joined the forces, though.' He got to his feet and stood in the light breeze drifting in through the window. 'You were right. We never should have brought him in.'

'What if he comes for me?'

'I remember it was Fletcher who gave me *The Art of War* by Sun-Tzu. I skimmed it, mostly to shut him up. But he's always tried to follow one of the core philosophies. "The supreme art of war is to subdue the enemy without fighting." That's how he thinks. He's more than capable of fighting, but he sees it as messy and unpredictable. So he tries to find more underhand, indirect ways of achieving his goal. That's why I thought he could deal with Sawyer for us, and leave no trace.'

Marco lowered his head. 'And how does this help me?'

Dale sat down. 'Stay sharp. Don't look for shadows in the street. Check under your bed, in your cupboards. Be careful what you eat or drink. Keep your gun within reach. And if you do get into a tangle with him, finish it quick. Don't make him angry.'

'Okay. So he's a ninja and the fucking Hulk.'

'We get the results of the mayor candidacy tomorrow. It's almost certainly Hogan's, but there will be plenty of attention. And Fletcher might come to the party.'

40

Sawyer opened his eyes and stared up at the rosy glow flushed across the ceiling. The heat made sleeping in the dark claustrophobic, and so he had got into the habit of setting his phone on the bedside table, with a night light switched on, and the ambient sound effect of a summer rainstorm on a loop: a constant crackle, like static, punctuated by occasional distant thunder.

It was too early to get up, but he forced himself out of bed, fed Bruce, and made himself a cup of tea. He worked out, and, as the early sunlight came to the boil behind the curtains, he stood topless before the mirror, and executed the second Wing Chun form: *Chum Kiu* ('Searching for the Bridge'). The form's emphasis was on stability, unity, and he moved through the one-hundred-and-fifty-two components with grade-perfect poise and precision.

He screwed in his earphones and walked along the lane, down into Edale village, under an immaculate blue sky. The sun showed no sign of softening; if anything, it was turning up the temperature, making it impossible to even conceive of a time when it might tire and retreat. But, his live radio app spoke of a 'break' coming; a swell of humidity, and an almighty popping of the bubble, and, at last, a drink for the cotton-mouthed land.

The Church of the Holy and Undivided Trinity was set in generous grounds, at the Southern tip of the Pennine Way, off the main lane which carried the walkers to the base of Kinder Scout. Sawyer padded along the path, gazing up at the Gothic spire. The open door beckoned, revealing the nave and aisle, but Sawyer turned away, and approached the vicarage: a modest, single-storey cottage, recently built in matching grey stone.

A short, jocular-looking man in a dark suit, matching shirt and white dog collar opened the front door before he could ring the bell. He stepped out onto the porch.

'Peter Plant?' said Sawyer.

The man nodded and offered a faintly quizzical smile. 'The very same.'

Sawyer stopped at the doorstep. 'You're the parish priest.'

'And you're rather perceptive, if you'll pardon the sarcasm.'

'Requirement of the job.' He flashed his warrant card.

Plant leaned forward and studied it. 'Detective Inspector Sawyer. Am I under arrest?'

'No. But I was hoping you could help me with my enquiry.'

Plant chuckled. 'Whatever you need, Mr Sawyer. I'm on the side of the angels. Would you come inside for some tea?'

Sawyer took out his phone. 'I don't think it's wise of you to invite the likes of me over the threshold.'

Plant bowed his head in thought. The sunlight shone through the thinning grey hair stretched across the top of his head, revealing a rash of lobster-red scalp. He looked up again. 'I'm assuming you mean that you're a non-believer, not a vampire?'

Sawyer smiled. 'I don't define myself by my lack of belief.' He scrolled through the image gallery on his phone, and found the PlayWithFire99 torso picture. 'Could you take a look at this, please?' He held up the phone for Plant to see, and zoomed in on the gap in the blind. 'This looks like a clock face to me. But I'm not sure where it could be from. I assume it's from a church steeple? Hopefully somewhere local.'

Plant took the phone from Sawyer and held it in the shade of the porch. 'Are you investigating the murders? So awful. A couple of my parishioners have told me about the unfortunate woman who is currently missing. We said prayers for her.'

'It won't help,' said Sawyer.

'Ah. I take it you're not part of the congregation. Do you have a faith yourself?'

Sawyer smiled. 'Nothing formal. I pick and mix. I like the Buddhist idea that man has no refuge in man. We can't just pray away our sins, sacrifice our Sunday mornings to a religion and assume all will be well. Our lives are in our own hands.'

Plant caught his eye, then looked back to the phone. 'Prayer isn't necessarily a direct appeal to a higher power, you know. It can also be a communion with one's self, often in times of adversity. A ritualised form of hope, if you like. Or acceptance.'

'I understand that,' said Sawyer. 'But I prefer to put my faith in hard evidence, direct action.'

Plant handed back the phone. 'Are you familiar with the agony in the garden, where Jesus prays and accepts that he is about to be betrayed? "The spirit is willing but the flesh is weak"?'

'I am,' said Sawyer. 'But, as I say, I don't accept the practical value of prayer, and when lives are at stake, hope is an expensive luxury.'

Plant regarded him, rubbing his hands together in a slow, lathering motion. 'That's a pity. I'm impressed by your sense of certainty, Mr Sawyer. I wish my own faith was so ironclad. For me, prayer is an integral part of the nature of faith. I pray with many things in mind. Better fortune, better health, deeper understanding. Lately, I've been praying for a relief from this weather.'

Sawyer looked up, to the stinging sun, the cerulean sky. 'I remember my assembly at school. It was an old building, and we had this oversized book of tatty paper suspended on a rope at the side of the hall. The teachers would lower it, turn the vertical pages to the words of the chosen prayer, and then hoist it back up for all to see. The teachers were strictly religious, and anyone caught not reciting the right words to the prayers, not bowing their head, or not keeping their eyes closed... They'd be in deep trouble. But it doesn't matter how low you bow your head, how tightly you close your eyes. And it doesn't matter what you're praying for. Salvation, forgiveness, better prospects, better weather.' He took a breath, smiled at Plant. 'There's nobody listening. The sky is empty. *We* do the forgiving. We make the good things start and the bad things stop. That's what we do. If there is a God, then he's pretty hands-off, wouldn't you say? And he's a lousy delegator.'

Plant's grin widened. 'That's not the God I believe in, Mr Sawyer. I must get you in to do the Sunday sermon sometime. It'll be fascinating food for thought. What it must be like to live in a world of such certainty. I'm afraid I only have my imperfect faith to guide me.' He nodded to the phone. 'I'm assuming you won't interpret this as divine intervention, but I can answer your question. The only local church with a clock face like that one is St Martin's, in Stoney Middleton.'

41

Shepherd opened the Mini passenger window and poked his head out.

'You remind me of Rufus,' said Sawyer, as he sped away from the mob of rush-hour traffic inching its way into Buxton.

Shepherd looked over. 'Friend or foe?'

'Dog.'

'I can't see how I could take that as a positive.'

Sawyer shrugged. 'It's an affectionate insult.'

'So, if I was a dog, what breed would I be?'

Sawyer frowned. 'Do you really want to hear this?'

'No.'

'Labrador. Steady and dependable. A bit too eager to please, but actually a lot deeper than it seems on the surface.'

Shepherd poked his head out of the window again. 'I've never been to Stoney Middleton.'

'It's not Machu Picchu. Couple of pubs, chippy.'

Sawyer turned off at the Sparrowpit crossroads and joined the slender two-lane connecting road to the Hope

Valley. On either side, the infinite farm fields braced for another day of unyielding heat and light.

'I saw Newton first thing,' said Shepherd. 'Still quiet.'

'We know he was at Mount's place, and the Angela Holt scene. Why would he walk into the police station, say he wants the killing to stop, but then lock up on us?'

Shepherd sipped from a bottle of water. 'Power play? He loves the idea that he can enter the belly of the beast, antagonise us, tease us, then walk right back out again. He knows we only have circumstantial evidence.'

Sawyer squeezed the accelerator. The road was straight and clear, but he was pushing seventy on a fifty limit. 'It's still not clear if he's referring to himself in some kind of schizoid third person, or someone else.'

'Again, though. If by "he", he means someone else, and he wants the killing to stop, then why not just tell us who's doing it?'

Sawyer overtook a post van, swerved back into lane. 'He's an art dealer. The bodies are presented almost artistically. Is it all a fucked-up situationist statement? Murder as art?'

'He could be everything or he could be nothing. Like Mount.'

Sawyer glanced at him. 'But why kill Mount? That's the big itch we need to scratch. If he's a misogynist psychopath, presenting his kills as grotesque art statements, then at least that's something to investigate and understand. It's joined up. But why kill the guy who found one of the bodies? Just some chancer trying to get a bit of attention, squeeze money out of the police.'

'We're still not a hundred per cent sure that Mount wasn't the killer. Maybe Stephanie Burns is just another misper, and Newton has succeeded in stopping the killing by finishing off Mount. And now he's handed himself in, he's trying to fudge things with this third person nonsense.'

'Or maybe the third person nonsense is real for him. And he's separating out the killing side of himself, as a way of coping. The only way he can stop that persona from continuing to kill is by handing himself in.'

Shepherd took out a handkerchief and dabbed at his brow. 'Walker is working on background. Whatever Newton is up to, we have to work it out before his custody time runs out at 9pm.'

They parked in Stoney Middleton village and walked along a cramped lane of stone terraces built along the edge of a depleted brook. A handsome church with a square clocktower sat at the centre of a gated graveyard.

'Fifteenth century,' said Sawyer. 'That's the original tower. See the blue clock face with white numbers? According to my local vicar, that's the only one of its kind in the area.' He took out his phone, opened the image from PlayWithFire99, and zoomed in on the gap in the blind.

Shepherd took the phone, looked from screen to church and back again. 'Looks possible. So, our *Secret Encounters* man took his photo in one of these houses facing the church.'

'Get the details of the male homeowners and tenants. Looks like a first floor shot to me, but find them all and cross reference with local gym memberships. He didn't get that body doing press-ups.' Shepherd nodded, sighed. 'Now you're reminding me of a Labrador who didn't get his walk. I know it's not much, but we saw this guy on the online chat. He's a fit. And we know that he had contact with Angela Holt.'

Sawyer's phone rang; Shepherd handed it back.

'Trace and eliminate,' said Sawyer, looking at the caller ID: *CHRIS HILL*. He answered. 'This is Jake.'

Hill caught his breath. 'Mr Sawyer. I'm so terribly sorry to be the bearer of bad news. But it's Michael. He's been taken to Cavendish. He's okay. But...'

Sawyer turned away from Shepherd and raised his eyes to the unclouded sky. 'What happened?'

'Your brother. He tried to take his own life, Mr Sawyer.'

Sawyer stumbled out of the lift at Buxton's Cavendish Hospital and sprinted along the corridor towards the acute care unit.

A fortysomething man in a blue surgical tunic stepped out from the nurse's station and held up his hand. 'Mr Sawyer? Could you please come with me for a second?'

They moved into a cramped, pastel-shaded relative's room. The man closed the door and turned to Sawyer with a look of sympathy. 'I'm Jim Matthews. I'm one of the senior ICU doctors.'

Sawyer spoke over him. 'Where's Michael?'

'He's stable, but I'm afraid you won't be able to see him at the moment. He was very lucky. It seems that the attendant at his facility found him shortly after...' He sighed. 'We call it a "near hanging". That is, there wasn't a body-length drop which could have resulted in spinal transection. I don't know the full circumstances, but as far as I'm aware, he used his belt and stepped off the edge of the bath.'

Sawyer felt himself drift slightly, as if the doctor was only speaking to a part of him, and the rest was struggling to calibrate to the scene.

'There's been some brain swelling, and so we've had to put Michael into a medically induced coma.' Matthews placed his palms together, as if in prayer. 'Now, that's not necessarily as bad as it sounds. It's merely a deep state of unconsciousness. A protective measure, while the brain recovers. The level below sedation, which is semi-conscious.'

Sawyer's knees buckled, and he flopped into one of the low cushioned chairs beneath the open window. 'What are the prospects?'

Matthews frowned. 'It's impossible to say at this moment. He could recover completely, or there may be irreversible... impairment. It's common for survivors of this kind of trauma to not even remember the incident.'

'Retrograde amnesia.'

'Yes. We'll monitor him for now. Obviously, he wasn't able to nominate next of kin, but you—'

Sawyer closed his eyes. 'I'm his only kin.'

Matthews dropped his head, and they endured a moment of silence. 'I'm so sorry, Mr Sawyer. We'll keep you informed of your brother's progress. The neurological team here are extremely good. He's in the right place.'

Sawyer stood up. 'Thank you.'

Matthews hesitated. 'There's a gentleman here, in the waiting room. Chris. He came with your brother in the ambulance.'

Sawyer sighed. 'That's the manager of his care home.'

'I could send him in?'

'Fine.'

Matthews left the room. Sawyer took out his phone. Message from Shepherd.

How is he?

Sawyer replied.

Stable. Don't tell Keating.

A couple of taps on the door. Chris Hill entered, looking flushed and sweaty in a white work shirt and green tie.

He strode over and placed a podgy hand on Sawyer's shoulder. 'Mr Sawyer, I am so sorry.'

Sawyer turned away, and stared up at the tiny muted television mounted on the wall in the far corner. Day-Glo daytime TV. 'Did you find him?'

'Ah. No. It was Victoria. One of the attendants. She had just cleaned Michael's room and heard a noise as she was passing back along the corridor after storing her items.'

On-screen, a young woman Sawyer didn't recognise sat on the far side of a plum-coloured sofa, opposite male and female presenters in awkward, cross-legged poses. 'So, he did it when he thought he might not be discovered.'

'It would seem that way. This is extremely rare for Rosemary House. In our twenty-five year history, we've only had one patient commit suicide—'

Sawyer turned and glared at him. 'Die by suicide.'

Hill hitched up his half-moon glasses. 'Sorry?'

'You don't "commit" suicide. It's not a crime.'

'Of course. It's odd, though. Michael did seem a whole lot brighter recently.'

'That's common, for someone who has made up their mind.' Sawyer walked to the window and gazed out at the heat-shimmer above the tightly packed car park at the back of the building. 'The conflict has gone. The struggle is coming to an end. They feel unburdened.' He turned to Hill. 'Was there any note? Anything addressed to me?'

Hill took a breath, bracing himself. 'No.'

42

Sawyer sat at his office desk, almost horizontal in his chair, with the blinds fully drawn. It was close to midday, and the world outside was a soup of humidity. But he had switched off his air con, and stewed in the enclosing heat, taking slow, measured breaths, tuning in to the office murmur beyond his partition.

He felt the ugly pull of self-pity. He had spoken to Alex about sitting at the centre of the storm, undamaged, while the suffering happened around him, to the people he was closest to. Suffering drawn from his own action, or lack of action. He knew it was absurd to blame his six-year-old self for not saving his mother from her adult assailant, but as his mind drifted back to that ruptured summer's day, he recalled how he had been running too far ahead, causing his mother to call for him repeatedly, warning him not to go too far ahead. She had been fixated on him, distracted, and therefore unaware of her killer making his move.

And his father, strait-jacketed inside his grief. His revenge on Caldwell had been monstrous and unlawful, but it had been Sawyer's relentless pursuit of the truth that had ultimately led to his father's end.

Now, his only brother lay in limbo, chemically preserved: another longstanding consequence of his mother's distraction, caused by his blindness to consequence. He had doomed his mother by running away, and in her dying moments, she had implored him to run, to not look back. But how could he move forward, forge a meaningful life, when all he touched turned to dust?

Sawyer startled as his phone buzzed. He took the call without looking at the ID.

'Have you arrested someone?' said Dean Logan.

'For what?'

'Really? A trip round the houses?'

'Tell me what you think you know.'

'You have someone in custody for the murders.'

Sawyer sipped from his bottle of water, taking his time. 'Even if we did, that's not news. It's only news when we charge.'

Logan laughed. 'Anything new is news. Even fucking fake news is news.'

'I thought you were a journalist. You sound more like a content strategist.'

'Nobody is one thing any more, Sawyer. That went out in the eighties.'

Shepherd knocked and entered.

'We're building a case,' said Sawyer. 'Questioning suspects, eliminating them.'

'I'll take that as a yes."

'I wouldn't expect anything more. You'll construct whatever story you think will sell newspapers.'

Logan sighed. 'You're no fun any more, Sawyer. Trotting out the old knee-jerk lines. And, anyway, it's all about page impressions. Unique visits. Monetisation.'

'Lying to advertisers.'

'That's more like it!' Logan spluttered.

Shepherd walked to the window and opened the blinds slightly. Sharp shafts of sunlight lasered through the gaps and Sawyer squinted and turned away.

'Can't you give me a bit more?' Logan persisted. 'I want you to catch the bastard who's doing this, you know.'

'If I had a bit more, I might be able to help. But at this stage, you probably know more than we do. Let me know when your next monetisable content drops.'

He hung up and kept his eyes on his phone.

Shepherd stood at the desk before him. 'Everything okay?' Sawyer looked up, shrugged. 'You missed the fun. Keating brought in two specialist interrogators to have a go on Newton. He gave them nothing.'

'Still no commenting?'

'Not even that. He's lost the third person schizoid thing. He's now just staring into space. I'm sure Whittingham is just writing his shopping list next to him.'

Sawyer sprang to his feet and walked to the door.

In the interview room, Sawyer ran through the initial formalities and sat back, facing Newton and Whittingham. Shepherd sat off to the side, blocking the breeze from the desktop fan.

Sawyer stayed silent, gazing at the desktop.

Newton picked up his glasses and put them on. He sat back and folded his arms.

Whittingham looked at Shepherd, who shrugged. 'Do you have a question for my client, Detective Sawyer?'

'Julius,' said Sawyer. 'You say that you want the killing to stop, and that he killed them. Is he inside you?'

Newton lowered his eyes on the desk.

'You said that you let the killings happen. Is he some

kind of inner voice that urges you to kill? Have you got him under control now? Was he controlling you before? Making you do bad things?'

Newton cleared his throat. 'I read about you.'

Sawyer nodded. 'And what did you think?'

'You had a tough start in life.'

'Yes, I did. A terrible thing happened to someone I love. Did that happen to you, too?'

Newton nodded. 'Yes. And it changed him.'

Sawyer leaned forward, jolting the desk. 'Him? You mean, you?'

Newton's voice was calm, unhurried. 'He is a psychopath, you know.'

'Do you mean yourself, Julius?' said Shepherd. 'Do you mean *you're* a psychopath?'

'He thinks he's in control,' said Newton. 'But he's not. He can't control himself.'

Sawyer leaned further forward. 'So, why now? Why do you want the killing to stop now? If he can't control himself, how do we make it stop?'

Newton's breathing quickened. For the first time, he looked up and locked eyes with Sawyer. 'It's a wonderful world, Detective Sawyer. Don't you think? So much beauty and vibrancy. But we fill it with hate and ugliness. We're all born into this magnificent paradise, and we pillage it and desecrate it, out of greed. And we visit so much personal hurt and pain on each other, all because of the hurt and pain that was visited on ourselves. From what I've read about you, this is something you know only too well.' Newton placed his trembling hands on the table. 'There's always neglect, pain, violence. Nobody wakes up one morning and decides to hurt other people. But the cycle continues. Individual lives may end, but the pain trickles on down through the generations. Stephanie Burns is the latest victim of this continuum of hurt, and until you find where it all began, you won't find Stephanie. Until it's too late.'

Sawyer rose to his feet and rested his hands on the desk, inches from Newton's. 'Or I could take the short cut and just ask someone who knows where she is.' He leaned forward, close to Newton's face. 'Where is she?'

Newton dropped his gaze. 'No comment.'

Sawyer grabbed the edge of the desk and dragged it to the side. It tilted on its end, sending the voice recorder and water bottles crashing to the floor. Newton scrambled to his feet and backed into the far corner. Sawyer approached him, eyes flashing with fury. Shepherd leapt up and grabbed Sawyer by the shoulder, but he shrugged him off.

Whittingham stepped between Sawyer and Newton. 'Detective! Get a grip on yourself. The PACE guidelines require you to—'

Sawyer stood over Newton as he sunk down into the corner, his entire body tremoring. He stared him out for a few long seconds, and then turned and crashed out of the room.

Back upstairs in his office, Sawyer closed the door, drew the blind on his partition window, and sat on the edge of his desk, covering his eyes with both hands.

Two taps on the door. Shepherd's signature knock. Sawyer walked to the window and fully opened the blinds. He turned to see Shepherd closing the door behind him. He walked to the chair in front of Sawyer's desk and sat down, keeping his eyes forward.

'I have twenty-two names,' said Shepherd. 'People who either own or rent the properties facing Stoney Middleton Church.'

Sawyer stayed by the window, and looked out across the car park and football stadium. Since his return, the sky had darkened, with dense smears of cloud muting the sunlight. He turned to Shepherd. 'Gym memberships?'

'Three of them. Two women, one man.'

'Let's go see the man.'

Shepherd nodded. 'Briefing in half an hour. Go after.' He paused. 'I squared it with Whittingham. Said you were under pressure. Family issues.'

Sawyer barked a laugh. 'Anything else?'

'Apart from your deteriorating mental state?'

Sawyer turned away again. 'I'm okay. I'm under pressure. Family issues.'

'It's okay not to be okay.'

'I understand that. But I am.'

'Okay?'

Sawyer looked over his shoulder. 'Yes.'

'Well. That's okay, then.'

43

Keating brought the briefing to order. Sawyer sat in his usual spot, flanked by Shepherd and Walker, with Myers and Moran at the other side of the conference table, and Stephen Bloom sat beside Keating. Farrell, Whittaker, McBride and Barlow stared out from inside their boxes on the shared Skype screen.

'Okay. As you all know, a thirty-four-year-old man, Julius Newton, entered the Buxton station yesterday, claiming a connection to the perpetrator of the murders.'

'Another attention-seeker?' said Barlow.

'Possibly. But he's been arrested on suspicion to give us time to formally question him.'

'So far,' said Shepherd, 'he's given us very little. But he is implying that he knows where Stephanie Burns is being held, and that he wants the killing to stop.'

'He seems to be referring to the murderer as himself, or "he", in the third person,' said Keating.

'Seems to be?' said Farrell.

'Trace evidence puts him at the Mount scene,' said Sawyer. 'And his DNA is on the cigarette end found near to Angela Holt's body. But if he is responsible for the murders of the women, there's very little in his background to suggest motivation. Even less for killing Mount.'

'On paper,' said Walker, 'he's pretty dull. Steady Eddie at school. Decent grades. Gravitated towards art. His old form tutor told me he was a bit of a loner, but it's a long way from a grumpy teenager to a multiple killer.'

'Family life seems pretty conventional, too,' said McBride. 'The HOLMES section says his father was a PE teacher and his mother hopped around in various clerk roles for shipping companies.'

'They're still together,' said Walker. 'They live in Hope.'

'Don't we all?' said Barlow.

Keating tapped the bridge of his nose. 'Anything else?'

'The *Secret Encounters* line,' said Sawyer.

'Ah, yes,' said Farrell. 'Fine work on snaring our last remaining connection to Angela Holt, Detective Sawyer.'

Sawyer glanced at Keating. 'Although the contact reacted badly, I felt it would be worth the effort to gain a facial image, and identify the potential suspect, rather than conducting another sting that may go nowhere. DS Shepherd and I are investigating possible locations for the flat in the PlayWithFire99 profile photo. There's a partial image of a clock face visible through the blinds, and the type is only found on one church locally. Stoney Middleton. We're looking into the residents of the houses facing the church.'

A moment of silence. Keating shared a web link via the chat system. A piece by Dean Logan, from the Derbyshire Times website, with a typically histrionic headline.

COPS MAKE ARREST IN RIPPER PROBE

'I'm going to run a short press conference this afternoon,' said Keating. 'To keep engagement. No confirmation or denial. Just an acknowledgement that we're speaking to a person of interest.'

'There's very little in the story,' said Bloom. 'Just speculation. But we need to get out there again. Show willing. I would suggest deflecting with an appeal for Stephanie Burns.'

'Good idea,' said Farrell. 'The victim profile is a perfect fit.'

Myers nodded. 'But we're still nowhere near the threshold for approaching the CPC. All the evidence is circumstantial. We can't back up Newton's presence at Mount's place with motive, and the blood from Laura Bertrand's dog bite doesn't match him. We won't get him anywhere near a court, let alone secure a conviction.'

Keating gestured to Bloom. 'We'll run the conference to address questions over the arrest, and we'll formally announce the urgency of finding Stephanie Burns.'

Sawyer shifted in his seat. 'Even if Stephanie Burns's disappearance is unrelated, which seems unlikely, there's no time to worry about a false connection now. We have to be direct, efficient. Whoever Newton is, and whatever game he's playing, we have to let him go in six hours.'

44

Sawyer and Shepherd climbed the external metal staircase to a short balcony at the front of the two first-floor flats whose back windows overlooked St Martin's Church. Sawyer stepped back, while Shepherd rang the doorbell.

'Interestingly,' said Shepherd, 'there's a place called Middleton Stoney down in Oxfordshire. Stoney Middleton, here. Middleton Stoney down there.'

'That's a charitable interpretation of the word "interestingly". Any more detail on the etymology?'

Shepherd shrugged, kept his eyes on the door. '"Middleton" is probably something to do with the middle town of a group. I'm not even looking at you, and I can tell you're glazing over.'

'It's too long ago. All that Domesday Book stuff. Also, I'm under doctor's orders not to fixate on the past.'

The door opened. A tall, powerfully built man in a sleeveless white vest stood in the hallway. He tilted his head forward, fixing them both with a quizzical stare. He had cropped his dark hair down to a shadow, leaving a slightly thicker patch front of centre. He folded his heavily worked out arms across his chest. 'It's a fair cop.'

'Sorry?' said Shepherd.

'You're coppers, right?'

'Is it that obvious?' said Sawyer.

The man grinned. 'Yeah. It is. What's up, lads?'

Sawyer caught Shepherd's eye. 'Mr Powell?'

The man held out a beefy hand. 'Malcolm.'

Shepherd shook, Sawyer did likewise. Powell's grip was so strong, Sawyer had to jerk his hand away. 'A pleasure to meet you, Mr Powell.' He wrung his hand. 'A pain, too.'

Powell laughed. 'Sorry. I'm not good at judging that kind of thing. And I was just working out. Bit of testosterone still flowing. What can I do for you?'

'I'm Detective Inspector Sawyer; this is Detective Sergeant Shepherd. Can we come in for five minutes? Just a few questions.'

Powell looked irritated. 'Do I have to let you in?'

'No,' said Shepherd. 'But—'

'I know, I know. This is the easy way, right? You can always go and get a warrant or whatever, and we can do it the hard way.' He grinned again. 'Just messing with you. Come in. No problem at all.'

They walked through to a neat sitting room: angular, dark-grey sofa and matching armchair with lime-green cushions; low white coffee table with stubby steel legs; enormous flat-screen TV and DVD player; workout bench pushed up against the open window overlooking the brook and lane winding through to the centre of the village. The wall had been knocked through to connect with a small galley kitchen, in white and chrome. Another door, ajar, revealed a glimpse of the bedroom on the church side. No pictures or ornaments. The place was unadorned, show-home tidy.

'Good to see a DVD player,' said Sawyer. 'I'm not a fan of streaming.'

'Me neither,' said Powell. 'I like physical objects. Not just noughts and ones. Annoys my missus. Probably a man thing. I stream my music, though.'

'Is your wife at work?'

Powell opened the fridge. 'Yeah. She's a Euro MP. Spends a lot of time in Brussels. You been there? Dull as fuck. Do you want a beer? Ice cold. Hoping this fucking weather breaks soon.'

'No, thanks,' said Sawyer. 'We can't stay long. Just a couple of questions. Routine elimination from an enquiry. Apologies in advance if the theme might seem a little indelicate.'

Powell closed the fridge and turned to face them, arms folded again. 'Sounds intriguing. Fire away.'

Shepherd stepped further into the room. 'What do you do for a living, Mr Powell?'

'Bits and pieces. Decorating, labouring. I mostly pay my way with personal training work. Freelance and local gyms. I qualified as a PT a couple of years ago.'

'Any kids?' said Shepherd.

'Nah. Hasn't really happened. Although I can't say we're that keen on the idea.'

Sawyer walked over to the armchair but didn't sit. 'Are you happily married, Mr Powell?'

Powell moved away from the fridge and rested his elbows on the wooden kitchen worktop. 'How do you mean?'

'Are you familiar with a website called *Secret Encounters*?'

Powell looked to Shepherd, back to Sawyer. A cloud passed over his sunny demeanour. 'What's that got to do with anything?'

'You used the site to make contact with a woman by the name of Angela Holt.'

Powell frowned. 'How the fuck do you know that? Are you hacking phones?'

'No,' said Shepherd. 'Angela was found dead five days ago, and her computer history shows that you made contact with her in the time just before her death.'

'She was one of the women in this Ripper thing?' Powell stared into space, shaking his head. 'I'm not... Look. It's just a bit of fun. Danielle's away a lot. I have a lot of free time. We're all red-blooded males, eh?'

'Does Danielle know about *Secret Encounters*?' said Sawyer. 'Does she share your opinion that it's a "bit of fun"?'

Powell took a step towards Sawyer. 'I don't like your fucking tone.'

'It's a simple question. No tone. Is your activity on *Secret Encounters* known to your wife? Some people are open about this kind of thing.' He smiled. 'I just wondered if you have an arrangement.'

Powell inched closer to Sawyer. 'No, we don't have an arrangement. It's private. I'm sorry that this woman is dead, but it's nothing to do with me. We just talked online, didn't meet in the end. That's it. Are we done now? Or do I need a fucking lawyer?'

'No,' said Sawyer. 'You don't need a fucking lawyer. You're not under arrest. Are you active on any other similar online sites? *Extramarital*? *Dark Strangers*?'

Powell took another step towards Sawyer. He lifted his arm and jabbed his finger close to Sawyer's face. 'What about *you*? Are you a member of the sites? What gives you the right to come here and judge me?' Powell stood his ground, in front of Sawyer, too close. He smelt of something sharp and citrus, and his teeth were unnaturally white. He smiled, gave a strangled little laugh. 'You're a cocky fucker, aren't you?'

‘Cocky?’ said Sawyer.

‘Yeah. Big lad like me. Squaring up to you. But you don’t even blink.’ He nodded to Shepherd. ‘Is he an android or something?’

‘It’s okay, Mr Powell,’ said Sawyer. ‘You’re not going to attack me.’

‘How do you know that? Just because you’re a copper?’

Sawyer shook his head. ‘I just know the clues. People need an emotional run-up before violence. Their inflections alter, their posture becomes sharper, more direct. Their bodies get bigger as blood flows to the muscles that they intend to use. You’re just puffing up. You’re not going to attack me.’ He smiled. ‘Can I use your toilet?’

Powell took a few breaths and turned away, heading back to the kitchen. ‘Corridor. First right.’

Sawyer moved away. As Powell opened the fridge, he snuck a look inside the bedroom. The blind was up, showing the church and blue clock face, and, although a few furnishings had been shifted around, the room looked the same as the one in the *Secret Encounters* photo.

He entered the bathroom. It was small and sterile, with a sink, over-bath shower, toilet and mirrored bathroom cabinet with surrounding lights. He checked the products arranged around the side of the bath: lemon shower gel, but no soap. A green toothbrush sat on the sink, below the cabinet. He took out a small plastic evidence bag and slipped the toothbrush inside.

On the way back to MIT, Sawyer turned off the main road to Buxton and drove into an ugly industrial estate with identical office buildings, all numbered and marked on a map at the entrance.

Shepherd turned to him. 'Is this the scenic route?'

'Quick stop-off. Five minutes. Wait for me.'

He parked up and entered a three-storey glass-fronted building with a sign above the main doors: *SCIENTIFIC SERVICES.*

Sally O'Callaghan sat on the sofa in the reception area, browsing a magazine. She stood as Sawyer entered and trotted over. 'We've reached peak fast-track, you know.'

'This is a new level. Ultra-fast-track. How quickly can you do it?'

He took out the evidence bag and handed it over.

'An hour. Bit more for the checks. Why the urgency?'

'I just want to cross him off. He was playing with us. Feigning outrage. That's always interesting. And he was aggressive, deflecting. Not watchful or wary. No goodwill, but plenty of authentic arrogance.'

Sally shrugged. 'It's not a crime to be a cunt.'

'No, but he's the last person from *Secret Encounters* who contacted Angela Holt. He might just be cheating on his wife, but I want to know for sure that he's not linked to any of the scenes. And I want to know quickly, before we have to release Newton and slide back down to square one.'

She smiled. 'You want?'

Sawyer stared her out. '*Please.*'

In the cellar, Stephanie Burns startled at the clunk of the door locks being released. The light streamed in behind the man as he descended the steps, threading what looked like a long tube in with him.

Stephanie tugged at the chain and scrambled out of the corner, squinting up at the silhouette. She tugged her matted hair off her face, and rubbed the dust and sweat from her eyes.

The man stopped and angled his head. 'Time for a change of scene. And since you've been a good girl, I'm going to let you take a shower first.'

He threw down a bar of soap, pointed the end of the hosepipe at Stephanie and released a valve, showering her with icy water. She gasped and shivered, scrubbing at herself, holding her head forward to soak her hair, lathering the soap. She was desperate to renew herself, to wash away the horror.

She cupped her hands and turned away from the stream to drink.

The man kept the water trained on her for a minute, then closed the valve. 'That's better, isn't it? What do you say?'

Stephanie raised her head; her blue eyes glittered in the light. 'Fuck. You.'

He laughed. 'Let's get you out of here. It'll all be over soon.'

45

Sawyer scrambled up the smooth slope of rock, his skin clammy and tingling. It seemed as if the ceiling of sunless sky had slipped lower, compressing the space, and his breath came in ragged gulps as he sank into the dank cocoon of Thor's Cave.

To his relief, the space was free of tourists, and he ducked through the narrow passage to the ditch beneath the slitted window in the cave wall. He dug beneath the overhang and shifted the large rock aside. The Glock was still there, inside the evidence bag.

He replaced the rock and walked back to the main chamber, taking a seat on the central stone that formed a natural viewing platform for the treetops and valley below.

Fifteen minutes in his childhood thinking spot. He had cleared his mind here many times, grappling with the puzzles of adolescence. Lately, he had re-adopted it, as a meditative touchstone, a place of peace and reflection where he could pass the elements of a case through the light of his quieted mind.

The disconnect between the bestiality and the artistry, between the ugliness of the violence and the beauty of its presentation. The women: all blonde, all achievers. Mount, Newton, Powell, Nash. The cleanness of the four main scenes, at odds with the evidence left at Mount's place. He thought of Ainsworth's idea: that the presentation could be part of the killer's remorse; an attempt to clean up and beautify the horror he'd created. But, why?

Nothing came. Nothing coalesced. A group of elderly walkers climbed up into the cave and he moved off, nodding to them as he crouched low to descend the slope.

'Excuse me.'

Sawyer turned. The lead walker—a grey-bearded man in a light purple waterproof—held an empty plastic bottle of Pepsi Max above his head. 'Is this yours?'

'No,' said Sawyer. 'Not me. I would have moved it if I'd seen it there.'

'Righto! Sorry to trouble you. Bloody litter louts.'

Sawyer made his way down the steps, his mind whirring. He hurried along the path and climbed into the Mini.

He rolled down the windows and sat there for a while, listening to the woozy late afternoon birdsong. His breath quickened as the thoughts converged, shaping themselves around the skeleton of an idea.

He started the engine and sped away, up the steep lane that led out of the valley and into the village at Hulme End, and the nearest phone signal.

At the lay-by near the Manifold Inn, he parked and checked his phone. Missed call from Sally. He returned it, and she picked up straight away.

'Go on,' said Sally. 'Do that thing you do.'

'What?'

'Tell me what I'm going to tell you.'

Sawyer smiled, and looked out across the fields, tumbling down to Alstonefield. 'Powell's DNA matches the Laura Bertrand dog bite but not the Angela Holt cigarette end.'

She sighed down the phone. 'Gold star. But it's better than that. I ran the toothbrush DNA through the national database. Got a hit on a "David Bowman". Looks like a routine sample, in 2009. He must have changed his name. Walker is looking into it.'

'Thanks for the quick turnaround. Speak later.'

Sawyer set the phone in the cradle and dialled Shepherd's number. The call connected as he pulled away from the lay-by, spinning his wheels.

'Sir.'

'What's our timing on Newton's release?'

Shepherd paused. 'Less than an hour. Sherman is finalising the paperwork now.'

'Keep him there. Get an extension if you have to. I think we're going to need him.'

46

Sawyer pushed out of the MIT lift and strode across the main floor. Walker jumped up from his desk and fell into step alongside him, carrying a sheet of paper.

'Any briefings planned?' said Sawyer.

'Haven't seen Keating this afternoon.'

Shepherd joined them as Sawyer entered his office. 'You spoken to Sally?'

Sawyer nodded and closed the door behind them. 'Tell me about Bowman. What happened in 2009?'

'He lived at a place in Sheffield,' said Walker. 'Fell out with a neighbour, who had a break-in. Accused Bowman. So, the police took his DNA. It's a match for the DNA you collected today. So, either David Bowman is a regular guest of Malcolm Powell—'

'So regular, he leaves his toothbrush there,' said Shepherd.

'Or,' said Sawyer, 'they're one and the same.'

Walker smiled. 'He changed his name by deed poll in 2011, just before he moved to the place in Stoney Middleton, and married a local councillor called Danielle

Duncan. Couple of years younger; she kept her name. She became an MP a year later.'

'He said she's now a Euro MP,' said Shepherd.

Sawyer nodded. 'Lots of travel. He has the place to himself regularly.'

Walker glanced at Shepherd. 'Here's the best bit. He's done time. For murder. When he was sixteen, in 2003, he strangled a young girl, Caron Patterson, nine years old. She was found on the stairwell outside his aunt's flat. Got ten years in HMP Ranby. Diminished responsibility and age. But he only did six.' He held up the paper. 'I got this from an interview with the prison psychiatrist.' Walker read out loud from the sheet. '"As a result of my examination, I am of the opinion that this prisoner is in urgent need of constant care, control and supervision. I do not think that any form of psychotherapy is likely to benefit his condition, and he will constitute a danger from now onwards. It is to be expected that, given the minimum of opportunity, he will repeat his offence."'

Shepherd glanced at Walker. 'Bowman's mother walked out when he was twelve, taking his two younger sisters. His father killed himself when he was fourteen, and he lived with his aunt until he went to prison.'

Sawyer closed his eyes, absorbing it all. 'Cross-reference the period his wife has been away with the times of the killings. Makes sense that he would time it all to give him space at home, maybe to hold on to the women. Then he can kill them and dump the bodies at leisure.' He turned to Shepherd. 'Get a team to his flat now. Section 17. Search, make the arrest. Let's build it from there.'

'What about Newton?' said Shepherd. 'I got a twelve-hour extension. But why do we need him?'

'Because I don't think Bowman will be at his flat. And Newton is the key to finding him, and Stephanie Burns.'

47

Sawyer sat down beside Walker in the interview room. Newton and Whittingham faced them across the table, Newton with his head bowed.

Sawyer turned to Whittingham. 'Apologies for the inconvenience. We needed a bit more time.'

Whittingham gave a curt nod and noted something in his papers.

Sawyer started the recorder and ran through the formalities. He sat back, and regarded the top of Newton's head.

The desktop fan chugged away in the corner.

Sawyer let the silence hang for a full minute. Whittingham leaned forward. 'Any questions, Detective?'

'The French have a phrase,' said Sawyer. '*Folie à deux.* You're an educated man, Julius. I'm sure you know what that means.' Newton didn't stir. 'It roughly translates as, "a madness shared by two". Bonnie and Clyde. Brady and Hindley. Fred and Rose West. Tell me about David Bowman.'

Newton raised his head slowly and fixed Sawyer with a wary glare. 'No comment.'

Sawyer smiled. 'With the couples I've just mentioned, both parties were fully aware of the shared madness. There's a bit of debate about who was dominant or whatever, but they were willing collusions. You followed him, didn't you, Julius? David killed, and he dumped the bodies. But you followed him, and you presented the bodies, and he doesn't even know you did it.' Newton looked over at Whittingham, but his solicitor was focused on Sawyer. 'Last week, you followed him and you saw him leave Angela Holt's body near Dovedale. And, like the others, you covered her with fabric, applied make-up, arranged her hair and limbs, crowned her with flowers. And, before you could get away, a dog walker came along. Damien Mount. And you dropped your cigarette, and you hid and watched. You saw him take photographs. You heard him call the police to report the body.' Sawyer leaned forward, drawing Newton's eye. 'And you heard him tell the police his name. And, later, when he shared one of the photos on the *Times* website, you realised that he might expose your presentation, and David might find out. So, you killed him. But you couldn't be intimate, like David. You couldn't strangle. So, you stabbed. Why didn't you present Damien Mount's body as you did with the women? Wasn't he worthy?'

Newton took off his glasses and stared down into the desktop.

Sawyer continued. 'We've been wondering how the killer could cause so much violence in one moment, and show tenderness and respect in the next. Did you start with Caron Patterson, Julius? Were you there when David murdered her back in 2003?'

Newton kept his eyes on the desk. 'David has suffered so much. I got to know him at school. I was the sensitive type, always getting bullied. Getting close to David made all of that stop. But he wasn't... like me. He was the eldest son, and when his mother had his sisters... He told me they were "spoiled, and his behaviour at school started to change. He started to do the bullying himself. First, other boys. Then girls. Inappropriate behaviour. I was always there with him. Looking out. Keeping watch. One day, I noticed a different woman bring him to school. His aunt. He told me he'd bitten one of his sisters, made her squeal. He was laughing about it. Like it was fun.' Newton unscrewed his bottle of water. 'It got worse. He missed a lot of school. Got sent home a lot. Formal suspensions. Then, his mother left, and his father...' He took a deep drink, gathered himself. 'He told me one day that he had found his father's body. He came home from a rare day at school and climbed up to the loft and found his father hanging from one of the beams.'

'What did David's mother look like?'

Newton scoffed. 'Do you really need to ask? He was growing, working on himself, becoming physically powerful. She took his sisters to protect them from him. He loved his father, and he blamed his mother for his death.'

'The key female figures in his life rejected him, abandoned him.'

Newton jerked his head up. 'Yes! I told you. He suffered. And I tried to reach him, get close to him. But while I was waking up, coming to terms with who I was, with my identity and sexuality, David was going the other way. Withdrawing, learning to show nothing, to *feel* nothing. I think he fed off my over-sensitivity, but he soon grew to reject that, too. So, he focused on building up his physical form.'

'Masking his inner turmoil,' said Walker.

Newton looked at him, startled. 'Of course. He transformed himself into something formidable.'

'Was your relationship intimate?' said Sawyer.

Newton smiled. 'No comment.' He shook his head. 'Briefly. But I never felt like he bought into it. I thought he was complying, for the comfort. Enjoying the novelty of acceptance, after all the rejection. And then, he began to slip away, and his behaviour with the girls at the school grew worse. Unsustainable. He started to reject me. I often told him that he was beautiful, and he started to hate me for that, telling me to stop it. I had a little artistic talent, and so I drew pictures for him, as a way of expressing my feelings. He soon rejected those, too. But I stayed with him, even after he was expelled.'

'Stayed with him?' said Sawyer.

Newton nodded. 'Today, you might call it stalking. But my intentions were good. I was concerned for him. Quite rightly, as it turned out. I didn't see him murder Caron Patterson, but I was there when it happened. And I saw how he left her, sprawled in that stairwell. I couldn't bear it. And so, I... made her beautiful again. I covered her up, gave her some dignity.'

'And when he came out of prison,' said Sawyer, 'you stayed with him?'

Newton nodded. 'He was the love of my life, Detective Sawyer. Have you ever heard the phrase, "love is blind"?' He sighed. 'I knew he would never change. I knew his marriage was just another attempt to compensate for the damage. And when I completed my university course, I started to follow him, to track him. I saw all of his indiscretions and infidelities. A couple of years ago, I saw him beat a man in an alley outside a pub. The beating went on for so long, I was convinced I was witnessing a murder. When David left, I checked on the man. His face was just... He could barely speak. I helped him, and he survived. Although I believe he lost his sight permanently. After that, I checked in on David from time to time, followed his car, marked his routines.'

'And last year,' said Sawyer, 'you found yourself in that park in Nottingham, standing over Laura Bertrand's body.'

'I hadn't expected him to do that. He kept the others at his flat for a day or two, and then stole cars to take them to dumping spots. I placed trackers on the cars when he parked them at his flat and went inside to retrieve the bodies. That's how I could get close to the scenes without being spotted. I just couldn't bear the idea of those poor women being found in such desperately undignified states.'

Sawyer's phone buzzed in his pocket. Message from Shepherd.

Flat is empty. Heading back.

Walker shifted his chair forward. 'You keep talking about dignity. If you were following him, then you presumably saw him bring these women back to his flat. Why didn't you give them the dignity of allowing them to live? Why didn't you intervene?'

'I did. I walked into this building yesterday. And I've struggled with my conscience. I wanted the killing to stop and that compulsion drew me here. But I've been having second thoughts. David has suffered so much. And, walking in here... It opened my eyes. I realised that I might be able to leave here and grow close to him again. Show him my work. What I did with Mount. What I did to someone who was trying to profit from his tragedy, from his sickness.' Newton dropped his head. 'I hoped I could give him a reason to stop.'

Sawyer rested his elbows on the desk. 'And the presentation of the bodies? You draw no pleasure from that yourself?'

'Only in the sense that I wanted the women to be discovered as women, not just as pieces of meat.'

'As you say,' said Sawyer, 'you made them beautiful again. But that's not about their dignity, is it? That's *your* pleasure. That's *your* sickness. You want us to see this as your benign intervention. Prettying up the mess left by a psychopath. But I think you're getting more out of it than you want to admit. You grew to enjoy it, didn't you? You became compelled by the artistry, by the immensity of the statement.'

Newton shook his head. 'No. I didn't enjoy it.'

'David's handiwork became the raw material for your art.'

Newton sneered at Sawyer; he had started to tremble again. 'What do you know about art?'

Sawyer leaned in. '"Beauty is the promise of happiness".'

Newton nodded. 'Stendahl.'

'And if that's true, and art is an attempt to create beauty, then art is also the promise of happiness. You talk about David's rejection. But you were rejected, too. By him. And the women he chose over you... You didn't care about them, did you? Your post-mortem presentation isn't about the women. It's about *you*. It's about you making yourself feel better. It's a rush of control, power. The most profound and shattering art statement.'

Newton dug his hands between his knees, trying to calm the trembling.

'And you killed Damien Mount because he had the nerve to share your work without your permission. So, this is your madness as well as David's. *Folie à deux*.' Sawyer sipped his water. 'I'm not sure who's worse, Julius. A killer, or someone who could prevent the killing but chooses not to, for the sake of his own vanity.'

Newton stared at Sawyer, dead-eyed. 'All is vanity.'

'That sounds like the Bible.'

Newton dropped his head again; the trembling had eased.

'But this is all for later. Right now, you can take the opportunity you've always ignored. You can save a life. If you help us find Stephanie Burns alive, then it will be taken into consideration.'

Newton coughed out a laugh. 'I murdered a man, and I abetted another with four murders.'

'Five, if we're counting Caron Patterson,' said Walker.

Sawyer nodded. 'We are.'

'Well,' said Newton. 'There's no consideration.'

'Do it for yourself, then,' said Walker. 'You're used to that. You can at least accept your fate knowing you did the right thing.'

Newton was silent for a moment. He looked up, from Walker to Sawyer. 'He took her to his flat. Yesterday.'

'She's not there now,' said Sawyer.

'He might already have murdered her, and taken her somewhere, to dump the body.'

'What if he'd been forced to leave the flat before murdering Stephanie?' said Sawyer. 'Is there somewhere he might have taken her?'

Newton pondered. 'The girl who was found in Saddleworth, near Manchester...'

'Hannah Lane,' said Walker.

'He took her to the flat, but then had to leave soon after, because his wife came home early. He took her to an abandoned place, up near Dovestone Reservoir.'

'That's in Greater Manchester,' said Walker.

'Yes. It's a big old house. Set down in the base of a valley. You can see it from a ridge overlooking the reservoir.' He looked at Sawyer. 'I could show you.'

48

Dale Strickland jinked through the crowd and climbed the three steps to a recessed VIP section, with several booth seats upholstered in padded, chocolate-brown leather. A titanic bouncer in a black tuxedo and white bow tie waved him through, and he slid in opposite Marco. Both men wore light blazers and T-shirts, on Dale's instructions. A little celebration would be acceptable, but there could be no sense of decadence or gloating.

Marco rattled the ice around his whisky. He spoke over the music: brassy lounge classics. 'Good speech. Short. Didn't steal the spotlight from Hogan, as the new mayor, but reminded the public of the subplot.'

Dale grinned. 'Brick by brick. We're going up in the world.'

'Seventh floor.'

'Only four hundred memberships here. Massively oversubscribed, of course. Russell assures me he can get me in.' He nodded to Marco. 'Guest privileges apply.'

'It's "Russell" now, eh? Already?'

'It is. And it's "Dale" for him. We're meeting on Friday to discuss the new campaign. A drive for more regulation.

More protection for young people, taking the supply and distribution away from the criminal networks.' He lowered his voice. '"The supreme art of war is to subdue the enemy without fighting". The message is clear. You'll never get rid of drugs, but you can reduce drug-related deaths, which are increasing. Focus on the human cost instead of plugging away at unwinnable battles.'

Marco nodded. 'Then what?'

Dale sipped his champagne. 'Then, we go to the communities. Bring in the campaigners and harm reduction workers. We *change the equation*.'

Marco took a drink and looked around the bar. 'Fitting that we're having this discussion in a place that looks like an old speakeasy.'

'Club Brass. The link isn't intentional, but it's a perfect backdrop. A reflection of how the US made such a mistake with prohibition in the twenties. Parallels with the Great Depression, too. Austerity measures, economic downturn. This building used to be a bank. Hence the polished brass tiles, the light fittings styled like money bags.' Dale drained his glass. 'Okay. Let's hear it.' He leaned back against the leather. 'I'm high. I won't shoot the messenger.'

Marco raised an eyebrow. 'Hector is dead. Fire at his flat. Took them a couple of hours to get it under control. Only Hector was there. Dental records, according to Mina.'

Dale drummed at the edge of the table. 'Accident?'

'Investigation ongoing. Could take a while. Not a lot left to investigate.' He caught Dale's eye. 'Fletcher.'

'We don't know that for sure.'

'Yes,' Marco leaned forward, 'we do. Dale. You know him. Call him. Give him what he wants. Let him see it through.'

'I can't. Especially not now. We don't know about Sawyer's insurance.'

'Then play the same game. Tell Fletcher if anything happens to me or you, then you also have insurance in place. Something that can connect the gun to him.'

Dale nodded. 'I'll talk to him soon. When all this calms down. Stop getting so nervy. I'm sorry about Hector, but... People die. New people come along. There are good times ahead, Marco. Look around you. We have... *insulation*.'

Marco got to his feet. 'I have to go. Need to get away for a few days, if that's okay.'

Dale stayed seated, squinting up at him. 'Walking in the Highlands?'

Marco forced a smile. 'Not a bad idea. At least you can fucking breathe up there.' They shook hands. 'Enjoy the party.'

Marco took the lift down to the hotel's basement parking garage. He lingered just outside the entrance door and watched as a man and woman in formal dress paused at the bottom of the far stairwell and indulged in a lingering kiss. They broke off, stumbled into a grey Audi SUV, and sped away up the exit ramp and into the street.

He waited for a minute or two, listening, straining to catch any movement in the shadows. Light traffic rumble from the street, a few shouts from the pavement drinkers on Chancery Lane. The air was thick and muggy, and as he approached the white Mercedes, his skin prickled with sweat.

He had parked the car facing forward in a bay close to the exit ramp. He approached around the back of the adjoining vehicles, giving him a good view of the Mercedes' interior. Empty. Front and back. Perhaps Dale was right, and he was overthinking everything. They were dealing with an aggrieved employee, not a vengeful bogeyman.

Marco froze, at the sound of the lift, clunking into gear and rising away from the garage.

He unlocked the Mercedes and stepped into the driver's seat, trying to slow his breathing.

Austin Fletcher lowered himself from the undercarriage of the car parked beside the Mercedes. He slid out and steadied himself behind the boot, keeping low against the wall. He opened the Mercedes back door and lunged down onto the back seat, pointing Hector's handgun up at Marco.

'Jesus Christ, Fletcher!' Marco held his hands up in front of the steering wheel. 'You trying to kill me with a fucking heart attack?'

Fletcher swatted Marco in the side of his head with the gun handle. The force was strong enough to bounce the other side of his head into the driver's door window. As Marco reeled from the blow, Fletcher reached into his trouser pocket and pulled out a short length of black cord with an oblong wooden handle at each end. He whipped the cord over the driver's seat and hooked it around Marco's neck, pulling back on the handles and forcing Marco's head back into the headrest. Marco grunted and gagged. He reached up for the cord, trying to loosen it. But Fletcher held it firm, pulling it taut by crossing over the handles behind. Marco's eyes bulged as he flailed his arms up and back, desperately trying to grab Fletcher. He reached down for the seat recline lever, but Fletcher anticipated it, and ground the heel of his boot into Marco's fingers before he could release the mechanism and drop the seat back.

Fletcher held the position, squeezing the handles at full strength, until Marco stopped moving. He raised his head, looking around the parking garage. Empty. After another minute, he pulled the cord away from the deep impression on Marco's neck, and pocketed the garotte. He checked Marco's pulse, and pulled his body into the back seat, flattening it down across both footwells. He took the key fob from Marco's pocket and climbed into the driver's seat, then took a few breaths, checking for any signs of activity by the lift or stairwell.

Fletcher swiped the sweat from his face and ran his hands over his hefty forearms, blackened with grime and oil from the underside of the car. He pushed the button ignition and eased the car out of the garage.

49

Sawyer bullied the Mini out of the northern suburbs of Buxton and joined the motorway that skimmed the western fringe of the National Park as it blended from tended farm fields to the rugged moorland of Greater Manchester. Shepherd sat in the back seat, alongside Newton, whose cuffed hands rested in his lap.

They passed the turning to Edale, and Sawyer switched off the air con and rolled down the window. As ever, the air outside was peaty and overbaked, but for the first time in weeks, it carried a hint of moisture.

'Storm coming,' said Newton.

Sawyer looked up. A vast bank of cumulus clouds had blossomed across the blue sky, eclipsing the low, early evening sun.

'Drinks are on the farmers,' said Shepherd.

Sawyer slowed at a junction. He attached his phone to the windscreen cradle and started an album: *Disintegration* by The Cure. The widescreen wash of the opener 'Plainsong' swelled through the car.

'Doesn't this break your nineties-only rule?' said Shepherd.

Sawyer squeezed the accelerator. 'It's from 1989. Near enough. I've just had this in my head all day.'

'Robert Smith wrote it when he was twenty-nine,' said Newton. 'In the grip of depression. It's a cliché, but a lot of great work has come from suffering. Damien Hurst said that you can always recognise fine art because you can feel the artist's struggle.'

Sawyer lowered the volume, glanced at Shepherd. 'Tell me about the house.'

Shepherd checked his phone. 'If it's the one he's describing, it's hardly a bothy. More like an abandoned manor house, partially dilapidated. The National Trust were planning to refurbish it, but it's structurally unsound, so they left it.'

'There's only the outbuildings and part of the main house still standing,' said Newton. 'It was a magnet for urban explorers. David does some decorating work and his firm was involved in assessing it. I'll show you where I saw him, with the other girl.'

Shepherd nodded. 'One of the urbex community fell through some rotten floorboards there a couple of years ago. Survived, but the accident tainted the place. The people on this forum mostly chase old hospitals and asylums.'

'Pre-made spookiness, I suppose,' said Sawyer.

A distant grumble of thunder, over the hills to the east.

Sawyer glanced over his shoulder. 'Let's be clear, Julius. You're here to help us find the place, and to show us where you saw David before.' He caught Shepherd's eye. 'If we see evidence that David is holding Stephanie Burns, then we may need to call in support. The main goal is to preserve life, and, regardless of your personal feelings, to apprehend a dangerous killer.'

Newton nodded, and gazed out of the window.

Guided by Newton, they parked in a side-road below the peak of a ridge that looked down on a wide, bowl-shaped valley, dominated by the depleted reservoir.

'I walked up into the trees on the left,' said Newton. 'You can see the house from round there. But I couldn't see any walking routes that would make it easy to approach the place without being seen. There's also a road that winds down to the house itself, but obviously that's pretty conspicuous.'

Sawyer opened the door and climbed out. 'Five minutes.' He made his way up and around the ridge, into a copse that fell away as they merged with the steep valley wall. The house was visible in the middle distance, near the foot of the valley, built on the hillside. It looked like a neglected old primary school: single storey; dirty grey brickwork; multi-pane windows, all smashed. The main house seemed intact, but the separate outbuildings were roofless, with the front walls eroded and exposed.

A grey car had been wedged into bushes at the near side of the house, just off the road Newton had mentioned, which rose up the valley wall until its path was obscured by overhanging trees.

Sawyer scanned the house and outbuildings for a few minutes, but could see no sign of movement. He headed back to the car and motioned for Shepherd to get out.

They stood near the bonnet, facing Newton, speaking in low voices.

'There's a car there,' said Sawyer. 'But it's impossible to tell if it's Bowman. And there's no obvious sign of life.'

Shepherd eyed him. 'You know what I'm thinking.'

'Of course I do. This is Farrell's jurisdiction. But it's time critical. Sometimes you have to improvise.'

'That doesn't sound healthy.'

'You know what will happen if we call the cavalry now. Apart from the time it will take them to get here and set up, we'll have Farrell pulling rank on the geography, all the process. The media might even get hold of it.' Sawyer moved around, facing Shepherd. 'While we have Newton on side and talking, we have to keep the momentum, keep it intimate. His connection with Bowman might help us to talk him out, and that's the best outcome for Stephanie, if she's here.'

'Talk him out? You mean, like Gazza and Raul Moat?'

'Newton is an asset, and we have to go softly because of the risk to Stephanie. It's like Newton says. The house is too exposed, with little cover. If Bowman is there, we run the risk of him seeing us, if he's looking out. The fewer people, the better.'

Shepherd flattened down his beard. 'I'll go. By myself. Get closer. I'm a walker. Just stumbled on the place. I might see something, hear something. Without spooking him.'

Sawyer shook his head. 'No.'

'Well, you can't do it. He'll recognise you. You're the most recognisable civil servant this side of Sheffield.'

Sawyer pondered. 'We need a long-range view, looking down from the trees, to get a closer picture of the house as you approach. You can't go down there without cover.'

He took out his phone.

50

'Did you see the house?'

Sawyer nodded. He turned to face Newton from the driver's seat. 'We're waiting for someone to help us get down there safely.'

'I could go with you. I could talk to him.'

'You could,' said Shepherd. 'But that's not happening. You'll stay here with Detective Sawyer until we have a clearer picture.'

'David is unwell,' said Newton. 'But there's no need to harm him.'

Sawyer looked at Shepherd. 'That's not the aim. As I said, we're here to preserve life. Stephanie Burns's life.'

'And to bring David to justice,' said Shepherd. 'It's up to him how that process goes.'

Sawyer's phone buzzed. He took it out and checked. 'Be right back.'

He got out of the car and walked to the end of the side lane. Tony Cross was climbing a steep section between the lane and the main road. He wore a black T-shirt and dark jeans, and carried a long, thin case over his back. He called up. 'Parked a bit further back. Since I'm not officially here.'

Cross pumped Sawyer's hand and took in the surroundings: the forests of pine and larch trees spread over the hillside; the water sparkling in the muted sunlight. 'This is positively...'

'Bucolic?'

Cross frowned, then smiled. 'Alpine.'

They walked up past the car and around to the spot in the trees where Sawyer had viewed the house.

'I saw a car hanging around near your place this morning,' said Cross. 'I was going to call you.'

'What kind of car?'

'Fiesta, I think. Old thing. Sort of light brown. Anyone you know?'

Sawyer shook his head.

'I was watching from a car by the Hayfield crossroads. Didn't have my nocks, but it looked like one fella. Just sat there for about half an hour, then drove away.'

'Thanks. Good to know.'

They reached the viewing spot. Cross crouched and surveyed the landscape. He pointed down to the house. 'So, you think your man is in there?'

'We hope so.'

Cross grimaced. 'I'm not keen on this.' He looked up. 'It's the way the sun is setting. It looks cosy and enclosed from where we are, but the line is too direct, and if he looks out of one of those windows, there'll be shine off the barrel. What's on the other side?'

They moved up around the ridge, and found an area with more trees and a more lateral, side-on sightline of the house and the crumbling outbuildings.

'This is better,' said Cross. 'Let's have a quick look.' He slid a dismantled rifle from the bag and slotted the pieces into place. 'M107. Fifty cal. Semi-auto. Day and night scope.' He opened out a V-shaped support with a spiked base and drove it into the earth. He positioned the rifle on the base, lay prone behind it, and pressed his right eye against the sight. 'I'm not trained in sniper fieldcraft, but I was a DM for a while before the Murphy op.'

'DM?'

Cross adjusted the sight. 'Designated marksman. This is the weapon I use for long-range security work, and it's adjustable for animal darting. Medium and long. Can you answer me a question?'

'Go on.'

'Why not bring in some authorised AFOs or marksmen for this?'

Sawyer crouched and followed Cross's line of sight, squinting down at the house. 'Jurisdictional issues. Multi-force op. And I want to know our man is definitely here. Once we're positive, then we'll make it official. And we believe he has a hostage.'

'Who's in the car?'

'My DS. Shepherd. And an acquaintance of the man we think is in the house. He might prove useful in talking him out.'

Cross glanced back at him. 'An acquaintance?'

'It's complicated.'

Cross smiled and went back to the sight. 'This is what I've been missing, Jake. A bit of drama.' He stiffened. 'Oh! There he is. Ground floor window on the right.'

Cross moved aside and Sawyer looked into the sight. David Bowman stood at the front of the room, to the side of the window. He was topless, with his head tilted down slightly, but the angle made it impossible to see what he was looking at.

'Can we draw him out?' said Sawyer. 'Get him near to the window?'

'I'll only take a shot if there's a risk to life, Sawyer.'

'There's risk at the moment.' Bowman walked off to the side, out of the scope image. Sawyer looked up at Cross; he was staring down at him.

'We need to go official, Jake. If you think he's got a hostage alive in there.'

'We can't risk storming in, but if he knows we're here, then it might buy us some time.'

Cross knelt down. He took up the rifle and began to dismantle it. 'Sorry, Jake. I'm not down with it. I haven't fired a shot in anger since the Murphy op, and even if I could get a clean sight through the window, I have no authority to take the shot.' He slotted the rifle back into its case. 'Now we've acquired the target, I suggest you talk to your DS and send for the cavalry. Negotiate with him.'

'I don't think he's the negotiating type.'

The sky had darkened, and another rumble of thunder shuddered overhead.

Sawyer felt a slight impact on the top of his head, and he looked up to the blackened clouds. A sprinkle of warm water spattered across his face, trickling down his cheeks.

'Terrific,' said Cross.

They moved down the ridge, heading back towards the car.

Cross darted in front of Sawyer and held up a hand for silence. 'What's that?'

They listened. A male voice: groaning, crying out.

Sawyer caught Cross's eye. 'Shepherd.'

They sprinted the rest of the way, through the gathering rain. At the car, Shepherd sat on the passenger seat: door open, with his legs outside, holding a handkerchief to the top of his head.

Cross went to him, and Sawyer angled his run to take him around the side of the car, to the back seat.

No Newton.

Sawyer moved round to Shepherd and lifted the handkerchief. A deep, jagged cut ran several inches across his scalp, and the cloth was matted with blood.

'I let him go for a piss. Kept him secured but he clocked me with the edge of the cuffs. He was fucking *strong*. He ran off towards the trees on the left of the ridge.'

Cross moved in to take a closer look at Shepherd; Sawyer stepped over to the other side of the car. 'Keep the pressure on it. You feeling okay? Any nausea? Double vision?'

Shepherd shook his head. 'I'm sorry, sir. Just underestimated him.'

The rain spattered on the ground around Shepherd's feet. 'Let's get you inside the car,' said Cross. 'You should get checked out.'

Shepherd shifted his legs around and Cross closed the door. He looked around for Sawyer, checked the back of the car, then the other side. He sighed and slipped into the driver seat.

Shepherd dabbed the handkerchief onto the wound. He winced and looked over. 'You're Cross, right?'

Cross nodded. The rain was raging now, clattering down on the windscreen and windows. 'Sawyer's gone. And so am I.' He opened the door. 'We saw your man in the house. DS Shepherd, you need to call this in. You need help. And I know he doesn't believe it, but so does your boss.'

51

Sawyer hustled his way through the trees at the edge of the ridge and found the spot where he and Shepherd had first spotted the house below. The hillside was steep, but he stayed low and scrambled his way down, squinting through the pummelling rain. He paused and looked up at the sky: a defiant shaft of sunlight seared through a crack in the midnight blue cloud.

A delicate roll of thunder, like an inhale. A flicker of lightning. The storm was teasing, holding back. It had been suppressed for so long, but wasn't quite ready to rage, to reveal its full power.

'David!'

Newton, calling from below. Sawyer pushed on, through the sopping grass, skidding and stumbling. He caught sight of Newton, at the bottom of the valley, rounding the near shore of the reservoir, heading for the house. He took a steeper route, almost tumbling forward, and found the shallow ground near the water's edge. He followed it round, staying low, covered by the bushes and the spray from the rain.

Sawyer followed a sparse clump of trees around to one

of the ruined outbuildings, and stopped, out of sight of the house. He dropped down low and peered around the wall.

David Bowman stood in the main doorway, holding something low in his right hand. He was still topless, and in jeans, barefoot. He stepped forward, staying under the porch. Newton was out in the open, on the path that led to the road beyond. He was bent over, breathing hard, doused by the rain. He shifted forward, towards Bowman, then hesitated as Bowman stepped closer to him. Now, Sawyer could see that Bowman was holding a short-handled axe.

'Who are you?' said Bowman. 'Are those *handcuffs*?'

'David...' Newton's shoulders rose and fell as he steeled himself. 'Don't you recognise me?'

Bowman took another step and squinted at Newton through the rain. '*David*?'

'We were at King Edward together,' said Newton. 'David, it's Julius.'

Bowman moved closer, into the rain, studying Newton. The water rattled on the blade of the axe. His face cracked, and transformed into a broad, beaming smile. 'Holy fucking shit. I haven't seen you for—'

'Sixteen years. But I've been watching you all your life, David. I've followed your work. I've displayed it for you.'

Bowman sank back into the shelter of the porch. 'What *work*?'

'The women, David,' said Sawyer, stepping out from behind the outbuilding. 'The women you brutalised and murdered. The proxies for your mother, who couldn't control you.'

Bowman squinted at Sawyer. 'I was just reading about you. I thought I recognised the name, when you came to my place.'

Newton stepped to the side as Sawyer approached. 'Your mother walked out, David. And you blame her for your father's death. But women don't walk out on you any more, do they? They don't reject you. You decide how long they stay, and when and how, they go.'

Bowman lowered his head, keeping his eyes on Sawyer. 'Well. We have one thing in common. Fucked-up and motherless.' He lifted the axe, resting the back side of the blade on his shoulder.

Sawyer stopped walking, glanced at Newton behind. 'Where's Stephanie? Is she inside?'

Bowman lolled the axe around in front of his face. 'I noticed the toothbrush had gone. That was a cunt's trick. Inadmissible, surely?'

'Probably. But then we have the tiny matter of the woman you've kidnapped, as well as plenty of other hard evidence.'

Bowman nodded, smiling. 'So, this is it. You're taking me in?'

Sawyer reached into his pocket and took out another set of handcuffs. 'David Bowman. I'm arresting you on suspicion of the murders of Laura Bertrand, Dianne Walton, Hannah Lane, and Angela Holt. You do not have to say anything, but anything you do say—'

Bowman launched himself from the porch towards Sawyer and raised the axe above his head. Sawyer backed away, trying to gain ground to counterattack, but stumbled in the saturated soil. He prepared to roll to the side, as Bowman bore down on him.

A distant crack, from somewhere high on the valley's edge.

The axe flew out of Bowman's grip and spun across the ground, into a gap between the outbuildings.

Bowman looked up, towards the source of the sound. He tried to turn and break for the porch, but Sawyer charged, head down, toppling him into the wall. Bowman roared with anger, and swung a heavy fist towards Sawyer, missing his head but landing a blow on his shoulder. They grappled, but Sawyer struggled to get a grip on the topless Bowman, as the rainwater showered them both.

Bowman shoved Sawyer away and wound up for another punch. But Sawyer read it, stepped to the side, and countered with a potent *biu jee* finger jab to Bowman's eyes. As Bowman staggered back, temporarily blinded, Sawyer lunged forward and hit him with a right cross punch, dropping him to his knees. Bowman steadied himself with a hand to the ground, but kept his head down, breathing hard, holding his other hand to his eyes.

Sawyer stood over him, saturated by the cascading water. He caught his breath. 'Where's Stephanie?'

A thick, heavy impact across the back of his head. A flare of agony.

His knees, squishing into the flooded soil.

Sawyer's vision tunnelled. He turned his head.

Newton stood behind, holding a heavy stone the size of his hand.

Sawyer tried to push himself upright. But his arms wouldn't move, wouldn't obey, and the image of Newton's astonished face shimmered for a while, then faded to black.

52

Rain. A constant crackle, like static. Then, less fuzz in the noise; more clarity. Splashing and spattering on the roof above. Sawyer opened his eyes, but kept his head down. He was sitting on a hard wooden chair, hands cuffed behind his back. A loud headache pressed on the base of his skull.

A soft keening, from somewhere to the left. Rhythmic and endless. He tilted his head, following its source. A woman sat crumpled in the corner, hands and feet bound with thick rope, dressed only in bra and briefs. Her face was bruised and swollen, and her skin slick with sweat. She had let her head flop down onto her shoulder, and her body heaved as she sobbed.

Sawyer raised his head and took in the room. It was bare and carpetless, with a blocked fireplace and an empty bookcase beside a glass-panelled door, hanging off its lower hinge. Filthy tartan curtains covered the main window, and a desolate old sofa sat in the centre, its arms leaning in at unnatural angles. Dark blotches of mould wept down from the ceiling, scarring the pattern on the ancient wallpaper.

The body of Julius Newton lay at the side of the sofa, face up, in a mire of fresh blood. One of Newton's arms lay at his side, while the other had fallen across his chest, as if he were taking a nap. Sawyer gazed into the space where his face had once been: now a bloody maw of meat and bone. He had a deep axe wound in his shoulder and several others across the front of his chest.

David Bowman stood at one of the curtains, peering around the edge. He turned, and walked towards Sawyer, grinning. 'Wake up!' He stopped, and leaned down, his face inches from Sawyer's. 'Time to die.'

Bowman raised his hand up to his head, paused, and swung it around, connecting square with Sawyer's cheek. It was an open-palm slap, but Sawyer reeled at the force of the blow.

Sawyer brought his head around and raised it towards Bowman, staring him down. Bowman's eyes were bloodshot, and a fresh bruise was forming around the socket edges.

'Trying to poke my eye out,' said Bowman. 'What are you? A fucking schoolgirl?' He jerked his head towards the window. 'Was that your mate, Shepherd? The shooter? Well. He can't get to us in here.' He walked over to the woman. 'Detective Sawyer, this is Stephanie Burns. Stephanie, Detective Sawyer.'

Sawyer sucked in a deep breath. 'You killed Julius.'

'I can see why you're a detective. Are you shocked?'

'I'm just making a mental note to add his name to the charge sheet.'

Bowman nodded and crouched down in front of Stephanie; she turned away, digging her chin into her shoulder. 'Detective Sawyer has come to save you, Stephanie. It's not really working out.' He stood upright and walked over to the sofa. He slid the axe out from the other side and switched it from hand to hand. 'You must have a headache. The queer boy caught you pretty good.'

He sat down, sending a puff of dust up from the sofa cushion. 'Maybe a bit of concussion. I can see it in your eyes. But, you know what? I don't give a shit. I'm not really interested in other people's pain. I hear all this rubbish about kindness being a "superpower". But I think it's the opposite. I used to go bird watching with my uncle. My favourites were the sparrowhawks. Amazing things. Pure predators. They have these needle-like claws, and they knead their prey, crushing and stabbing. But there's no eye contact, no emotional connection to the act. It's as if the claws have a life of their own, and they're just getting on with the business of killing. They sometimes eat their prey while it's still alive. Now, we look on that with horror, through a lens of empathy. But when you start to feel sorry for things... That's not a strength. It's a weakness.

'Julius always used to go on about the beauty of nature, the wonders of the natural world. But nature isn't beautiful. That's just us projecting onto it. Nature is functional. It does what it needs to do and no more. And we're part of nature. Conditioned and socialised and judgemental. But, deep down, we're all killers. If we're pushed to the limit, we're all capable of killing. It's a survival impulse, and it's much closer to the surface than we like to think.'

Sawyer worked his hand into his back pocket and pulled out a paperclip. 'Is this a rehearsal for your speech in court?'

Bowman set the axe down on the floor and got up from the sofa. He stepped over Newton's body and strolled over to Sawyer. 'Hero cop. Do you feel like a hero now?'

'No. I'm just trying to do the right thing.' Surreptitiously, Sawyer unfolded the paperclip and worked the end into the handcuff lock, bending it to form an 'L' shape. 'I assume you don't buy into that idea?'

Bowman scoffed. He turned and walked back to the sofa. 'Right and wrong, good and evil. You sound like a fucking witchfinder or something.' Sawyer rotated the clip, pushing down the cuffs' inside ridges, feeling for the bite. 'I have a problem. Kill you first and make her watch, or kill her and make you watch. I'm erring towards the latter. Mainly because I suspect we're running out of time.'

'The cavalry is on its way,' said Sawyer, as he turned the clip and unlocked the cuffs. There was a slight click, but Bowman wouldn't be close enough to catch it.

Bowman turned, smiling. 'The cavalry are already here. Up on the ridge. Quite a few cars. Lights. Looks like a van. They're not hiding, but I doubt they'll be crashing through the doors with both you and the woman in here.'

'Specialist firearms unit. Assault team.'

Bowman nodded. 'It's... a fair cop.' He picked up the axe and walked to the window again, peering round the curtain. 'I heard the handcuffs click. That's okay, though. I read about your talents. How you got that boy out of the cave. See, this is the problem with fame.' He turned. 'You get *worked out*. Your tricks become part of the package. The old extraordinary becomes the new ordinary.'

Sawyer rose up from the chair. The room dipped a little as he walked over to Stephanie. He crouched in front of her and she lifted her faraway eyes. She had been badly beaten; her jaw sagged at the right side and the bruising around one of her eye sockets had forced the eye half-closed.

Bowman moved back to the centre of the room and tossed the axe onto the sofa. 'The truth is, I'm bored. I need a challenge. The women have hardly been worthy opponents. And...' He gestured towards Newton's body, shrugged. 'I accept that you won't fight fair. But you've already showed me one of your tricks. So I'm expecting the unexpected. And, yeah. You might be a bit slow because of the head injury. But, what can you do? You can only play the hand in front of you.'

'*David Bowman*.'

A call from outside. The voice was distorted, spoken through a megaphone.

'*This is Detective Chief Inspector Robin Farrell of the Greater Manchester Police. All possible exits from the house are covered by trained firearms officers. I urge you to leave by the front door, with your arms raised above your head. You will not be harmed.*'

Sawyer turned away from Stephanie and stood upright, facing Bowman. The room swayed again, and he took a steadying step to the side. He looked down at Newton's pulverised face, then back at Stephanie.

The dank room became a façade, a backdrop. In the centre, ahead of Bowman and the sofa, he saw the grass, shining in the sun, dripping with his mother's blood.

Newton's face: eviscerated by the axe.

His mother's face: shattered by the hammer.

Stephanie's sobbing, louder now.

His mother, crying and screaming, reaching out to him.

Farrell's voice again from outside: jagged, distorted.

His mother's shout, tearing through the burning air. 'Don't look back!'

Bowman moved for Sawyer and struck him with a brutal haymaker punch, sending him wheeling to the floor.

Sawyer's hand dug through a grainy layer of dust. He clenched his fingers into a fist, keeping his head low.

Bowman moved forward, standing over him. He leaned down, and Sawyer felt the splat of warm of saliva on his cheek. Bowman raged. '*Come on*! Hero cop. You keep preaching about the "right thing". So, what is it? Show me.'

Sawyer pushed himself to his feet, but as he turned, Bowman struck him with a fierce punch to the stomach.

He doubled over and slumped down into the dust, choking, gasping for air.

Bowman gave another laugh. 'Try again!'

Sawyer looked over to the corner, where Stephanie watched, her head raised higher, her eyes red and raw. But there was no fear there; only defiance, outrage.

His father, his parting words. "There is nothing in darkness that will not be disclosed. Nothing concealed that will not be brought to light."

His father, telling him to look after his brother, then extinguishing himself, snuffing out his light.

His brother, half alive.

Bowman grabbed Sawyer by the shoulders. 'Come on. I'll help you up. I'll give you a free shot. This is too fucking easy.'

Sawyer stood before him, mouth wide open, sucking in air, riding the pain from the stomach punch. He tipped back his head and stared up at the rancid ceiling. 'Your mother was a whore, David. That's what you thought, anyway.'

'Yes. I thought it because it was true.' Bowman released Sawyer, and he slumped to the floor again.

'You're right,' said Sawyer, looking up at him. 'We're both motherless, both fucked up. But I had something you didn't have. My mother's love. Your sisters took all of that, didn't they? Nothing left for you.'

Bowman raised his foot and stomped it into Sawyer's shoulder, tipping him onto his back.

Sawyer lay there. 'Your mother was a whore, David. She rejected your father and she gave her love to other men.' He raised himself onto his knees. 'And you know why? Because of you. Some people just don't deserve love. It's wasted on them.' Sawyer was upright now, braced. 'And your mother recognised you as one of those people. So she gave you the flipside. The gift of hate. And you've been repaying her for that ever since, and Stephanie is just the latest to bear the cost.'

Bowman backed away to the sofa and laid a hand on the axe, keeping his eyes on Sawyer. 'I was hoping for a good fight, you know. Not a fucking therapy session.'

'*David Bowman. I repeat. Come out of the front door with your arms raised above your head.*'

Bowman moved away from the sofa, leaving the axe. He lunged at Sawyer and struck him with another mighty punch, into the side of his face. Sawyer stumbled to the floor and stayed down, on one knee. Bowman slid a hand around his neck and raised him up. Sawyer's green eyes were murky, fading. He slumped in Bowman's grip, and spat blood onto the floor.

Bowman slapped Sawyer in the face with his free hand, jerking his head to the side. He swung the back of the hand into Sawyer's other cheek, then repeated both blows. He paused, stared at Sawyer's bloodied and swollen face for a few seconds, then repeated the side to side slapping, twice, three times.

Bowman paused again, relaxing his grip on Sawyer's neck. Sawyer dropped his head forward and his shoulders rose and fell, shuddering. Bowman smiled. 'Don't fucking tell me that the hero cop is *crying*.'

Sawyer raised his head, as a broad grin stretched across his battered face. The noise swelled, from a rumble in Sawyer's chest, to full-throated belly laughter, as if Bowman had just told him a hilarious joke. He opened his mouth and drew in rasping breaths, feeding the mirth, raising the volume.

Bowman brought his other hand around and held Sawyer by the neck, squeezing slightly, dampening the laughter. 'You're confusing me, Sawyer. I'm not sure which one of us is the psycho.' He raised Sawyer up by the neck, a few inches off the ground, and squeezed his hands tighter around his throat. 'This is a familiar sensation. You've got quite a feminine neck.'

Sawyer opened his mouth wide, gagging like a beached fish, straining for air. Bowman smiled and squeezed even tighter, draining the life out of him.

Sawyer felt a tingling sensation in his fingertips, spreading up his hands and arms, into his body. He was trembling all over, spasming, as a fuzz of darkness spilled around the edges of his vision.

In the corner, Stephanie cried out, wriggling against the rope.

'Are we done, then?' said Bowman, lifting his elbows, bracing himself to finish the job. 'You're really giving up?'

Sawyer jerked his dangling body to the left and drove his right elbow into the side of Bowman's face. The impact was enough to force Bowman to release his grip, and Sawyer dropped to the floor, struggling to stay upright.

As Bowman staggered back, Sawyer stepped to the side and drove his forehead into the top of Bowman's nose, cracking the bone and splashing blood into his eyes. Bowman howled in pain and reeled back, flailing for balance, crashing to the floor in front of the sofa.

Sawyer snatched up the axe and walked to Bowman, following him as he kicked his feet against the floor, pushing himself away from Sawyer, trying to find the balance to stand. But the headbutt had dazed him, and he backed into the wall by the bookcase.

Bowman hitched himself up and lifted his head, trying to focus on Sawyer. 'I'll give you that one.' He held his hands high, seemingly in surrender, but then brought them together in a slow handclap. He wiped the blood from his face. 'So, you're the hero again. You saved the girl. You brought the bad guy to justice.' He shrugged. 'I'll be okay, though. I mean, look at me. I'll be the alpha in whatever prison you bury me in. And, as I was saying, I'm bored with it, anyway. It's all too easy. Killing women. I'm a fucking lion. A lion stalking lame horses.' He looked up at Sawyer, standing before him, holding the axe in his right hand, blade resting against the floorboard. 'Get on with it, then. Finish my rights. Call in the supercops. Bring 'em in out of the rain.'

Sawyer stared at him, slowing his breathing.

'Fuck's sake. Forgotten your lines?'

Sawyer reached his left hand down and gripped the end of the axe handle, holding it firm now with both hands. He swung the blade out to the right, then stepped in towards Bowman and pivoted to the left, bringing the blade down into the side of his neck. It impacted at a downward angle, and penetrated several inches, slicing through Bowman's trachea.

From the corner, Stephanie screamed, loud and shrill.

Sawyer dug the axe out of the wound and let it clunk down onto the dusty floorboards. He stepped back and watched.

Bowman's eyes bulged, and he tumbled forward, groping at his neck, desperate to staunch the blood cascading down over his torso. He opened his mouth wide, and spat out a strained, gurgling sound. He gave up on holding his hands to his neck and reached out to his assailant. But Sawyer took another step back, and glared into Bowman's eyes as he gulped and gasped for air. He fell down onto his front, convulsing.

Sawyer turned to Stephanie. She was sobbing hard, hiding her eyes, muttering to herself, soothing herself.

He walked away from Bowman and crouched down,

undoing the rope around her ankles. Behind, Bowman's feet ground and thumped against the floor.

'It was the right thing to do, Stephanie,' said Sawyer. 'I just made the world a bit better. And I saved your life. So, here's what I ask in return.'

She uncovered her eyes and looked at Sawyer.

'He attacked me. He almost killed me. And I have the wounds and bruises to prove it. I got hold of the axe and I used it on him, in self-defence. It's almost the truth. And that's more than he deserves.' Sawyer checked behind him; Bowman was face down, still. 'Your scream will probably trigger the assault team. They will have a unit around the back, near the road.'

He held out his hand. Stephanie hesitated, then lifted her bound wrists for him to untie.

Sawyer dug through the knots. 'His time is over. He can't kill anyone else, and he can't infect others with his poison in prison.' He pulled away the rope, freeing Stephanie's hands. She pushed herself against the wall and sat upright.

A crash from the back of the house.

'*Armed police*!'

Stephanie startled, and Sawyer moved in closer. 'It was the right thing. It was him or the both of us. It was self-defence.'

Boots, crunching across the floorboards.

She looked up at him and nodded.

53

THREE DAYS LATER

Sawyer knocked twice on the door of the interview room, and entered. Keating and Farrell sat on the far side of the desk, both in full uniform. Two other men sat, side by side, at a temporary desk by the window. One was slight and bearded with rimless glasses; he was suited but not uniformed, and around Sawyer's age. The other was older and wider, with a cheap-looking suit that matched his wispy grey hair. Keating and the third man were busy scribbling notes; Farrell typed into a laptop.

Sawyer stepped up to the desk. He wore a navy suit, white shirt, orange tie. Most of his facial swelling had eased, but he was still heavily bruised around the forehead and eyes, and his movement was stiff and stilted.

'Detective Sawyer,' said Farrell without looking away from his laptop. He smiled and gestured to the chair. Sawyer took his seat, and turned slightly towards Keating.

'You're still under caution,' said Keating, looking up.

'We've reviewed your report, and the video interview you gave under caution two days ago.' He nodded to the two men. 'This is Federation rep DC Simon Gail and IOPC Lead Investigator Callum Whitehead. I would like to briefly cover a few points, and then we'll formalise the situation moving forward. On a positive note, it's clear that the man you apprehended, David Bowman aka Malcolm Powell, was responsible for the murders of Laura Bertrand, Hannah Lane, Dianne Walton and Angela Holt. Analysis of his computer and devices shows clear contact, the timings of meetings, and clarifies Bowman's movements around the times of the murders. In addition, we're satisfied that Julius Newton was involved in the presentation of Bowman's victims at the deposition scenes, and was also responsible for the murder of Damien Mount, the IT worker who discovered Angela Holt's body, and who attempted to blackmail police with photographs from the scene. In addition, evidence given by yourself and Bowman's abductee, Stephanie Burns, confirms that Julius Newton was murdered by David Bowman, shortly after you were incapacitated.'

'By Newton,' said Sawyer.

'Indeed.'

'It's our position,' said Farrell, 'that you acted irresponsibly by pursuing Bowman to the abandoned house at Dovestone Reservoir. We believe that two people would now be alive were it not for your actions, and that your pursuit of Bowman was both outside the Operation Orca protocols and, given that the location was not within the Derbyshire jurisdiction, constitutes gross misconduct.'

Sawyer took a breath. 'If we had pursued Bowman according to PACE principles, there's a good chance that we would now be looking at five murdered women instead of four.'

'Are you saying that PACE doesn't matter?' said Keating.

'Yes.'

Whitehead stirred in the corner.

'I'm saying that there are situations where you might be forced to choose between potentially saving a life and following conduct guidelines. And this was one.'

'The end justifies the means?' said Whitehead.

Sawyer nodded. 'Sometimes, yes. I believe it does.'

'This is Death Following Contact With Police,' said Farrell. 'And, as you know, the IOPC may choose to conduct its own further investigation.'

'In your video interview,' said Keating, 'you said you had started to make the arrest on Bowman. Had you actually finished reading him his rights?'

'Practically, yes. I outlined the crimes, but I hadn't quite completed the final line when Bowman attacked me.'

Whitehead piped up again. 'So, Bowman was officially under arrest.'

'Yes,' said Sawyer. 'Barring the final few words. He was absolutely aware of my identity, and aware of his rights.'

Farrell looked at Keating. 'Sounds like a Category Three.' He turned to Sawyer. 'Just take us back through the events, briefly.'

'From when I apprehended Bowman?'

'From when you took the decision to bypass your superiors and conduct an operation outside your jurisdiction.'

Sawyer looked to DC Gail. 'I hope I'm not being too sensitive, but that does sound a bit like a leading question.' He paused. 'I *took the decision* that while we had Newton willing to show us Bowman's potential location, we had to follow that up there and then, or risk him freezing up later and putting Stephanie's life at risk. His behaviour up to that point had hardly been consistent. I travelled to the location with DS Shepherd. Newton escaped our custody, and when I followed, I discovered Bowman and Stephanie Burns. Newton overpowered me, and when I came to, I discovered he had been murdered by Bowman. I fought with Bowman, and he got the upper hand. I managed to grab the axe and struck him in self-defence. I believe that if I hadn't done this, he would have murdered both me and Stephanie Burns.'

'And Stephanie saw this happen?' said Farrell.

'Yes.'

'She's still recovering,' said Keating. 'But we will be talking to her.'

Farrell nodded. 'You mention the axe. Did Bowman bring the axe to the location himself?'

'He had it in his possession when he came out of the house, yes.'

'We've determined that he bought the axe new at a hardware store in Ashbourne, three days earlier. So, can you explain why a section of the blade was damaged, and carried traces of a metal alloy consistent with that used in bullet manufacture?'

Sawyer caught Keating's eye. 'No, sir. I can't explain that.'

Farrell forced a smile. 'I'd assumed that might be the case. So, I've called in a forensic firearms team. Hopefully, they'll be able to complete the picture.' He nodded at Keating.

The senior officer sat upright. 'DI Sawyer, I'm sorry to have to confirm that you are officially suspended from duty on the grounds of gross misconduct, pending the outcome of the investigation into the death of David Bowman while in police custody. The initial period of the suspension will be twenty-eight days, but this is dependent on the investigation's findings and may be formally extended. You are not to leave the United Kingdom in this period. I'm not going to force you to sign in regularly, but you must make yourself available for further interview within a period of forty-eight hours. Your salary will be paid in full, but you will be required to surrender both your warrant card and your key card to this building.'

Sawyer took out his warrant card and key card, and passed them across the desk to Keating, who looked round at Whitehead and Gail. 'Is there anything more to add?' Both shook their heads. Keating turned back to Sawyer. 'Is there anything you need to collect from your office?'

'No, sir.'

'Then we're done. We'll speak soon, Detective Sawyer.'

Sawyer got to his feet and headed for the door.

Farrell followed him. 'I'm sorry to be a stickler, but, since the suspension is with immediate effect, you'll need to be escorted from the building. I'll do the honours.'

Sawyer exited the interview room and Farrell used his key card to open the connecting door to reception. Sawyer glanced at Sergeant Gerry Sherman as he turned into the ground floor corridor, past the evenly placed lime-green doors with yellow frosted windows.

Farrell stopped at the custody desk and called after him. 'Two suspensions within a year, Sawyer. If you come back, you'll be on a hat trick.'

Outside, a mid-morning shower had dampened the air, and as Sawyer strode across the car park to the Mini, a thickset man in an ill-fitting white polo shirt approached him from the side gate. He was balding, with grey hair at the temples, and he looked at Sawyer with tired, uneasy eyes.

'Detective Sawyer? My name is Jordan Burns. I'm sorry to disturb you, but I saw you arrive and... I waited. I just wanted to...' He held out a hand, and Sawyer shook. It was damp, with a swollen palm. 'I'm Steph's husband. Stephanie Burns. It's wrong what they're saying about you, in the paper. It says you're being investigated, because of that... Because of what happened. To that man.' He shook his head, and finally let go of Sawyer's hand. 'You don't deserve that. You deserve a fucking *medal*, mate. Taking bastards like that out of the world. Excuse my language. I'm... It's been like a living nightmare.'

'How is Stephanie doing?'

Burns shook his head. 'Ah. Steph's not right. She might never be right again.'

'I'm sorry to hear that.'

'Apart from anything else, she's under pressure from the police to tell them what happened, and I'm worried that reliving what she went through might break her entirely. But... she's alive. Thanks to you.'

Sawyer nodded, and moved off. 'I was just doing my job. I'm glad we got Stephanie back safe.'

Burns fell into step with Sawyer, but then hung back as he climbed into the Mini. 'Listen. I...' He hesitated. 'I know you went above and beyond to save her. If ever you need anything, Detective Sawyer. I mean, I haven't got much. But it's yours, mate. You hear me? I don't care what they say. You did the world a favour. You did good.'

54

Sawyer climbed up onto the mobile gantry of the MRI scanner and lay on his back, resting his head in the padded support. He held a wired panic button in his right hand, and had been told not to move his head and to keep his eyes closed throughout the process, which would last around forty minutes.

The gantry slid back, slotting him into the cramped tube, head first. The white ceiling of the room was replaced by the beige plastic interior of the scanner, and Sawyer closed his eyes.

'You okay in there, Jake?' The operator's voice came through a loudspeaker, just about audible beyond his protective headphones.

'All good,' said Sawyer.

The scanner began its work, magnetically interrogating the atoms in Sawyer's brain tissue, alchemising them into meaningful differential imagery. He listened for a while: the insectoid whirring; the rhythmic clunks and clangs; the tantrums of buzzing followed by pregnant pauses, as if the machine were drawing breath, gathering itself for the next phase.

After twenty minutes, they wheeled him out, injected a contrast dye into his arm, and posted him back in again. This time, he took himself away, hiding in the peace of the past: helping his mother spread jam on a sponge cake; watching his father laugh at a TV comedy he didn't understand; throwing a blue rubber bone toy for his endlessly enthusiastic Jack Russell; using a matchstick to gouge a mashed-up pea out of a chunk of his brother's Lego. He replayed a match-winning penalty save from his time as a goalkeeper in his teenage Sunday league team. He revisited scenes from simpler times: police training; martial art study; university girlfriends; a summer picnic with Maggie, cut short by persistent wasps.

Bowman's neck wound, pulsing as he tugged out the axe.

A school trip to the tram museum, drinking dandelion and burdock.

His father, pushing the barrel of the shotgun under his own chin.

The scanner saw it all: reading him, capturing him. He ached for a machine that could blur out the damage, or at least fade it down. But lately, the horrors had risen in volume and contrast, forcing his pleasant memories into the corner. It was as if the mere act of reaching for the positives only served to trigger the negatives.

Sawyer left the hospital at Chesterfield and drove the Mini down to Matlock. He walked between the manicured flowerbeds of Hall Leys Park, past the boating lake and bandstand, heading for the tree-lined path that led up the high tor, away from the town. The park was trim and tidy, ablaze with mid-summer colours, and crammed with tourist families sunbathing, playing football and frisbee, splashing in the water play area, riding the miniature train. But Sawyer passed through like a phantom, dressed in his long jacket, despite the warmth of the day.

He scaled the path, winding his way up the three hundred foot limestone crag, an inland cliff where his father had told him eagles once nested. He stopped at an open meadow just before a split in the path to the summit, and took out his phone, turning it on for the first time in two days. Missed calls, unread emails, unattended messages. Eva, Maggie, Shepherd, Tony Cross. There was care out there for him, but it was all too much: the thought of acknowledging it, returning it. To take such action would be irresponsible, given the fate of those who had formed him, and the suffering caused by his apparent blindness to consequence. The thought that had once nagged him now followed him with every step: he was only doing what he *knew* to be right, not acting on any kind of moral compulsion or instinct. Had he lost his capacity to care? To feel?

He turned off his phone and walked on, towards the hillside path known as Giddy Edge, a narrow path along the cliff face created by the Victorians for their amusement. He paused at the sign, with its falling man icon.

WARNING! SHEER DROP
KEEP WELL BACK FROM THE EDGE
KEEP CHILDREN UNDER CLOSE SUPERVISION

Sawyer edged along the path, holding the metal bannister. There was barely enough room for him to stand square, and after a few steps, he stopped, took a breath and looked down at the vertical drop.

And he felt it.

A lurch in his core. A warning from his limbic system, wrestling with the call to the void.

He looked up from the cliffside, across to the opposite hill, at the cable cars gliding up towards the Heights of Abraham. And in the beauty below—the sway of the treetops, the sunshine sparkling on the River Derwent—Sawyer felt the promise of happiness, and a fear of non-existence.

Bowman was right. Nature was neither good or bad; it just *was*. Getting on with the process of surviving, feeding itself, passing through the cycle of life and death. The animal side, the killer instinct, was always there, just below the surface. But that was why it was up to us, the most evolved member of the natural world, to transcend that, and make our unlikely lives more liveable.

There is nothing in darkness that will not be disclosed. Nothing concealed that will not be brought to light.

He moved along the path and rested on a bench, in a small grotto carved into the limestone. Above, the cloud cover shifted, and the sunlight flared across the trees, lighting the way. In recent weeks, he had fought his fantasies of self-destruction and craved instead a great cleansing: to have his old toxic self washed away, revealing something new and hopeful.

'Don't look back.'

Sawyer thought of Kierkegaard and his line about how life can only be understood backwards, but it must be lived forward.

And in his epiphany, the core truth sang like a songbird: he could never reinvent himself from scratch, in denial of what had shaped him, what had gone. He would need to use the past as foundation to rebuild. He would have to go back to go forward.

55

Alex Goldman sank back into her mauve armchair and reached for the tea tray on the curvy-legged side table. Sawyer watched from the black *chaise longue*.

Alex lifted her eyes, caught him spying. 'Am I really such a specimen?'

'Sorry. Just daydreaming.'

She poured the tea. 'I'd like to say that you look well, but we both know that wouldn't be true.'

He shrugged. 'You should see the other guy.'

Alex shook her head. 'I'll have to take your word for that. I've stopped reading your press. It doesn't feel healthy.'

'Same here.' He raised a hand as she finished filling her cup. 'No tea for me.'

She nodded. 'Biscuit?'

Sawyer took a custard cream and set it down on the chair arm. He dug a paper bag out of his pocket and opened it. 'Sweet? They're a bit sharp. Got them from a place in Matlock.'

Alex smiled. 'I'm seventy, Jake. Not seven.'

'How are you feeling? The aches and pains.'

'It's okay. You can say the V-word. The veins are still varicose. I use compression stockings. You don't get used to it.'

Sawyer placed the bag of sweets by his side, along with his wallet.

They shared a moment's silence.

'I went for the MRI. Takes them a while to prepare the report, though.'

'That's good. It'll be helpful to see if there's anything physical that's compromising your behaviour or impulses.' Her eyes moved to the bag next to him. 'When was the last time you bought sweets, Jake?'

'Apart from those... I don't know. A few weeks ago. But it's okay. I know we've talked about me being frozen in the moment of my mum's murder. And all that worry about how I hide in the nineties, in the era I was relatively happy. But...' He took a bite of the biscuit, halving it. 'I'm not concerned about that now. I know I need to live for the future. But that's only a part of me. You can't just close the door on something, separate yourself. It's more about finding a fresh joy in the moment. You don't need to deny the past. We've tried to do that with Michael, my brother. It didn't work. He's... pretty poorly at the moment.'

Alex rubbed at her leg, wincing. 'Sorry to hear that. So, how are you finding this fresh joy for yourself?'

'I'm not supposed to talk about the case—'

'So, don't.'

He smiled. 'It's no big secret that I've been suspended, pending an investigation. I cut a few corners. It'll work out. But I've been thinking of doing some freelance. Nothing stopping me from working a couple of jobs on the side.'

'With your latest case, did it end well for... all the good people? Remember, we were concerned about your actions endangering those close to you.'

He waved a hand. 'Everyone was fine. I... know all of this. I don't need this.'

'This? You mean therapy?'

'Yes. You've helped me to embrace more self-knowledge, but I don't need to relive what happened in order to mend myself from the trauma of it. I don't want to set it aside that way, turn it into something else. It's part of me, and I have to accept that I will always carry it around. I can't just wait until I've cast it off before I can live my life.'

'The Americans call it closure.'

He scoffed. 'Of course they do. It's nonsense. This idea of moving on. I don't want to *move on*. That would be like denying that my mother and father ever existed. It feels disloyal, to just pass them into memory.'

Alex sipped her tea. 'Denial, anger, acceptance.'

Sawyer sighed and slumped forward, elbows on knees.

'Do you think you're grieving, Jake?'

'Of course I do.'

'And do you accept there may come a point when you stop grieving?'

He looked at her. 'No, I don't. I owe my parents my life, and that will always be true.'

She set down her cup. 'But you can't live out your life as a memorial to them. Don't die with the dead. If you would indulge me in a metaphor for a second... One way of looking at grief is that it's like a balloon in water. You have to keep it below the surface in order to function in your daily work, when you have to deal with others, be professional. But you *can* let go when you're at home or by yourself. You can let it rise above the surface. And that's a form of acceptance.'

He sprang to his feet, gathered up the sweets and wallet. 'I'm sorry. I feel like I'm wasting your time here. I'm grateful for your help and guidance. But I have to work on myself, by myself. I need to give thanks for what I've got, rather than desire what I don't have.'

Alex smiled. 'You're paraphrasing one of your great Stoic thinkers. Epictetus.'

He laughed. 'See, this is another problem with coming here. You're wiser than me. It's not good for my self-esteem.' Sawyer headed for the door.

Alex stayed in her chair and took another sip of tea. 'Short and sweet. We have another forty minutes if you need it.'

He smiled. 'I don't.'

Sawyer hurried out to the car and drove away. The roads were heavy with teatime traffic, and he sat in a queue for a while on the road into Stanshope, before turning off along a single-track lane that snaked around, back past the other side of Alex's village.

The lane was quiet, and he slowed to a stop and slotted his phone into the windscreen mount. He was cueing up some music, when the Spotify app was overridden by an incoming call, from Alex.

He connected. 'Missing me already?'

'I'm sorry, Jake. I forgot. I need your signature for the last two sessions. It's a new electronic payment system. Sorry. I should have asked at the start. Are you still nearby?'

He looked out across the fields. There was a tone to Alex's voice he'd never heard before: something clenched and icy. 'Of course. Five minutes?'

'That's fine. See you soon. Just come straight in. I'll leave the door unlocked.'

She disconnected.

Sawyer drove back down to the bottom of the road in

front of Alex's row of houses. He parked, took the phone out of the dock, and navigated to his photo and video files. He found the video he was looking for, typed a short message, and sent it.

At the front door, he paused, turned the handle, and walked inside.

As Sawyer entered, Alex's dog, Molly, fussed and scrabbled behind the closed kitchen door.

He called out to Alex. No answer.

The door to the consulting room was ajar, giving him a view of the left side of the black *chaise longue*. His uneaten custard cream still sat on the arm. He pushed the door open and walked in.

'I'm sorry, Jake.'

Alex sat in her armchair, with her head down. Austin Fletcher stood at the side, aiming a handgun at her head. He probed Sawyer with his black eyes and nodded towards the *chaise longue*. 'Sit.'

Sawyer took his usual seat. He kept his eyes on Alex, willing her to look up so he could offer some reassurance. But she kept her head low, with her trembling hands resting on one knee.

'Gun,' said Fletcher.

Sawyer looked at him. 'Is this word association?'

'Where?'

'In your hand?'

Fletcher cocked the gun and pointed it down at Alex's knee. 'Last chance.'

Alex looked up in alarm. She caught Sawyer's eye and he nodded.

'I take it you mean the gun I took from you last year,' said Sawyer. 'The one I assume either you or Dale used at the club in Manchester?'

Fletcher nodded. 'Where?'

Sawyer smiled. 'I'll show you. But I need to get my phone out.'

'Slowly,' said Fletcher.

Sawyer slipped his phone out of his pocket and navigated to the photos and videos. He found the video and pressed play, then held it up for Fletcher to see.

The screen showed Sawyer, filmed from a low angle, sitting on his sofa at the Edale cottage. 'Hello, Dale. Firstly, congratulations on the new role. We hear so much talk about the toxic political climate, these days. But the appointment of a violent career criminal with connections to county lines drug operations as a new northern drugs czar... That really is beyond satire. Now, I'm afraid I do have the Glock that you, or one of your associates, used to kill Shaun Brooks last December. It's in a safe place, with your fingerprints all over it. And, as I'm sure you know, the rifling will connect the bullet used to kill Shaun to the specific gun. At best, that will lead to a pretty embarrassing start to your political career. At worst, we'll use it to build a case for murder, and you'll be convicted, and your public-spirited chain of youth-friendly social clubs that definitely aren't a front for county lines recruitment... that will all be over before it's even begun.'

A phone rang in Fletcher's pocket; he ignored it, fully focussed on the screen.

'Now, I've briefed a trusted friend on the significance and whereabouts of the gun, and if anything should happen to me or to someone personally connected to me, then he's under strict instructions to blow the whistle. Bye now.'

Sawyer pocketed the device. Fletcher's phone continued to ring. 'I just sent that video to your employer. I'm guessing that's him calling to confirm.'

Fletcher dug his phone out of his pocket, looked at the

screen, and answered it. He listened for a few seconds, then switched the phone to speaker.

'Am I on?' said Dale.

'You certainly are,' said Sawyer. He nodded to Alex again.

Dale sighed. 'Sawyer. I take it your superiors know nothing about the gun?'

'If they did, they'd have already built a case against you. It can be our little secret, Dale.' He picked up the custard cream and crunched into it.

A pause, at Dale's end. Fletcher switched the phone to private and stalked out into the hall. Sawyer stood up and walked over to Alex. He lifted her hands from her knee and squeezed. She didn't look up, and Sawyer kept his eyes on the door, listening to Fletcher's voice, sharp and angry as he spoke to Dale. They heard him stomp down the hall and slam the front door.

The trembling in Alex's hands spread to the rest of her body, and she began to weep. Sawyer folded an arm around her shoulder, but she pulled away.

56

'This is a new one,' said Maggie. 'Meeting where the grown-ups play.'

Sawyer looked around the busy main bar of The Prince of Wales, a traditional old pub on the edge of Baslow, recently refitted to lure upscale tourists and local foodies. 'Fish and Chips Night. Catnip.'

He sipped his Diet Coke and broke open a packet of cheese and onion crisps, spreading them over the wrapper.

Maggie smiled. 'That's okay. I won't be partaking.'

'All the more for me.' He munched on a crisp. 'Is this where you tell me that I'm a man-child?'

'No point. You seem to be owning it.'

He shrugged. 'I don't really understand this obsession with "adulting".'

'You mean, behaving like an adult?'

'The moment you grow up, that's when you start to grow old.'

Maggie laughed. 'Is that on a sign above the toilet?'

'I honestly just thought of it.'

She leaned in. 'How is your brother?'

'I went to see him yesterday. He's still in a medical

coma, but he's stable, and they're confident he'll recover. He's being cared for. Fed, watered. He doesn't speak. Not a lot has changed.'

'Apart from the fact that he tried to kill himself.'

Sawyer sighed. 'I'm getting him out of that place the moment he wakes up. He can come and live with me if he wants to.'

'You won't sleep on a sofa.'

'I'll build an extension.' He looked at her. 'Whatever it takes.'

She nodded. 'And you have some time on your hands now.'

'The suspension is for the brass's benefit.'

'Not everybody sees it that way. Some are calling you a liability. The more you get away with this kind of thing, the more you feel like the rules don't apply to you. Sounds dangerously close to populism to me. Shaking up the system, a law unto yourself.'

'Other people's opinion of me is none of my business.'

Maggie sipped at her wine, nodding. 'Stoicism dot com?'

'Pretty much. I'm thinking of doing some work for myself, anyway. Freelance investigation. PI instead of DI.'

'We talked about this last year, remember? PI work isn't glamorous. It's serving papers, tracking parole infringements, divorce disputes.'

'Like I said, that's the old model. I'll find my own way. Already got a possible case. Have you heard of Darren Coleman? Fifteen-year-old from Matlock Bath. Went to a party seven years ago and never came home.'

Maggie shook her head. 'Yes. But surely that's just a cold case? Leave it to the misper teams. It'll drive you crazy. It's incredibly rare to find someone after so long. You know that.'

Sawyer took a drink. 'I know. On the surface, it's a standard misper. Horrible, but boring. He's probably dead. But, there's a trainee journalist, Virginia Mendez. I bet you haven't heard of her.'

'No.'

'A few months ago, she started an independent podcast project, based on the case. Investigative journalism, really.'

'Like *Serial*?'

Sawyer smiled. 'Yeah. And about a thousand others. She's already broadcast three episodes. And here's the thing.' He leaned in close. 'She hasn't been seen for two weeks now. Could be coincidence. Could be interesting.'

Maggie sat back. 'How are things with Alex?'

He frowned. 'I'm taking a break from that, at least until the suspension is sorted.'

She studied him. 'I sent her an email before I came out tonight. A referral. Got her Out-of-Office. When I saw her a few weeks ago, she said she wanted to see family in France for the summer, but she was probably too busy. Seems quite sudden. We were also due to have dinner next week.'

'She's struggling a bit,' said Sawyer. 'Physically. Probably decided she needed the rest.'

Maggie gazed into her wine glass. 'How are things with Eva?'

'You'll have to ask her.'

She looked up. 'I thought...'

He shook his head, smiling. 'It's been a busy time. It's all a bit hands-off.'

'Great. You're stopping your own therapy but now you need relationship counselling.'

He laughed. 'It's not that bad. But the last time we went out together—'

'You almost started a fight with a bear.'

'Exactly. It's hard to keep up that level of intensity. She's a demanding woman.'

'Yes, but you do actually have to *see* your girlfriend from time to time, you know.'

He finished the crisps, dabbing at the shards with a wet finger. 'I'll bear it in mind.'

Sawyer drove with the Mini's top down, way too fast for the narrow lanes on the outskirts of Bakewell. At Hulme End, he dropped down into the valley, through the late evening twilight, and parked at his usual verge near Ecton Mine. He sat for a while with the engine running, tasting the zesty air, basking in the bird calls. He turned the key and raised the roof, then made the call.

'You're very welcome,' said Tony Cross.

'Sorry to be quiet. Had a few things to sort out.'

Cross laughed. 'I saw. One or two. They suspend you?'

'Twenty-eight days minimum. Investigation pending.'

Cross whistled. 'Welcome to my world. Feels strange to do a good deed and be labelled an outcast, doesn't it?'

'I think I've moved beyond the need for blanket approval. Nice shot, though. Did you take up at the second position?'

'Thanks. And, yeah. Couldn't get a line when you went behind the building. I saw him drag you inside but... there wasn't a definite shot. So, do you owe me your life, or did you have the mad axeman covered? Gearing up a roundhouse kick?'

'Dragon whips his tail.'

Cross laughed. 'Did they get the bullet?'

'Not sure. They're interested in damage on the axe

blade. Haven't spoken to Shepherd yet. I'm assuming he saw the shot, or at least heard it.'

'Will he help them?'

'If they put him in a chair and ask the direct question, then yes. But I doubt he'll volunteer anything.'

Cross sighed. 'I suppose that's the best we've got. I had a couple of checks around your place over the last day or two. No sign of Mr Fiesta.'

'That might have gone away. But I could be looking into something else. Freelance. Might need a bit of help.'

'Is there danger and excitement involved?'

'You know me. Never a dull moment.'

'I hope that's in your will, as your epitaph.'

'You're the second person who's said that recently.' Sawyer looked out through the trees, along the walking track. 'I'm not planning my funeral yet.'

He followed the path to the steps, up to Thor's Cave. The sky had grown dusky, but he still had to linger at the entrance as a teenage couple skittered their way down the rock and left him alone.

He climbed into the cave and shuffled through the narrow passage towards the far end. He paused, and listened.

Nothing.

At the ditch below the slitted window, he crawled deeper into the cave and pulled away the large, smooth rock, embedded deep beneath the overhang.

He pulled the rock aside and aimed his phone light into the space.

No evidence bag. The gun had gone.

BOOK FIVE IN THE **JAKE SAWYER** SERIES

JAKE SAWYER is in limbo. Facing an internal enquiry into his capture of a vicious killer, he turns private detective, and takes the seemingly hopeless case of a teenage boy, missing for seven years.

When a young woman podcaster investigating the boy's disappearance also goes missing, Sawyer is drawn into the secretive and treacherous world of urban exploration.

But then an adult male body is found, showing signs of extreme torture, and the murder reminds Sawyer of an unsolved case from his early career. He connects the past with the present, uncovering a terrible truth which could hold the key to the disappearances.

http://books2read.com/chasethedevil

JOIN MY MAILING LIST

I occasionally send an email newsletter with details on forthcoming releases and anything else I think my readers might care about.

Sign up and I'll send you **a Jake Sawyer prequel novella**.

THE LONG DARK is set in the summer before the events of CREEPY CRAWLY. It's FREE and totally exclusive to mailing list subscribers.

Go here to get the book:
http://andrewlowewriter.com/longdark

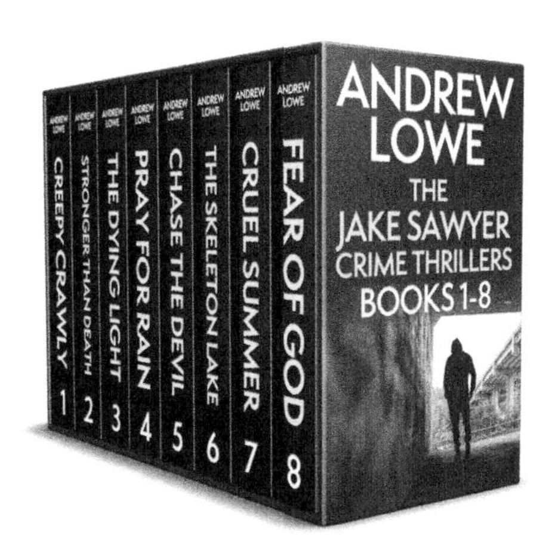
ANDREW LOWE
THE JAKE SAWYER CRIME THRILLERS
BOOKS 1-8
CREEPY CRAWLY 1
STRONGER THAN DEATH 2
THE DYING LIGHT 3
PRAY FOR RAIN 4
CHASE THE DEVIL 5
THE SKELETON LAKE 6
CRUEL SUMMER 7
FEAR OF GOD 8

ACKNOWLEDGMENTS

Detective Constable Ralph King and Detective Constable Simon Albrow for their help with police procedural issues.

Professor Sube Banerjee for his neurological expertise.

Bryony Sutherland for keen-eyed editing and creative steerage.

Book Cover Shop for cover and website design.

Special thanks to **Julia** for listening to me go on about it all.

Andrew Lowe. London, 2020

PLEASE LEAVE A REVIEW

If you enjoyed **PRAY FOR RAIN**, please take a couple of minutes to leave a review or rating on the book's **Amazon** page.

Honest reviews of my books help bring them to the attention of others, and connecting with readers is the number one thing that keeps me writing.

Go here to leave your review:
https://books2read.com/prayforrain

THE JAKE SAWYER SERIES

THE LONG DARK
CREEPY CRAWLY
STRONGER THAN DEATH
THE DYING LIGHT
PRAY FOR RAIN
CHASE THE DEVIL
THE SKELETON LAKE
CRUEL SUMMER
FEAR OF GOD
TENDER IS THE NORTH
BLOOD NEVER SLEEPS (2025)

BOOKS 1-3 BOX SET
BOOKS 4-6 BOX SET
BOOKS 1-6 BOX SET
BOOKS 1-8 BOX SET

GLOSSARY

ACT – Acceptance and Commitment Therapy. A form of psychotherapy that uses acceptance and mindfulness strategies along with commitment to behaviour change.

AFO – Authorised Firearms Officer. A UK police officer who has received training, and is authorised to carry and use firearms.

ALF – Animal Liberation Front. A political and social resistance movement that promotes non-violent direct action in protest against incidents of animal cruelty.

ANPR – Automatic Number Plate Recognition. A camera technology for automatically reading vehicle number plates.

AWOL – Absent without leave. Acronym.

BSE – Bovine Spongiform Encephalopahy. Colloquially known as 'mad cow disease'. A neurodegenerative condition in cattle.

CCRC – Criminal Cases Review Commission. Independent body which investigates suspected miscarriages of justice in England, Wales and NI.

CI – Confidential Informant. An individual who passes information to the police on guarantee of anonymity.

CBT – Cognitive Behaviour Therapy. A form of psychotherapy based on principles from behavioural and cognitive psychology.

CID – Criminal Investigation Department. The branch of the UK police whose officers operate in plainclothes and specialise in serious crime.

COD – Cause of Death. Police acronym.

CPS – Crown Prosecution Service. The principle public agency for conducting criminal prosecutions in England and Wales.

CROP – Covert Rural Observation Post. A camouflaged surveillance operation, mostly used to detect or monitor criminal activity in rural areas.

CSI – Crime Scene Investigator. A professional responsible for collecting, cataloguing and preserving physical evidence from crime scenes.

CSO – Community Support Officer. Uniformed but non-warranted member of police staff in England & Wales. The role has limited police powers. Also known as PCSO.

D&D – Drunk & Disorderly. Minor public order offence in the UK (revised to 'Drunk and disorderly in a public place' in 2017).

Dibble – Manchester/Northern English slang. Police.

EMDR – Eye Movement Desensitisation and Reprocessing. An interactive psychotherapy technique used to relieve psychological stress, particularly trauma and post-traumatic stress disorder.

ETD – Estimated Time of Death. Police acronym.

FLO – Family Liaison Officer. A specially trained officer or police employee who provides emotional support to the families of crime victims and gathers evidence and information to assist the police enquiry.

FOA – First Officer Attending. The first officer to arrive at a crime scene.

FSI – Forensic Science Investigator. An employee of the Scientific Services Unit, usually deployed at a crime scene to gather forensic evidence.

GIS – General Intelligence Service (Egypt). Government agency responsible for national security intelligence, both domestically and internationally.

GMCA – Greater Manchester Combined Authority. Local government institution serving the ten metropolitan boroughs of the Greater Manchester area of the UK.

GMP – Greater Manchester Police. Territorial police force responsible for law enforcement within the county of Greater Manchester in North West England.

GPR – Ground Penetrating Radar. A non-intrusive geophysical method of surveying the sub-surface. Often used by police to investigate suspected buried remains.

HOLMES – Home Office Large Major Enquiry System. An IT database system used by UK police forces for the investigation of major incidents.

H&C – Hostage & Crisis Negotiator. Specially trained law enforcement officer or professional skilled in negotiation techniques to resolve high-stress situations such as hostage crises.

IED – Improvised Explosive Device. A bomb constructed and deployed in ways outside of conventional military standards.

IDENT1 – The UK's central national database for holding, searching and comparing biometric information on those who come into contact with the police as detainees after arrest.

IMSI – International Mobile Subscriber Identity. A number sent by a mobile device that uniquely identifies the user of a cellular network.

IOPC – Independent Office for Police Conduct.

Oversees the police complaints system in England and Wales.

ISC – Intelligence and Security Committee of Parliament. The committee of the UK Parliament responsible for oversight of the UK Intelligence Community.

MCT – Metacognitive Therapy. A form of psychotherapy focused on modifying beliefs that perpetuate states of worry, rumination and attention fixation.

MIT – Murder/Major Investigation Team. A specialised squad of detectives who investigate cases of murder, manslaughter, and attempted murder.

Misper – missing person. Police slang.

NCA – National Crime Agency. A UK law enforcement organisation. Sometimes dubbed the 'British FBI', the NCA fights organised crime that spans regional and international borders.

NCB – National Central Bureau. An agency within an INTERPOL member country that links its national law enforcement with similar agencies in other countries.

NDNAD – National DNA Database. Administered by the Home Office in the UK.

NHS – National Health Service. Umbrella term for the three publicly funded healthcare systems of the UK (NHS England, NHS Scotland, NHS Wales).

NHSBT – NHS Blood and Transplant. A division of the UK National Health Service, dedicated to blood, organ and tissue donation.

OCG – Organised Crime Group. A structured group of individuals who work together to engage in illegal activities.

OP – Observation Point. The officer/observer locations in a surveillance operation.

Osman Warning – An alert of a death threat or high risk of murder issued by UK police, usually when there is intelligence of the threat but an arrest can't yet be carried out or justified.

PACE – Police and Criminal Evidence Act. An act of the UK Parliament which instituted a legislative framework for the powers of police officers in England and Wales.

PAVA – Pelargonic Acid Vanillylamide. Key component in an incapacitant spray dispensed from a handheld canister. Causes eye closure and severe pain.

PAYG – Pay As You Go. A mobile phone handset with no contract or commitment. Often referred to as a 'burner' due to its disposable nature.

PM – Post Mortem. Police acronym.

PNC – Police National Computer. A database which allows law enforcement organisations across the UK to share intelligence on criminals.

PPE – Personal Protective Equipment designed to protect users against health or safety risks at work.

Presser – Press conference or media event.

RIPA – Regulation of Investigatory Powers Act. UK Act of Parliament which regulates the powers of public bodies to carry out surveillance and investigation. Introduced to take account of technological change such as the grown of the internet and data encryption.

SAP scale. A five-point scale, devised by the Sentencing Advisory Panel in the UK, to rate the severity of indecent images of children.

SIO – Senior Investigating Officer. The detective who heads an enquiry and is ultimately responsible for personnel management and tactical decisions.

SOCO – Scene of Crime Officer. Specialist forensic investigator who works with law enforcement agencies to collect and analyse evidence from crime scenes.

SSU – Scientific Services Unit. A police support team which collects and examines forensic evidence at the scene of a crime.

Tac-Med – Tactical Medic. Specially trained medical professional who provides advanced medical care and support during high-risk law enforcement operations.

TOD – Time of Death. Police acronym.

TRiM – Trauma Risk Management. Trauma-focused peer support system designed to assess and support employees who have experienced a traumatic, or potentially traumatic, event.

Urbex – urban exploration. Enthusiasts share images of man-made structures, usually abandoned buildings or hidden components of the man-made environment.

VPU – Vulnerable Prisoner Unit. The section of a UK prison which houses inmates who would be at risk of attack if kept in the mainstream prison population.

ALSO BY ANDREW LOWE

A WOMAN TO DIE FOR

AN EX WHO WOULD KILL TO GET HER BACK

Sam Bartley is living well. He's running his own personal trainer business, making progress in therapy, and he's planning to propose to his girlfriend, Amy.

When he sees a strange message on Amy's phone, Sam copies the number and sends an anonymous threat. But the sender replies, and Sam is sucked into a dangerous confrontation that will expose his steady, reliable life as a horrifying lie.

https://books2read.com/dontyouwantme

ALSO BY ANDREW LOWE

WHAT IF THE HOLIDAY OF YOUR DREAMS TURNED INTO YOUR WORST NIGHTMARE?

Joel Pearce is an average suburban family man looking to shake up his routine. With four close friends, he travels to a remote tropical paradise for a 'desert island survival experience': three weeks of indulgence and self-discovery.

But after their supplies disappear and they lose contact with the mainland, the rookie castaways start to suspect that the island is far from deserted.

https://books2read.com/savages

ABOUT THE AUTHOR

Andrew Lowe was born in the north of England. He has written for ***The Guardian*** and ***Sunday Times***, and contributed to numerous books and magazines on films, music, TV, videogames, sex and shin splints.

He lives in the south of England, where he writes, edits other people's writing, and shepherds his two young sons down the path of righteousness.

His online home is andrewlowewriter.com

Follow him via the social media links below.

Email him at andrew@andrewlowewriter.com

For Andrew's editing and writing coach services, email him at andylowe99@gmail.com

facebook.com/andrewlowewriter

x.com/andylowe99

instagram.com/andylowe99

tiktok.com/@andrewlowewriter

bookbub.com/profile/andrew-lowe

amazon.com/stores/Andrew-Lowe/author/B00UAJGZZU

Printed in Great Britain
by Amazon

42721647R00209